I0680589

A ROMANCE

A BLOOMING AND VERDANT

Home

Newton's Crossing Series Book 4

JEAN-PAUL PARE'

A
Blooming
And
Verdant
Home
By
Jean-Paul Pare'

Copyright © 2025 by Jean-Paul Pare'
All rights reserved.
ISBN: 979-8-9914994-3-9
This is a work of fiction. Any similarities to people, places, or events is entirely coincidental.

Acknowledgments

As always, my first reader Alexis. She helped me take a horrible first draft where awful things happened to good people and turn it into this. Trust me, you want to thank her. The first draft was way darker than what you read here. My mistake for starting a novel right after awful things happened in the world.

For my beta readers who gave me a lot of good suggestions.

Dedication

For all you fans of cozy summer reads with a desire to read a heart felt romance with a smattering of spice, this one's for you.

Trigger Warnings

Talk of addiction and relapse

Mentions of adultery, indirectly.

Death of a parent, Indirectly

Death of a child, indirectly

Without giving any spoilers, the above warnings are part of the conflict, and I've tried to minimize the effects of certain things. But I try to stay true to real life.

About the Addiction, if this triggers you, or you see yourself in certain characters from this book, I would encourage you to seek help from your local state or public recovery resource.

Chapter 1

Tommy Richards

"Are you gonna take the exit?" Arlene asked, pointing to the green Newton's Crossing sign.

Tommy blinked, pulling himself out of a cowboy movie daydream, and nodded.

He said, "Yeah, I am."

He guided the truck into the turn lane, slowing as the light changed. Ahead, the outskirts of their small North Carolina hometown unfolded—strip malls, a gas station, and three fast-food joints, all conveniently crammed into the same block. Classic Newton's Crossing.

The truck slowed onto Highway Thirteen. He'd driven this route more times than he could count, the scenery blurring into fields and faded billboards. In the distance, he could see the taller buildings of the downtown city center through gaps in the tall pines dotting the two-lane road. Near the center of town was a low rise called Mission hill, and a large bronze statue atop it of a civil war cavalry officer charging with saber drawn.

Yet another piece of decoration created for the town by Gideon Rittermark, in honor of the man's great grandfather Josiah, who died there in 1865.

He shook his head, throwing off the echoes of the past.

"Where is this place again?" he asked, mostly to fill the quiet.

Arlene didn't even look up from her phone. "Downtown. Right next to the bookstore—Cassandra's, remember?"

Her voice was calm, easy. A soft contrast to the hum of the engine and the churn in his chest.

He grunted, picturing the bookstore, that stuffy little place with its shelves overflowing and the scent of old paper hanging heavy in the air. Not exactly his scene. But then again, he wasn't an art connoisseur, either.

"Who is this woman, anyway?" he asked,

Arlene sighed, tucking a stray strand of hair behind her ear. "She's a friend from a long way back," she explained, a hint of nostalgia in her voice. "We met again a week ago, hit it off, and she wants to have a showing."

"For your art?"

"Yes, for my art."

He snorted. "Is she cute?"

Arlene shot him a playful glare. "Not your style cute."

"She's ugly, then."

"Meghan is not ugly," Arlene corrected, her voice firm. "You just have poor taste."

He scoffed. "I've got great taste. But if she owns an art gallery, I'm imagining an old gray-haired woman in tweed skirts with a bun, like Aunt Georgia.

"Stop it," Arlene laughed. "She's our age."

"Ugly, then." He joked back.

"Shut up," Arlene said, rolling her eyes. "She's cute. Why are you asking?"

"Just curious.. I want to know ahead of time what to expect."

"Yeah, right."

He shrugged, trying to appear nonchalant.

"She's cute," she admitted. "And try to be nice."

"I'm nice."

"In a gruff, overprotective way."

"That's nice," he countered. "And I'm not gruff."

"You're a regular grouch," she teased. "Tell that to Cathy. She almost cried when you made her get out of bed for chores on Saturday."

"Six o'clock is too late to sleep, especially when there's work to be done on the farm."

"Six o'clock is too early for a twelve year old who goes to school."

"Tell that to Dad," he said, a familiar ache settling in his chest.

"I would," Arlene replied, her gaze drifting out the window.

He reached over and squeezed her hand. "Me too, Sis."

They both missed Thomas Richards, Senior, who had died three years ago. The silence stretched between them, heavy with unspoken grief, until Arlene cleared her throat and announced, "Here we are. Be nice."

He pulled into the diagonal parking spot, his gaze sweeping over the gallery. It was a white building tucked between a bookstore and a closed Bagel King. Through the double plate-glass windows, he could see all manner of art. Paintings, pottery, and statues of half-naked women adorned the displays.

"Think she would like me?" he asked, a flicker of doubt creeping in.

Arlene laughed. "Not hardly," she said, shaking her head. "That'd be a regular Beauty and the Beast situation."

"So you're telling me she's the beast?"

"You do have a high opinion of yourself, don't you?"

"Hey, chicks dig me," he said with a grin. "I can't be that bad."

"She's not one of those chicks who's going to dig you," Arlene said, her voice firm. "Meghan is cultured."

Right, he thought. One of those places.

"And I'm not?" He shoved a handful of Cheeto's into his mouth, cheese dust coating his lips.

Arlene stared at him, her expression a mix of amusement and exasperation. Without saying anything, she handed him a napkin from the center console. "Got some on your cheek there, bro."

"Oh." Sheepishly, he wiped his mouth, feeling a blush creep up his neck.

They climbed out of the truck, and Tommy stretched, his muscles protesting the long drive. He glanced at his reflection in the truck's window, rumpled shirt, hair sticking up at odd angles, a faint orange stain lingering near his mouth. Great, he thought. Just great. A stray lock of black hair spiked off his head.

Hope she's at least decent to look at.

As if summoned by his thoughts, the gallery door swung open, and Meghan stepped out. Tommy froze, his breath catching in his throat.

Damn.

She was more beautiful than he'd imagined; tall, with a cascade of blond hair that tumbled over her shoulders and a figure that made his heart do a wild jump. She wore a white tank top under a pale yellow spring blazer and jeans that hugged her curves. Her blue eyes sparkled with intelligence and warmth.

Arlene gestured toward him. "This is my brother, Tommy."

Tommy's palms were suddenly slick with sweat. He fumbled for words, his usual confidence deserting him. "Hi," he managed, his voice a raspy croak.

Meghan smiled, her gaze sweeping over him with a hint of amusement. "Hi, Tommy," she said, her voice warm and inviting. "I hear you're the labor today."

He felt a blush creep up his neck. "I am," he mumbled, shoving his hands in his pockets. "Yes, I am."

Arlene rolled her eyes. "Tommy, get the stuff out of the back seat first and bring it in," she called over her shoulder as she led Meghan inside.

Tommy lingered a moment, his gaze trailing after Meghan as she walked away. He couldn't help but admire the way her hair bounced with each step. And the way her blue jeans held tight legs that went on for days. Oh shit. This is going to be interesting.

He straightened his shirt, ran a hand through his hair, and took a deep breath. The stray lock went down. For a second. He wet his hand and tried again. This time it stayed. Good. Time to get to work.

He carried the first load of art into the gallery, his eyes wide with wonder. It was exactly what he'd expected, pristine shelves, vases, and cups arranged perfectly. A mix of impressionist, landscapes, and nautical paintings lined the white walls.

He paused in front of one of a fishing boat. A grizzled captain stood on its deck, blue and white clouds in the background, and seagulls flew overhead. He could almost imagine the man, and what it felt like, being on the open waters, wind at your back, looking out at a sun streaked horizon. The sea salt spray splashing his face, the horizon stretching to infinity.

"Take them to the back, please," Meghan said, her voice cutting through his thoughts.

"Sorry, got distracted," he grumbled, hauling the artwork through a back door and setting it down. He glanced around at the delicate pottery and expensive looking vases on shelves in the back room before heading back outside for another load.

As he passed through the gallery, a vase caught his eye. "You're really charging two hundred bucks for a vase?"

"Which one?" Meghan asked, her brow furrowed in concentration.

"The one with the rooster on it." He pointed to the vase with a black and red rooster on a brown painted vase.

"Oh, that's a Reynaldo Cruz," she explained, her voice softening. "He's well known in these parts. He has another one back there for two thousand." She pointed to the back room he'd just come out of. "It's on hold for a special buyer."

"Remind me to stay away from there, then," Tommy said with a nervous laugh.

He grabbed a large canvas from the truck and brought it in. Arlene was showing Meghan one of her drawings, a full length charcoal of their father standing at a fence, gazing out at the pasture, a couple of horses in the background.

"This is exquisite," Meghan said, her voice filled with admiration. "It looks like every whisker in his mustache is hand drawn."

"It is," Arlene said. She was happy someone had noticed the detail.

"He's the spitting image of Tom Selleck."

"That's what Mom says," Arlene replied, a hint of pride in her voice. "He was a handsome guy, for sure."

Meghan's gaze flickered toward Tommy, a playful smile tugging at her lips. "Now I see where your brother gets his good looks," she teased.

"Don't let him hear you say that," Arlene muttered, rolling her eyes. "It'll go straight to his head."

Tommy reappeared from the back, unable to resist a smirk. "Too late."

"Damn your supersonic hearing," Arlene grumbled. "And stay out of this. We're talking prices here."

"Well, if a vase goes for two hundred dollars, that picture of Dad should go for two thousand," Tommy said, flexing his negotiating skills.

"That is the asking price," Meghan said, her eyes twinkling with amusement. "Will you take offers?"

"Depends on the offer," Arlene replied, her voice firm.

Tommy's gaze locked with Meghan's for a moment. A spark of something, interest, challenge, maybe even a hint of attraction, passing between them. He tore his eyes away, feeling a warmth creep up his neck, and returned to the truck to grab more art.

As he returned to the shop with a large piece, his elbow clipped a shelf stacked with pottery. The shelf wobbled, and Tommy lunged to steady it, but instead sent it toppling. Dozens of plates and cups went crashing to the floor, the sound echoing through the gallery like a gunshot.

"Damn it! Ow!" Tommy shouted, falling and slicing his hand on a shard.

Meghan's voice rang out, sharp with panic. "Oh my God, my Reynaldos!"

Tommy sat on the ground, surrounded by shattered pottery, his hand bleeding. "I'm fine, by the way," he muttered, yanking out the shard.

Meghan rushed over, ignoring him as she inspected the broken pieces. "A year's worth of work," she said, her voice filled with despair. "Oh my God, he's going to kill me." She turned on him, eyes blazing. "What happened?!"

"I was moving artwork and bumped the shelf," Tommy explained, his voice tight with frustration. "It was an accident."

"An accident? Do you know how much this stuff is worth?"

"I'm fine, by the way," he said again, grabbing his hand with a shard of pottery lodged in his palm. He shook it, and it fell bloody to the ground. Broken pottery lay strewn about him, cups and plates chipped and smashed into pieces.

"To hell with your hand, this stuff is worth over four thousand dollars!" she cried.

"If it's worth so much, you shouldn't have had it out like that!" Tommy barked.

"You shouldn't have been bumbling around like some big, dumb, oaf!"

"Oaf ?!" he shouted, his temper flaring. "I said it was an accident. I'll pay for it!"

"Do you even have four thousand dollars?"

"I do, in fact! You want a check or cash?!"

Their faces were red, inches away from each other as they glared, neither backing down. The air crackled with tension, the scent of blood and anger filling the air.

"Alright, you two, break it up!" Arlene snapped, stepping between them. She turned to Meghan, her voice placating. "It was an accident. Megs, I'm so sorry. I'll pay for the damage."

"No," Meghan said sharply, eyes still locked on Tommy. "He pays."

"I'm sure you have insurance," Tommy grumbled, holding his bleeding palm and pulling a bandanna from his back pocket.

"They don't insure art, you moron!" Meghan shot back.

"Fine." Tommy dug into his back pocket, pulling out a thick wad of cash. "Here's a grand," he said, his voice tight with annoyance. "I'll give you the rest in a check."

Arlene blinked at the money. "What are you, carrying your life savings in your jeans?"

Tommy ignored her, his gaze still locked on Meghan. "Arlene, go get the checkbook," he said, his voice firm.

Arlene let out a heavy sigh, muttering to herself as she left the room. "Lord help me, I'm going to kill him."

For a moment, the room was silent except for Meghan's sharp breathing and Tommy's slow, deliberate movements as he crammed the cash into her hand. The tension lingered, electric and stubborn, until Meghan finally broke it.

"Let me see your hand," she said, her voice softening, disarming him.

Tommy frowned, but held out his injured palm. "It's nothing," he said, trying to brush it off. "Don't fuss."

"Don't fuss? You're bleeding all over my gallery," she said, exasperated. She tugged on his wrist. "Come on."

He allowed her to lead him to the small bathroom in the back. She rummaged through the first aid kit, pulling out gauze and antiseptic.

Tommy sat down on the closed toilet seat, his gaze wary. "I'm really sorry for the damage," he muttered again. "I got distracted by that fishing captain picture."

Meghan didn't answer right away. She turned on the sink, wet a cloth, and cleaned the cut on his hand. Her movements were gentle despite her frustration. "It's from Harold Carver," she said, her voice quiet. "He used to live on the Eastern Shore. He calls that one 'Eddie.'"

"It's a good piece," Tommy said, his gaze drawn to the painting. "I can almost see the movement." He watched as she took a gauze strip and placed it over his cut. "Sorry again," he mumbled. "I didn't mean to mess up your store. Not the best first impression, I guess."

"It's fine," she said after a beat, a small smile gracing her lips. "It just means I have to call Reynaldo, and he's an even bigger hothead than me."

"Let him talk to me," Tommy offered, his voice gruff but sincere. "I'll smooth it out with him."

Meghan glanced up at him, arching a brow. "You'll smooth it out?"

"Yeah." He gave her a lopsided grin. "I can be persuasive."

Her gaze lingered on his face for a moment, then dropped to his hand as she examined the gash. His palm was rough and calloused, a working man's hand. She frowned. "This is deep," she said, her voice laced with concern. "You'll need stitches."

"No, I won't," he said, trying to wave it off. "It'll be fine. I'll slap a Band Aid on it and get back to work."

"You are impossible," Meghan muttered, shaking her head as she wrapped his hand in gauze.

Tommy grunted, watching her close. "Like I said, I got distracted."

She froze for a beat, her cheeks flushing. "Oh."

Before either could say anything else, Arlene's voice rang out from the doorway. "Hey, I got the checkbook."

Both Tommy and Meghan looked up abruptly, the moment broken. Meghan stepped back, pulling her hands away as if burned.

"Hey, Sis," Tommy said, clearing his throat. "Write her a check for four thousand."

Meghan shook her head. "You already gave me a grand. It should be three."

"You patched me up," Tommy said with a smirk. "That's medical services. And it might be more than that," he added, his gaze lingering on hers. "We'll square up next time I see you."

"If there is a next time," Meghan shot back, lifting her chin.

"We'll see," Tommy replied, a faint smile playing on his lips. Why did he hope there would be a next time?

Arlene muttered something about stubborn fools as she scribbled the check and handed it to Meghan. "Thanks for understanding," she said, her voice laced with relief. "My brother is a bull sometimes. Again, I'm so sorry this happened."

Meghan looked at Tommy, eyes narrowed to slits. "Bull? That's putting it mildly."

Tommy stood, towering over her. "Do you need help cleaning up?" he asked, his voice softer now.

"No." Meghan sighed, shaking her head. "It gives me something to do," she said, her voice just above a whisper. "I may have overreacted." She glanced at the remaining intact pieces, a flicker of relief crossing her features. "But thanks for the offer."

Tommy nodded, shoving his bandaged hand in his pocket, , sending a tinge of momentary pain through his palm. "Again, sorry," he mumbled, the words catching in his throat.

Meghan met his gaze, her expression softer now. "It's just clay," she said, a hint of sadness in her voice. "I'll be fine in a few days." She turned to Arlene, her voice regaining its usual firmness. "Arlene, take him to the hospital, would you?"

Arlene raised her hands in mock surrender. "I'd rather jump out of a plane without a parachute," she said, her voice laced with playful dread.

Meghan blinked, her eyebrows furrowing in confusion. "I'm sorry, what?"

Arlene smirked. "You ever heard the story of the farmer going to the ER?" she asked, a mischievous glint in her eyes.

"No," Meghan said, bewildered.

Arlene's smirk widened. "They get the crash cart out when a farmer comes in on his own," she explained, "because he just said, 'I'm here, ain't I?'"

"Oh dear Lord," Meghan muttered, rolling her eyes.

"That's my brother in a nutshell," Arlene said, shaking her head. "He could get crushed by a barn and still get up to do chores." She turned to Tommy, her voice softening. "Come on, bro," she said. "Let's get you home. Mom'll patch you up." She turned back to Meghan, offering a quick explanation. "We've got everything we need at the farm."

"A doctor should really look at that palm, though," Meghan insisted, her brow furrowed with concern.

"Our mom's a nurse," Arlene explained. "She'll know what to do."

Meghan still looked skeptical, but nodded. "If you're sure."

"I'm sure," Arlene said, her voice firm. "Guy's strong as an ox. Doesn't feel pain."

"Why do I believe you?" Meghan said, her gaze shifting to Tommy with a playful smirk.

They said their goodbyes, and as they walked out to the truck, Tommy shook Meghan's hand one last time. She held it a second longer than necessary, her touch gentle despite the rough bandage. He felt a warmth spread through him, a strange mix of comfort and longing.

Tommy climbed into the truck, sneaking one last glance over his shoulder as Meghan disappeared into the gallery. He couldn't shake the image of her, her blond hair, her bright eyes, the way her jeans hugged her curves.

"Beast," Arlene muttered under her breath, a hint of amusement in her voice.

Tommy grinned. "That means she's the beauty, then," he said, a warmth spreading through his chest.

Arlene shot him a sidelong look as she buckled her seat-belt.

"Don't give me that look," he warned, her voice playful but firm. "I can see that look."

Arlene shook her head, muttering something unintelligible as they pulled away. She turned back to her brother, her expression softening. "You know, I appreciate your help," she said, "but next time try not to help me into a coma."

"I got distracted, that's all."

"By what?"

"The painting," he said, his gaze drifting toward the window. "The one of the ship captain."

"Sure it wasn't something in blue jeans and a tank top?" Arlene teased, a knowing smile playing on her lips.

"Never," he said, a little too quickly. "She's not my type."

Arlene chuckled, but stayed quiet. She knew what his type was, and it was standing in an art gallery miles behind them, cleaning up her brother's mess.

Tommy stared at the road ahead, feeling the dull sting in his palm. But the cut wasn't the only thing tingling, there was something else, lower and harder to ignore. A warmth that spread through his chest, a longing he couldn't quite explain.

Arlene broke the silence. "I hope my art does well."

"I'm sure it will," Tommy assured her. "There's a lot of great stuff there."

"It's good getting back into it, after all these years. You have no idea."

Tommy did have an idea. For the last twelve years, she'd been married to a guy who didn't appreciate what he had and left when things got too hard for him to deal with. He could still remember the day he'd picked her up from Joe's house, the hurt in her eyes after finding out about the affair. Some flooring customer. He could still punch that guy in the face.

"Awfully quiet, there," she said, her gaze intense.

His voice softened. "Just thinking, that's all." He smiled. "Glad you're here, doing what you love."

"You could put some of your carvings there, you know," Arlene said at last. "I'm sure Meghan could do something with them."

"Nobody wants that shit," he said. Scars of childhood words coming back to him.

"It looks like a turd," Ralphie Cousins had said. A ten-year-old putting down his first carving of a sea captain, much like the art in the shop they'd just left. Fucking show and tell. Never again.

He was silent about it for the rest of the trip home. When they got near the driveway, the green sign showed Two Bears Ranch in white block letters. Nearby was a small white cross, and as they pulled down the dirt and gravel drive, Tommy rapped his knuckles on the steering wheel, turned, and drove back home.

Chapter 2

Meghan

Bull? Hell, that man was a literal Minotaur. Broad shoulders, flannel shirt, and a lumberjack beard. He was everything she shouldn't like—but in Tommy Richards, all those things came wrapped in a package that made her sigh.

She knelt on the gallery floor, carefully gathering shards of pottery. Reynaldo Cruz would have her head when he found out what happened. He was temperamental and demanding, but he'd understand once she handed him the cash. Money usually fixes things. As much as the man was an Artiste, he would appreciate the cash regardless of how it came.

Still, the sight of all that shattered work made her stomach twist. Those shards represented more than broken clay. They represented time, months worth of labor. And to an artist, time was their most precious commodity.

Meghan sighed, dropping the shards into a small box. "Minotaur," she muttered to herself again. "A clumsy, infuriating Minotaur."

She finished cleaning, salvaged what she could, and put the wooden shelf back up. Thank god it was built well, otherwise, she'd have to buy a new one. When all was straightened and the remnants of Tommy's mishap were arranged, she realized it wasn't as bad as originally thought. She'd have to give Tommy and his sister some of the money back. "I'll have to wait 'til the show is over, though," she said.

She busied herself with Arlene's artwork, looking over every piece. She could tell that some of the paintings mimicked the Bob Ross style of landscapes, and they would go for a moderate price. But the ones of the father? She'd make those an exhibit of their own.

He must have been something. Because every painting and drawing of the man was detailed in a way that made him feel alive. Tall, white cowboy hat crooked on his dark-haired head, broad shoulders, rugged chin, black mustache, and deep, soulful eyes.

If Tommy shaved just to the mustache, he'd look just like his handsome father.

But Tommy was a slob. Unkempt. Rude.

Thomas Senior was probably nothing like that. How could two men look so similar but have such different lifestyles?

The rest of the day was spent tending to the few customers who came in to browse and buy mugs and small pieces. Meghan took the downtime between customers to price Arlene's work and store it in the back room.

If every piece sold for the prices she and Arlene agreed upon, the woman would walk away with over forty thousand dollars. But that was a big if.

At closing time, Meghan locked up and drove three blocks away to her apartment. She climbed the steps, unlocked the door, and changed clothes. She had to jog, cursing the extra few pounds around her hips that refused to go away.

Her phone rang. Unknown number. She almost let it go to voicemail but instinct told her to pick up.

"Hello? Galleria Fine Arts, this is Meghan."

There was a pause.

"Hello?" she said again. Great, another telemarketer.

Then, a voice she'd rather forget.

"Hey."

Her body went rigid. What the hell does he want?

"Hello, John," she said aloud, frost icing her tone.

"Hey," he hesitated. "It's good to hear your voice."

"I wish I could say the same."

"Don't be so mean. I just wanted to chat."

She cut straight to the point. "Is there a reason you're calling me out of the blue?"

"Geez," he laughed awkwardly. "Trying to be polite here."

"What do you need?" she asked, already exhausted.

"Who said I needed anything?"

Meghan rolled her eyes. She knew his games.

"Well, I assume it's not for money. Unless your movie bombed and you need to pay back investors."

"Stop being so pessimistic."

She exhaled sharply. "Then what is it?"

John hesitated before answering. "I was cast in a movie that's filming in Wilmington. Figured since I was in the area, maybe we could have dinner."

"A movie?" Meghan nearly laughed. "I thought you'd had enough of movies after that space epic tanked last year."

"It did well overseas," John countered. "This one's about a superhero named Diamond Girl. I play the handsome scientist who gives her superpowers but turns into the villain in the third act."

Perfect role for him.

"Where's the writer you've been shacking up with?" Meghan asked flatly. "Candace, wasn't it?"

"Yeah. She's back in the city. Working on a kids' show now."

Meghan smirked. "Cute."

"I figured I'd have some free time next week," John continued. "Maybe I could drive up, take you to lunch. You know, reminisce."

She barked out a laugh before she could stop herself.

"John," she said, straining to keep her voice level, "there is nothing I want less in this world than to sit across a table from you."

"Oh, come on," he groaned. "I just wanted to talk, you know, explain things. See how you were doing."

Meghan clenched her teeth. Ten years of marriage. Ten years of her putting up with his selfish bullshit. And the second she wasn't "red carpet ready" anymore? He'd replaced her.

"John," she out a hand to her face, exasperated. "I already heard you explain things. Any more would be talking to a wall."

"I've been working on myself. Doesn't that count for anything?"

"No," she said, voice flat. "It doesn't count for anything. And I'd appreciate it if you lost this number."

John sighed heavily. "Fine. I get it. You're still angry, but—"

She ended the call.

She ignored the three times he tried calling back and pounded down the steps to start the run.

The spring air was mild, and it would be hot soon, but her body burned with anger. It would take a couple of glasses of wine to cool her rage after the double dose of men she'd had to endure today. Running always helped her mood. She decided to go an extra two miles, hoping to rid her mind of the male species. That turned out to be impossible.

She came back in, and pulled out a half full bottle of Rose'. She poured it into a wine glass and drank three quick gulps

She heard her roommate Trina's voice—loud, frustrated, and already in mid-rant.

"Fucking people and their fucking tipping habits," Trina stormed in, tossing her purse onto the couch. "If one more person gives me fifty cents on a twenty dollar order, I'm going to scream. It's like these assholes are still in the fifties or something. 'Here's a quarter for your trouble, girly.'" She mocked an old man's voice.

Meghan smirked. Same old Trina.

Trina was a whirlwind of motion, flying around the small apartment, kicking off her shoes, peeling off her uniform shirt, and disappearing down the hall. A second later, her bra came sailing through the air, landing in a heap on the floor.

The door slammed behind her.

Meghan shook her head, sipped her wine.

A few minutes later, Trina reappeared, now in an old t-shirt and sweatpants, rubbing at her face. "God, I hope you had a better day than I did."

"Nope," Meghan held up her glass. "Started without you."

Trina grunted, grabbed a beer from the fridge, popped the tab, and chugged half of it in one gulp.

"There," she sighed, setting the can down. "Just caught up. So, tell me about your day. Because it had to be spectacular compared to mine."

"Not at all," Meghan said, swirling her wine. "And I don't want to talk about it."

Trina's eyes narrowed. "Oh, come on. I need to hear your drama before I launch into mine."

"I'd rather not. Let's just say I've had my share of men today."

Trina winced. "Oof. Okay, then I'll shut up."

She grabbed the remote, flipping through channels. Meghan finished her glass of wine and poured another.

"Another glass?" Trina arched an eyebrow. "That's rare." She went to the couch. "So who are the men?"

"John, and some other guy at the gallery." Meghan explained. "He called today. Before I went jogging."

Trina clicked her tongue. "John?"

"Said he's been working on himself. Like that'll ever happen." Meghan scoffed, taking another sip of wine. "And that he's in Wilmington for a stupid superhero movie."

"Oh shit, that's too close."

"Yeah, he asked me to lunch," Meghan mimicked his voice, high and reedy, "'Why don't we get together, reminisce?'" She sat down on the couch, "Men, boy can I pick 'em?"

"I hope you told him no."

"I hung up on him."

"Attagirl." Trina found a late night show she liked and hit play. The gray haired comedian started in about some Hollywood scandal and she tuned it out. "So what else?"

"No," Meghan leaned back, the wine loosening her tongue. "What about you? If it involves a man, maybe I'll feel better about mine."

"Oh, you know it does," Trina groaned, stretching out her legs. "So, you know Donny? The day cook?"

Meghan wrinkled her nose. "Yeah. He hit on you again?"

"Worse. Grabbed my ass during lunch. I slapped him so hard I think I rearranged his teeth."

Meghan winced. "Ugh."

"I wish Scrambles had an HR department." Trina scoffed. "Rob won't fire him. Donny's his best cook. I just wish for one day the asshole would keep his hands to himself."

Meghan's fingers tightened around her glass. Calloused hands. Strong grip. A farm boy who possessed them.

She swallowed, pushing the thought aside.

Trina tilted her head. "So who's the guy at the gallery?"

"Oh, some client's brother. He's clumsy and smelled like chicken shit. You know if you're going to come to a marble floored art gallery, least you could do is dress the part. "

"Men," Trina gulped. "So clueless."

"Tell me about it." Meghan looked out the window. If he cleaned up though, maybe there was something there.

Trina gave her a pointed look. "Meghan?"

She set her wine glass down and leaned back, then hesitated. Maybe it's not really worth talking about after all, she thought. "Nah, it's no big deal, I guess."

"Oh, just give me the fucking dirt already," Trina huffed. "Well?"

Fine. Maybe talking it out would help.

She sighed. "So, I'm helping a friend with an art show. Her stuff is really good, but her brother was helping and knocked over a vase."

"Shit."

"Yeah. Couple thousand dollars' worth."

Trina whistled. "Damn."

"So now I have to go tell Reynaldo tomorrow and give him the money."

"What's the guy look like?"

"Reynaldo?" Meghan smirked. "You interested? He's got a girlfriend. But knowing Reynaldo, that changes from day to day."

"No, the guy who broke the pottery."

Meghan paused, the memory flashing through her mind.

"A minotaur," she said finally. "Big. Tall. Dark hair. Strong hands."

"Is he hot?" Trina asked, reaching for her phone. "Give me his name. I'll look him up on Facebook."

Meghan laughed. "I doubt this guy has social media. He's a farmer."

Trina got a quizzical look on her face. She took a sip of beer. "Strong jaw?" she asked. "Gruff and hard headed?"

"Yeah," Meghan laughed. "But he had a bushy beard, like he hadn't shaved in a few days."

"How old is he?"

"I don't know, our age? Early forties?"

Trina paused mid-sip. "Huh."

Meghan narrowed her eyes. "What does 'huh' mean?"

Trina waved her hand. "Nothing. Just reminds me of a guy I dated a long time ago."

Meghan tilted her head. "Who?"

Trina said, "Tommy Richards."

Meghan went still. "...Oh."

"Yeah," Trina went tot he fridge, got another beer, and cracked it open. "Tall, dark, cute, farmer. Kinda clumsy. Huge asshole."

Meghan sipped her wine in silence. Fuck.

Trina squinted at her. "Meghan?"

"Yeah?"

"Was it Tommy?"

Meghan sighed, running a hand through her hair. Trina was going to press her for info so she may as well spill the tea.

"Yeah," she admitted. "It was."

Trina's jaw dropped. "Oh, fuck off! No. I forbid you to think about that asshole. Stop while you're ahead."

Meghan laughed. "Why?"

Trina slammed her beer down. "Oh, he's all charm, that one. 'Til he gets what he wants, then he turns into a cold-ass motherfucker. Leads you straight down Heartbreak Lane."

Meghan raised an eyebrow. "Been down that road, I gather?"

Trina exhaled. "Yep. And it's a road I wish had a 'Closed for Construction' sign over it."

She leaned forward, pointing a finger at Meghan. "He's broken more than a few hearts in this town, and I refuse to let yours be next. Me, my cousin Callie. And several others."

Meghan lifted her wine glass. "Well, you can rest easy. He's not my type. So don't worry."

Trina studied her. "Good. Just don't. 'Cause I don't want to pick up your heart after he shatters it."

Meghan rolled her eyes. "Fine. But it's not going to happen, so don't worry."

"Good. Make sure it doesn't."

Silence stretched between them as the late-night show droned on in the background. Then, out of nowhere, Meghan muttered—

"Still... he's got big hands. And you know what that means."

Trina whipped her head around. "Don't. You. Fucking. Dare."

Meghan smirked. "What? Just saying."

Trina shot her a warning glare.

"Don't."

"You still like the guy?"

"No. I don't. Listen it was just a fling. He took me to prom, and then he had to meet my grandfather Gideon. That was a mistake." She rolled her eyes.

"Oh no, you've told me about him before. Head of the family, right?" Meghan stretched back to when Trina first moved in with her several months ago, answering a Craigslist ad. They'd become fast friends.

"Yeah, my grandfather. I'm too exhausted to explain. It's just stupid southern men being stubborn southern men. The whole thing is ancient history, Tommy included."

"You'll have to regale me with your stories another time," Meghan grinned, drained the rest of her wine and stood. "And you know what they say, After all tomorrow's another day."

Trina smirked. "Okay, Scarlett." She pointed at her. "But remember—Tommy Richards? Trouble with a capital T."

Meghan grinned. "And that rhymes with P, and that stands for pool."

Trina snapped her fingers. "Exactly."

Meghan bent down, pressing a quick kiss to the top of Trina's head. "See you in the morning. I filled the pot—just hit the button."

"Bless you."

Meghan padded toward her bedroom, her mind still spinning with thoughts she shouldn't be having.

She shook the thought of big strong hands out of her head and drifted into sleep.

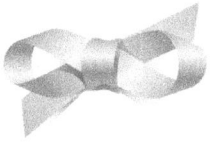

Chapter 3

Tommy

The old John Deere tractor engine groaned and sputtered to a halt. It sounded to Tommy like the death cry of a favorite animal.

"Shit!" he said. He looked up from the open casing and told George, the foreman of the farm, "Try it again."

"She ain't going anywhere, Tommy," the man said. He got down from the seat and looked around at the field they were just fertilizing. The earthy, pungent smell of fertilizer hung in the air, and it was a smell Tommy hated. It smelled like rotting meat in the summer, and the stink of it clung to his skin and clothes for weeks during the first part of the year.

But to his father, it was ambrosia. It was money. It was the best smell there ever was, and Thomas Senior could tell you where it came from like a sommelier with a fine wine.

Tommy said, "We'll have to walk back to the farm and get the tools." They were several hundred yards away from the house, and the white clapboard gleamed far away in the sun, with the red-roofed barn not far away.

"When are you going to put that thing out of its misery?" George asked, wiping his sweaty brow with a white bandanna. The spring sun was already past noon, and the heat had begun to bake them in the field. By two o'clock, the temperature would rise to above eighty. Nothing like summer, but they didn't want to be out here all day baking, trying to fix a forty-year-old tractor that had seen more than its fair share of seasons on Two Bears Farm.

"Just as soon as we have enough to buy one outright," Tommy answered. "I don't want to have to pay thousands of dollars every month." Especially if I don't need to, he thought. For years, Tommy had thought about giving up the farm, but it was his home, and his life. In another world, he'd be far away from the land, far gone from tractors, barns, horses, and harvests. But he was the son of Thomas Richards Senior, a man of the land, who'd been raised by his grandfather Old Tom to be a steward of the land. His father had embraced the lifestyle from day one. Tommy never did. And when his father had died three years ago, he was left the sole responsibility of the land, a job he'd never wanted in the first place.

"Let's go, then," George said. "You okay, buddy?"

"Yeah," Tommy answered. "Why?"

"You've been quiet a lot today, is all. Not your usual chatty self."

"I've got a lot to think about, that's all."

"Like what?" George and Tommy started walking back to the farm, their pace quickened by the pungent fertilizer smell. Neither of them wanted to be out in the middle of the field if they could help it. "I'm your best friend, spill it."

"Nah, you don't want to hear my troubles."

"We're going to be walking for the next fifteen minutes or so, we gotta fill the time, and I don't want to complain about my life, so go ahead."

"So you want me to complain. I see how it goes."

"Listen, for the last three days you've been quiet. Even when we were at the tonk the other night I noticed it. You usually go around and glad-hand everybody, but that night you were just drinking and looking off in the distance like your life was about to end."

"Oh, I wasn't," Tommy said ruefully. "I just got a lot on my mind. It's been a struggle the past few days, and I just had to pay out four thousand dollars for a dumb mistake, and then I got Arlene with this art show thing, and I'm going to have to be around rich people, and the kids, and Mom. It's all adding up, is all."

"Back up," George said, putting a hand on Tommy's arm. "Four thousand dollars, for what?"

"None of your business."

George laughed. "No, man, I gotta know. What did you pay for?"

"Some pottery," Tommy looked sheepish. "I messed up at this art gallery Arlene's got a show at. Knocked into a bunch of handmade cups and plates and it went all over the place. The lady was broken up about it, kept calling them her 'Reynaldo's', like it was some million-dollar designer or something."

"Oh, shit," George chuckled, then guffawed. "You? In an art gallery? Why didn't you stay in the car?"

"I had to help Arlene with her paintings. If she didn't paint these big canvases all the time it would have been easy. But here she was, talking to the chick, and I saw a painting and got distracted. That's all."

"So what did the chick look like?" George scoffed. "Because I know you didn't get distracted looking at no painting. Tommy Richards? Looking at a picture? No. More like you were looking at her."

"What makes you think I wouldn't like a pretty painting?"

"I've known you for twelve years. The only painting you'd ever look at is if it were a naked lady, like some of those Rembrandts or something in a museum," George explained. "So what did the girl look like?"

"I don't want to talk about it."

"Tom," George said. "We've got another ten minutes of walking, and I don't want to do it in silence. So tell me, what did she look like?"

"Fine." Tommy slowed his gait and started describing Meghan. "So she's a hotheaded bitch. I barely broke a half dozen things, and you'd'a thought I'd cracked up the world. She's got these blue eyes and pretty blond curly hair. And a dynamite figure. Like Marilyn Monroe or something."

"She sounds hot," George said. "She got big ones?" He mocked breasts in front of his chest.

"Stop it," Tommy grinned. "Yes. Not really though, I don't know, it just went with the whole package. She's cute. That's the best I can say."

"You gonna ask her out?"

"No, God no."

"Why not? I would."

"No," Tommy said. "Besides, she's not my type. And I'm definitely not hers."

"Why not? Doesn't hurt to ask."

"This one would hurt. I don't want to get my hopes up. She's doing business with my sister. And since Arlene's going through stuff of her own, I don't want to get involved with her business, so let it go."

"Still, though, you going to see her again?"

"Yeah, I got to help out at the show next week. Gotta serve canapés or some shit."

They were nearing the farm now, and the house rose from the horizon, bold and white.

"It's canapés," George said. "Appetizers, caramelized onions and little finger sandwiches, shit like that."

"How do you know what they serve at these things?" Tommy looked at the burly man in disbelief.

"I had a job working for a catering friend of mine one summer a long time ago. Had to walk around in a tuxedo and carry trays of ugly food to ugly rich people."

"Great. Exactly what I want to do—carry trays of food for art snobs."

"So get the girl alone and talk to her, ask her out."

"Not my type, remember?" Tommy said wistfully. "It's complicated. Besides, I like single life."

"Tommy, you're forty-two, you need to settle down eventually."

"Haven't found anyone to settle down with yet."

"So ask this girl out. You know what they say—opposites attract."

"She's no more attracted to me than the man in the moon."

"I don't know, what's the harm in asking?"

Tommy sighed. "You're going to be insistent on this, aren't you?"

"Yeah, and you want to know why?"

"Why?"

"The way you looked when you were describing her just now. Like a puppy dog. I've never seen you sound so mushy over a girl before."

"Because I've never talked to you about a girl, that's why," Tommy said. They had finally reached the farm and headed for the barn. The mid-spring sun beat down through the slats in the roof and highlighted dust motes in the large, cavernous space. The light coming from the open double doors illuminated the white Corvette, making it gleam in the sun.

"When are you going to fix that up? Or sell it?" George pointed at the vintage car.

"Ask my mom," he said. "I've been trying to get her to sell it for years. It's a classic, and she'd get a lot of money for it. But she refuses."

"I don't know why. She'd get a mint for it, and if you fix it up? Shit, the thing would go for thousands."

"Mom said no," Tommy said. "And you know how that goes."

"Unfortunately I do," George laughed.

Tommy went to the red toolbox in the corner of the barn's workbench space and started getting out wrenches, spark plugs, and other implements necessary for the tractor repair. He walked back to the entrance and said to George, "Let's drive back out there. I don't want to walk anymore, especially with you asking about my love life."

"Fine by me," George agreed. "But I'd ask her out, just sayin'."

The rest of the afternoon, Tommy and George did everything they could to get the old tractor running, and finally succeeded around five o'clock. They talked about college sports, girls, the tractor, the farm, family, and a host of other things. They got it running enough to get back to the barn, but several parts would need to be replaced before it would go a full day of planting or hauling fertilizer. But even during their chats about meaningless topics, Tommy found himself distracted by tight jeans, blond hair, and pretty blue eyes that seemed to light up like the beaches of Fiji.

Catherine fixed dinner that night, and Tommy noticed she was moving a bit slower as she prepared the hamburgers and oven-baked fries for the kids. There were a few times she'd coughed, and Tommy asked, "Mom, you okay?"

She waved a hand, put her Kleenex to her mouth to wipe away spittle, and said, "It's the pollen, son. Nothing to worry about. You know how I get this time of year."

"Okay," he said. "Just worry about you, is all."

She went to him, kissed him on the top of his head, and said, "I know, son. Don't worry, I'm fine."

"You'd tell us if you were sick, though, right?"

"Of course, baby." She turned back to the stove, put some cheese on the burgers in the cast iron skillet, and said, "Go get the kids, and knock on Arlene's door. Tell her dinner is ready, okay?"

"Got it." He'd been poring over the ledger for the farm, trying to do the math and make up for the debits and credits. Accounting was never his strong suit, but he tried anyway. Arlene and his mother had always had to come back later and fix his mistakes, but they let him try anyway, hoping it would come to him eventually.

He walked down the hall, hardwood creaking underfoot. There's something else, he thought. Going to have to get the flooring done one of these days, he thought. He sighed, went to the door to Arlene's room, and heard crying and muffled voices.

"Hey, Sis? You okay?" he called through the door.

"Yeah, bro," he heard his sister say. "Kind of a situation here."

"Don't tell him!" he heard his niece say, a sob in her voice.

He instantly went into protective uncle and older brother mode. He knocked.

"Don't tell me what?" His voice was a bit more gruff than he wanted to sound.

"Nothing, bro, don't worry about it," Arlene said, and he heard her stomp to the door. It opened slightly and he saw young Cathy, now thirteen, crying in a handkerchief.

"What's wrong? Is she hurt?" He wanted to barge through the door and find out who had hurt her, but Arlene put a hand on his chest and moved into the hallway. She smiled and pushed him back from the door.

"Chill out, Tommy. It's nothing," she said warmly. "She's just going through some girl stuff." She cocked her head, as if to think how much to tell a man. "Or woman stuff, now."

"I don't understand," he said, a question in his voice.

"She's started her monthlies," Arlene said, beaming. "She's scared. I'll have to go to the store with her, and we'll have to have the talk. Go get Mom for me, will you? The girl is practically inconsolable, she thinks she's dying."

"Oh," Tommy said. Shit. He remembered when his sister started that process—he was thirteen, and she cried for a week every day, and her temper got the better of her when he would ask her to do anything to help around the house. Welcome to teenager life, he mused.

"I'll be right back." He turned and went back down the hall to the kitchen. Catherine sat at the table, looking over the black ledger.

"You forgot to add the last parts charge from Bennet's, son," she said, not looking up.

"Can we talk about that later? Arlene needs you, and little Cathy too."

Catherine stood up, fear etched into her face. "What's wrong?"

He knew what the fear was about. Arlene had been sober for a few months, and they were both aware she could slip back into drinking at any moment. He put a hand on his mother's arm, smiled.

"No, it's nothing like that," he sighed. "The girl started her period. Thinks she's dying."

Before he could finish, Catherine had already sped halfway out of the kitchen, making a beeline for the hall and Arlene's room.

"There goes dinner," he mused. He went to the stove, turned off the gas under the frying pan, and sat back down at the table.

Joey came into the kitchen.

"Hey, Uncle Tommy," he said. The boy had taken to wearing a white cowboy hat, just like the one his grandfather had, but shaped for his eleven-year-old head. He took off the hat, remembering the rules about no hats in the house, and straightened his hair. "I thought I smelled hamburgers."

"You did," Tommy said, standing back up. He went to the pantry and got some buns off the shelf. "What do you want on them?"

"Where's Mom and Gramma?"

"They're in your mother's room, doing girl stuff with Cathy," Tommy explained, fixing his nephew a burger and putting it on a plate. He went to the oven, pulled out a pan of fries, and scraped them off with a spatula.

Joey put mustard and ketchup on his burger and started eating.

"What girl stuff?" he asked between mouthfuls.

"It's complicated," was all Tommy could say. "Let's just say your sister is going to be crying and moody for the next few weeks."

"Like she isn't already?" Joey joked.

"It's gonna be worse. Just be patient with her, would you?"

"Okay," Joey said, stuffing his mouth with fries.

"Whoa, cowboy, go easy there," Tommy told his nephew and handed him a napkin. "You got mustard on your cheek."

Joey wiped it off.

"Tommy?" he heard Arlene call to him. "We're going to the store." She came out of the room, Cathy behind her mother, her face blotchy from crying, with Catherine behind them both.

"You going too, Mom?" he asked.

"Yeah, moral support." She looked at the two younger women in her life. "I see you started dinner without us."

"Yeah, Joey was hungry. Famished by the looks of it." He looked at his nephew, who had already eaten one burger and dipped his fries in messy ketchup. "I'll clean up. You want us to wait?"

"We're getting something out," Catherine said. Arlene was already out the front door, walking toward her minivan, Cathy following close behind.

"Okay, I'll take care of things here," Tommy said.

"Thanks, son," Catherine sighed, then coughed again. "Damn pollen." She walked out the door, shutting it behind her.

Pollen my ass, Tommy thought.

Chapter 4

Meghan

Arlene sat on the couch, sorting through a stack of canvases, while Meghan stood by the display table, arranging a few pieces of pottery she planned to highlight in the gallery show.

"How's Cathy doing?" Meghan asked, glancing up.

Arlene sighed heavily, setting a canvas aside. "She's okay. But it's hard, you know? Being a teenager is tough enough without adding my mess on top of it."

Meghan gave her a sympathetic smile. "She'll get through it. She's a good kid."

Arlene nodded but didn't seem convinced. Meghan walked over and studied one of the paintings Arlene had set aside. It was a soft, moody landscape of a field at sunset.

"This one's beautiful," Meghan said.

"Thanks." Arlene tucked a loose strand of hair behind her ear. "It's one of my favorites. You think it'll sell?"

"If it doesn't, I'll buy it myself."

Arlene chuckled. "I wouldn't let you. But thanks."

She paused, then asked, "Tommy's still planning to help with the show."

Meghan rolled her eyes. "You're sure he knows what he's doing?"

Arlene smirked. "It's not rocket science, Meghan. He'll carry trays and hand out drinks. Even he can manage that. He's also still upset he destroyed half your shop and wants to make up for it."

Meghan tilted her head. "He doesn't have to do that."

Arlene said, "He's one of those guys that does something wrong to a person and spends years making it up to them." She thought for a second. "Unless you don't want him to be there."

"It's fine," Meghan said too quickly. "He can be there."

"You aren't crushing on my brother, are you?"

"No." Meghan said just as quickly. She turned back to the paintings.

"Come on," Arlene smirked. "You totally are."

"Not at all," Meghan said. "He's not my type."

"Why not?"

"He's big, brutish, and a klutz," Meghan said, ticking off the reasons on her fingers.

Arlene smirked. "Yeah, but he's got a heart of gold. Get underneath that gruff exterior, and he's one of the kindest men you'll ever meet."

"I don't want to get underneath that exterior," Meghan said firmly. "It's not going to happen."

Arlene raised an eyebrow. "You sure about that?"

"Yes." Meghan folded her arms. "I need someone intellectual. Someone who can talk about art and literature, who can quote Frost or Shakespeare. Not someone who's going to ramble on about corn futures all day."

The women burst into laughter.

"Fair enough," Arlene said. "But I still think you're wrong about him."

Meghan waved her off. "We'll agree to disagree."

Arlene set another canvas aside. "So, if everything goes right and we sell all this artwork like I'm hoping, you'll come out with quite a bit of cash. Not too shabby."

"You're really good, Arlene," Meghan said sincerely. "You could make a lot of money doing this full-time."

"Thanks," Arlene said softly. "It's been a passion of mine since I was a kid. I just wish I'd done more with it during my marriage instead of... you know."

"How's that going?" Meghan asked gently.

"Six months sober this Tuesday," Arlene said with a small smile. "I'll be getting my chip. Dana and Christa can't wait."

"Who are they?"

"Dana's my sponsor. She's been helping me through the process. She's also the one telling me not to date."

"Who even wants to date anymore?," Meghan said wryly.

"Right?" Arlene laughed. "Like Joe didn't kill my attraction to men."

"I feel the same way about John,. And that was three years ago," Meghan said. "Why are all asshole men named with a J?"

"It's a curse of the letter, I suppose," Arlene joked.

"Must be. I've dated a Justin, a Josh, and even a Jason. They were all assholes."

"You've got that right." Arleen stepped back to survey the paintings. "Do yourself a favor. Stay single. Enjoy your peace. God knows I am."

The women laughed again, their shared commiseration lightening the mood.

"So, I'll see you Thursday night to set everything up?" Meghan asked. "I've invited a lot of people I know who'll love your style. Sent some pictures of the Thomas Richards drawing, too. There might be a bidding war over it."

"Good," Arlene said. "The farm needs it right now. How did it go with Reynaldo?"

"All that fretting, and he didn't care," Meghan said with a smile. "He took the check, gave me half of it back, and laughed. He even said I should ask the klutz out on a date."

Arlene grinned. "And what did you say?"

"I told him no, I'd rather have a root canal. We laughed, and that was it. He's real chill about the whole thing. It helps that he has a girlfriend, and he's getting it on the regular."

"Lucky guy," Arlene said.

Thinking of guys, Meghan's thought. Her face flushed slightly as her mind wandered to calloused hands and strong arms. She shook her head. Focus, girl. Gallery, show, not the handsome farm boy.

"Does he have a nice suit?" Meghan asked, trying to steer the conversation back on track.

"A black one, yes," Arlene said. "I'll give him a nice tie and tell him to clean up. He might smell like fertilizer, though, so we'll have to do something about that."

"Yeah, please do," Meghan said with a laugh. "I don't need my guests smelling cow shit all night while they're eating finger sandwiches and drinking champagne."

"I'll do my best," Arlene promised.

They shared a warm smile before saying their goodbyes.

Chapter 5

Tommy

He stepped into the house, wet, sweaty, and exhausted. Arlene sat at the kitchen table—the same one their father had built years before she was even born. She was scrolling through her phone but looked up when she saw him enter.

"Hey, bro." She smirked. "Whatcha been up to?"

"Finished that tractor. Again." He yanked open the fridge, peering inside. "I swear it's held together with more baling wire and duct tape than actual parts at this point." He grabbed the almost empty pitcher of iced tea and held it up with a knowing look.

"Let me guess," he said flatly. "Joey's been here."

Arlene grinned, unapologetic. "You know how he loves Mom's iced tea. Says it's better than mine."

"Because yours comes from a can, and you have to add water."

"Hey," she defended, "when you've got kids who drink it like they've been stranded in the Sahara, you learn a few mom hacks."

Tommy poured the last pitiful amount into a glass and leaned against the counter, taking a sip. That's when he noticed the scattered paperwork—lists, menus, notes in Arlene's neat handwriting.

"What's all this?" he asked, nodding toward it.

Arlene sighed. "Meghan sent over the final menu for the opening tomorrow. I can't decide if I want caramelized onion crostini or cucumber finger sandwiches. Or maybe both?"

Tommy downed the rest of his meager portion of tea and turned for the stairs, hoping to escape before—

"So... you coming to the gallery to help?"

Fuck. Here we go.

"I'd rather have a root canal."

Arlene turned in her chair, raising an eyebrow. "Don't want to help your sister, huh?"

"I help my sister enough, thank you."

"Oh, come on," she coaxed. "It'll give you a chance to get out, meet people, build your people skills."

Tommy snorted. "Like I said—"

"Root canal. Yeah, yeah, I get it."

She tapped a fingernail against the table, pretending to consider something. Then, casually—"Meghan will be there."

Tommy froze mid-step. "Why do you think that'll change my mind?"

Arlene grinned, knowing she had him. "Just remembering what you said the other day. Thought she was cute, huh?"

"Whatever." He made for the stairs again.

"Probably be in a tight dress," she added as an afterthought.

He stopped on the first step.

Arlene hid her smile behind her hand. "You know, hugging all those curves."

He exhaled hard through his nose. Let it go. Go upstairs. Don't think about it. You have better things to do on a Friday night.

"I go dancing on Friday nights," he lied. "So, no. I can't make it."

"Okay." Arlene shrugged, then casually added, "But we were talking the other day, and Meghan asked about you."

He turned back around. "She did?"

"Yep. Asked if you were single."

Tommy narrowed his eyes. "She asked if I was single?"

"Mmhmm. I told her yeah, but that you don't date, so she let it go."

Tommy folded his arms, thinking.

Arlene grinned. Hook. Line. Sinker.

"So... what do I have to do?"

She feigned innocence. "Oh, nothing big. Just walk around, serve finger food, wear a nice suit."

"And she's going to be there?"

Arlene rolled her eyes. "Yes, Tommy. She owns the place. What did you think, she'd just open the doors and disappear?"

He scratched at his beard, glancing at the menu. The food looked fancy. "Why not just do chips and dip?"

Arlene scoffed. "Chips and dip? This isn't a college frat party. There's expensive wine, a violin trio, sophisticated guests—"

"Great," he deadpanned. "So I get to serve froufrou food to uptight art nerds in stuffed suits."

"So you'll help?"

Tommy eyed her suspiciously. "And Meghan's going to be there?"

Arlene smirked. "In a tight dress."

He sighed heavily, looking at the papers again.

"It's almost like you're trying to set me up," he told her.

"Nah." She smiled slyly. "Just need your help." She patted the seat next to her. "And... You do need to kind of make up for almost destroying her shop the other day."

Yeah. About that, he thought. He sighed.

"Fine." He dropped into the chair next from her. "Where do we start?"

Arlene's smile widened. Gotcha.

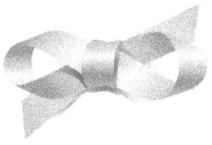

Chapter 6

Meghan

Tommy arrived in his black suit, beard neatly shaved, looking unexpectedly polished. His strong arms were evident under the fabric, and Meghan found herself momentarily distracted before she snapped back to the task at hand. She walked him through the setup of plates, drinks, and trays.

"All you need to do is go around the room and hand out hors d'oeuvres and drinks," she instructed.

"So, I'm a servant then?" Tommy quipped, raising an eyebrow.

"No, you're helping your sister."

"Okay, but still, a servant."

"Tommy, can you not be such a stubborn ass?"

"Who's a stubborn ass?"

She sighed, exasperated. "Do you want to do this or not? Because I don't have the patience or time to argue with you about it."

Arlene stepped in. "Tommy, chill out and do as you're asked."

"I just wanted to get under her skin, that's all."

"Don't," Arlene said firmly. "She's stressed out enough as it is."

"Okay, dim just playing around. Trying to lighten the tension," he said, raising his hands in surrender. Then, with a mischievous grin, he added. "Ready to serve the cans of peas."

"It's canapes," his sister corrected.

"I know," he smirked. "Just wanted to get under your skin, too."

"You're doing a great job of it," Arlene said, rolling her eyes. "Now behave."

"Best behavior," Tommy promised, a teasing glint in his eyes.

Meghan caught the way Arlene swallowed hard, her fingers wringing together as the first guests stepped inside.

She moved closer, slipping a steadying hand around her friend's back.

"How you holding up, kid?"

Arlene let out a choked laugh. "I need a drink." She exhaled. "This is more stressful than my divorce."

"It's okay," Meghan assured her. "You'll be fine. I've got herbal tea in the back if you need a breather."

Arlene shook her head. "No. I just—Jesus, I can't believe so many people showed up."

"Of course they did." Meghan gave her arm a squeeze. "They saw what you've done and wanted to experience it in person. You should be honored."

"I am." Arlene's voice was tight. "But this is too big."

Meghan turned to face her fully. "You're big. Get used to it."

Arlene let out a breath, like she was trying to absorb that truth.

"You're acting all calm," she muttered. "Me? I'm a bundle of nerves."

Meghan smirked. "You think I wasn't every time I had to walk a red carpet with John? Everybody gets stage jitters."

"You can keep them." Arlene's eyes flicked toward Tommy, who was wobbling under the weight of a champagne tray, jaw tight with focus as he tried not to soak the guests.

She chuckled. "Even he's got the shakes."

Meghan's smile grew. "I'll have to go see to him then. Maybe I should let him carry the appetizers instead."

"That may be a good idea." Arlene smiled for real this time, her shoulders relaxing slightly.

Meghan leaned in, voice dropping lower. "Listen to me—you're going to be okay. Your work is beautiful, and it will sell. But even if it doesn't, you've already won tonight. You're here, you're doing this, and you're surrounded by people who care about you. So take a breath, be charming, laugh at their stupid jokes, and trust me—you'll get through this."

Arlene inhaled slowly, nodding. "Okay," she murmured, though her voice still shook. Then she glanced toward the door, watching as more guests stepped inside—a blur of silk dresses, tailored suits, and champagne glasses.

"God," she whispered. "I should've worn something dressier."

Meghan gave her a once-over, taking in the red cocktail dress, the careful curls in her hair, the nervous way she held herself. Then, with a sigh, she said, "You look beautiful, Arlene. And don't let anyone tell you different."

"I wish I could believe you."

Meghan squeezed her forearm gently, her voice softening. "And if it gets too much, remember—your brother's here. Lean on him if you need to."

Arlene let out a breath, rolling her shoulders. "Not having a glass of champagne is making it worse," she admitted. "I normally would've had two drinks by now to take the edge off."

Meghan just smiled. "You don't need it."

Arlene exhaled, nodded. "God, I hope you're right."

Meghan walked beside her toward a group of patrons gathered around a portrait of her father.

"Here's the artist, folks," Meghan said, introducing her friend.

Arlene smiled, as gracious as she could manage, but Meghan felt the slight tremor in her movements.

She stepped a little closer, grounding her. "Arlene Richards, everyone."

A woman in a sleek navy dress studied the painting, tilting her head thoughtfully.

"This is charming," she said. "So delicate. So detailed."

Arlene swallowed, cheeks heating. "Thank you."

The woman turned to her. "The emotion in it is incredible. Is this based on someone in particular?"

For the first time that night, Arlene didn't hesitate.

She looked at the painting—really looked at it—and answered, "Yeah. My dad."

The gallery buzzed with soft conversation, the gentle clinking of champagne glasses punctuating the air. It was an elegant affair—polished, refined, the kind of event Meghan had spent half her life attending and the other half avoiding.

But tonight? Tonight was different.

She wasn't the center of attention. She wasn't here to promote a movie, charm the press, or play nice with people who smiled to her face and trashed her in the tabloids the next day. Tonight, she was just here. Supporting Arlene. Supporting Tommy.

Speaking of which—

Her lips twitched as she caught sight of him across the room.

Tommy was a bear in a suit.

He was moving through the space like a man twice his size, nearly tipping over glasses but catching them just before they spilled. Tugging at his collar like it was choking him. He was uncomfortable as hell—his body stiff, his eyes scanning the room like he was looking for the nearest escape hatch.

And Meghan?

She was enjoying every second of it.

God, this is the greatest show on earth.

She chuckled inwardly, watching him try to navigate this world that wasn't his. He was a fish out of water in a very big pond, and it secretly amused her to no end.

She had to admit, he was delicious in a suit.

The man cleaned up dangerously well. Gone was the scruffy beard from days ago. Now, clean-shaven, his sharp jawline on full display, he smelled like coconut and citrus. Fresh. Clean. Like home.

He caught her staring.

She smiled.

He smiled back.

And just as the warmth spread through her chest—

CRASH.

Well. Almost crash.

Tommy had turned directly into someone, nearly knocking them over.

"Oh, sorry, ma'am," he said quickly, steadying them both.

Trina stood in front of him, hands on her hips. Neither of them spoke.

Trina's eyes darkened, her posture stiffening. Her lips parted like she wanted to say something—then snapped shut.

"Trina," he said.

"Tommy," she nodded as she took a glass from his tray and stormed toward Meghan.

He watched her go, his expression a mix of confusion and exasperation.

Meghan smirked, shaking her head as Trina beelined straight for her.

And here we go.

Trina fumed. "He's here," Trina muttered under her breath, Taking a large swig of champagne.

Meghan blinked, shaking her head. "Who?"

Trina huffed, tilting her head toward Tommy. "Him."

Meghan bit back a laugh. "Trina, you do realize you're at his sister's showing, right?"

Trina glared. "Yes, but why him?"

Meghan just smiled. "Okay. Want to tell me what's got you wound tighter than a watch spring?"

Trina exhaled sharply, running a hand through her hair. "I don't know, alright? I just—I see him, and all I can think about is..." she trailed off, frustration evident. "Everything."

Meghan nodded, understanding. "Have you two actually talked?"

"He's helping his sister with the show."

"Whatever," she took another sip. "As long as he stays as far away from me as possible, I'll be okay."

Before Meghan could reply, a familiar voice cut in.

"Well, well, well—"

Both women turned.

Impeccably dressed, all smooth confidence, Reynaldo Cruz had arrived.

Meghan's lips turned to a mischievous smile.

Reynaldo's gaze flicked between them, sensing the tension. Then, smoothly, he extended his hand to Trina.

"You must be Trina," he said with a warm grin. "I've heard quite a bit about you."

Trina blinked at him, startled. "You have?"

"Of course." He gestured at Meghan. "This one talks about you all the time."

Trina shot Meghan a look.

Meghan sipped her champagne, saying, "Yes. Thought you two should meet."

Trina raised a brow. "Meet this one? I'm not desperate enough for that." But Meghan noticed Trina was taking him in a bit too much.

Reynaldo Cruz was tall, dark-haired, and a little too damn pretty for his own good. Dressed in a coal-black Armani suit that fit him like a second skin, an open white shirt with gold buttons, and a single red rose pinned to his lapel like he walked straight out of a goddamn romance novel.

He turned, and his smoldering dark eyes locked onto Trina's.

Oh, this is going to be fun, Meghan thought. She'd been trying to get these two together for a while now. And she would watch their first meeting with delight.

"Oh, mi amor," he purred, taking Trina's hand in his. He bowed slightly, lips brushing the back of her knuckles. "Pleased to meet you."

Meghan watched as Trina looked like she'd forgotten how to breathe.

Trina snapped back to reality, yanking her hand away like she'd just touched a hot stove. "Yeah, no. Don't do that."

"Do what, exactly?" Reynaldo's lips curled into a slow, knowing smile.

"That." She waved a hand in his general direction, as if that explained everything. "I'm not interested."

Liar, Meghan thought. She knew this is how Trina flirted. She noticed how her eyes widened at Reynaldo's soft touch.

Reynaldo's smirk deepened. "So, the mouse does not enjoy the game of the cat?" he murmured.

"Jesus," Trina narrowed her eyes. "I'm no mouse, Cruz."

"Ah." Reynaldo leaned in, voice dropping like a promise. "Then I shall have to find another name for you."

Trina turned to Meghan. "So this is the guy? The one who thinks he's got every woman eating out of his hand?"

Meghan grinned. "Yep."

Trina glanced back at Reynaldo. "Good luck rooster. Not happening. Move on to another one of your hens."

Meghan choked on her drink.

Reynaldo chuckled, unfazed. "Ah, you're my hen, then," His voice dropped into a wicked purr. " And I'm the one ready to fertilize the egg, huh, mi amor?"

Trina nearly inhaled her own spit.

Meghan lost it. Full-on cackling.

"You did NOT just say that," Trina glared at him.

"Oh, but I did," Reynaldo grinned, slow and cocky as hell.

Meghan could see the betrayal happening in real time.

Trina's brain? Absolutely not. Trina's face blushed and said, "I really need another drink."

Meghan noticed Trina's body shudder.

She did need another drink if she were going to talk to Reynaldo all night, which looked like it was going to happen. She could tell Trina's body was betraying her mind.

Reynaldo's fingers brushed Trina's as he took her hand and kissed it again. Trina didn't pull away this time. Smooth as hell.

"Ah, my hen needs a drink. I shall bring it to you," he said smoothly. Then, with a little cock-a-doodle-doo, he turned on his heel and walked away.

Trina stood there. Blinking. Processing. Malfunctioning.

Meghan was wheezing.

Trina turned to her, slow as hell. "What the fuck."

Meghan wiped a tear from her eye. "You are so screwed."

No. I'm not. He's cute, I'll give him that," Trina smiled. "As an arrow to the heart."

"Your Cupid returns, mon ami," Meghan said gleefully.

"Oh, please."

Minutes later, he was back.

Meghan watched him approach. There was a shift in the air, and warm Spanish hands pushed a new glass into Trina's hand. She blushed as his fingers grazed his. He nodded to her.

"I am sorry," he said, voice low, thick as sin.

Meghan arched a brow. Since when did Reynaldo Cruz apologize?

He turned to Meghan, nodding politely. "But I must leave you."

Then—the smirk.

"But I shall return to my hen a bit later," he continued, glancing back at Trina with pure, undiluted mischief. Reynaldo walked away, a satisfied smile on his face.

"I hate him," Trina said. Her face and the way she breathed rapidly betrayed her.

Meghan just laughed, "Really?"

"Yeah, he's an asshole."

"I have to go check on Arlene and the other guests," she said, eyes dancing with amusement. "You gonna be okay by yourself here?"

"I'm going to mingle."

Meghan smirked.

"Well, you may want to tear your eyes off the rooster while you're at it."

Trina's face darkened red. "Am not."

"Tell that lie to the paintings, maybe they'll believe you." Meghan teased her friend.

Trina swatted her playfully on the arm. "Stinker."

Meghan threaded through the crowd, expertly mingling and checking on everything. At one point, she stopped to chat with Derrick and Carrie, a pair of newlyweds. The two were looking at another painting of birds flying over a farmer's field. They were in conversation with a couple of other guests, a woman in a blue frock and an older gentleman in a grey suit that looked like he wanted to leave already.

"Remind me," Carrie teased Derrick. "Who chased who?"

Derrick flushed, embarrassed, which made everyone laugh. They had apparently told everyone about a half-naked man chasing Carrie down in the rain, trying to explain how a lingerie-clad woman from his long past had tried to destroy their relationship before it had even started.

As Meghan turned, she unexpectedly collided with Tommy, who was standing right behind her with a tray of champagne flutes. The glasses tipped over, spilling champagne all over her and clattering to the floor. Thankfully, they were plastic and didn't break, but the noise drew the attention of the crowd.

"Damn it, Tommy!" she hissed under her breath.

He crouched to pick up the fallen glasses at the same time she did, and they bumped heads.

"Oaf!" Meghan yelped, clutching her forehead. The crowd fell silent.

Derrick moved to Meghan, "You okay?"

Tommy said, "Sorry!" and rubbed his head as well. "Dammit!"

She only stared at him, stunned. Her head ached. She had to get out of her wet dress, or dry it off as quickly as she could. Without thinking and red-faced, she grabbed his arm and hauled him toward the back room.

"Shouldn't be right behind me!" she snapped as they entered the storeroom.

"I didn't know you were going to turn!" he shot back.

"You should watch where you're walking!"

"I got distracted!"

"By what?" she demanded, whirling around to face him.

He opened his mouth, then closed it, clearly unsure what to say. "I don't know," he mumbled, following her further into the room.

Arlene poked her head in. "Are you two quite finished?"

"Give me a minute," Meghan said through gritted teeth, glaring at Tommy.

He glared right back. She grabbed his arm and hauled him to the back room, anger shooting through flared nostrils. She turned to look at him, finger pointing up at his face.

She noticed he hadn't gotten any champagne on himself. "Perfect!" she cried.

"Listen, I didn't even want to be here tonight, but my sister talked me into it." He stepped to her, clean face red with heat.

"Well, you're free to go any time, farm boy!" Their faces were inches apart.

"Farm boy!" he said. "That's it, that's all you see me as, isn't it!"

She stopped. That was unfair of her. She waved her hands in the air and stepped away. She sputtered. "Just! Just...Let me clean this off."

He went to the table and waited. They were like two heavyweight boxers going to opposite sides of the ring.

Meghan dabbed at her dress, relieved the wet spots weren't noticeable against the black fabric. He took a calming breath and turned back.

"Sorry," he said. "It won't happen again."

"It's okay," she answered. "And I'm sorry I called you farm boy."

He tugged at his too tight collar. "If the shoe fits."

She paused, taking him in. She put a hand on his forearm, noticed it flex under her touch. "For what it's worth?" she smiled, trying to calm him down. "You look nice in a suit."

Tommy blushed. "Thanks."

She smoothed her hair, took a calming breath, and returned to the main room to mingle with the guests and answer questions.

She noticed Arlene in conversation with several people around a painting of the farm, and one younger woman with a goth hairstyle and chains as a belt, talking to Arlene excitedly about the composition. "It's amazing how the colors all work together. you have a real eye for the subtlety of nature."

Arlene just beamed and said, "Thanks."

The girl said, "You're a natural. Have you had study?"

"In college, for a bit. then life took over." Arlene said.

"Damn if i would let life take over if i was this talented. hell, i can't even draw a stick figure.

Meghan glanced over at Tommy, now holding a tray of hors deuvres. he was calmer now, but she noticed how he dwarfed most of the gallery patrons. He also moved more deftly around shelves of artwork, owing to his original sin of breaking her shop.

Trina and Reynaldo were in a corner all their own, flirting. apparently the two had formed some kind of peace treaty and were starting to get along well, from what she could tell with Reynaldo's hand on Trina's forearm and the girl laughing animatedly at something the handsome Spaniard had said.

Everything was going perfectly. she sighed, relaxing. it looked to be a successful night after all. many of the guests she had invited had shown up, and already people were putting bids into envelopes for the artwork on display.

That all changed when she noticed the door open and saw him.

Standing in the doorway, in a blue suit, trying to look dapper and smug as he always did, was John Masterson. Her ex-husband.

She shot him a look. He smiled, confident and warm, charming as always. She stood there, not knowing what to do. Her heart hammered in her chest, and the world went blank and almost dark.

As if this night couldn't get any worse. He walked to her, same old walk, same old charm. Blond hair, confident smile, and blue eyes that caught her in his trap to begin with. "Hey," he said. "Nice gig you got here."

"What are you doing here?" she stammered.

John smiled smoothly. "I was in the area and figured I'd stop by. You look good."

"What do you want, John?" Meghan snapped.

In LA, she'd tried so hard to be the dutiful, thin wife who looked perfect on her actor husband's arm. She'd struggled. Her body just didn't conform to his Hollywood ideal, always carrying a little extra weight. Divorce and stress had done what dieting couldn't—she'd lost the extra pounds over the last three years.

John seemed to sense he'd hit a nerve. "Sorry. Look, I just wanted to say hello. Maybe we can catch up after your show?" He stepped closer, reaching for a hug.

"Not a chance," she said. "I'm busy after."

"Busy with what?"

"Me," a deep voice said from behind her.

Meghan turned to see Tommy towering over both of them, tray in hand.

John raised an eyebrow. "Is that so?"

"Yes, it is," Meghan said, her voice shaky but firm. She took a deep breath. "John, this is Tommy, my boyfriend. Tommy, this is John, my ex-husband." God, she hoped Tommy would play along just this once. Tommy took the hint.

The two men shook hands, tension crackling in the air. Meghan noticed Tommy's grip linger a little too long, and John flinched slightly.

"Is this man bothering you, hon?" Tommy asked, kissing her cheek with deliberate ease.

Meghan straightened, her confidence bolstered. "No," she said firmly. "He was just leaving."

"Good," Tommy said. "Didn't see him on the guest list."

"Hon?" John asked with a disarming smile. "Listen, I just came to see my wife."

"She said ex," Tommy replied, his voice low and steady, his stance unyielding. "And yes, she's with me."

John's gaze flicked between them. Finally, he nodded. "Right. Well, it was nice seeing you, Meghan. Enjoy the rest of your evening."

As John walked out the door, Meghan let out a ragged breath and stormed back into the storeroom. Tommy followed her.

"Hey," he said softly.

She stood in the center of the room, her hands trembling. Without a word, she grabbed a glazed rooster cup from a shelf and hurled it against the wall. It shattered into pieces.

"Fuck him!" she yelled, her voice thick with anger. Tears streamed down her cheeks as she choked on a sob.

Tommy caught her as she reached for another cup, holding her wrist gently.

"Reynaldo, remember?" he teased softly.

"I don't give a fuck!" she shot back, but her anger wavered.

"If you're going to throw something, throw a punch at me," he said, lowering his face to hers.

Her breathing hitched, and she softened, her shoulders slumping. "I couldn't," she murmured. "Why would I?"

"You want to owe Reynaldo more money over him?" Tommy asked, nodding toward the main room.

Meghan sighed, her anger draining. "No, I don't."

"Okay," he said, stepping back, but not before placing a hand on her shoulder. "You gonna be alright?"

"I'll be fine. Just go smooth things over with Arlene, would you?"

Tommy nodded, leaving her to collect herself. The telltale sound of breaking pottery crashing against a wall came from the back room doors. Moments later, she walked out, her black dress smoothed, her flushed face wearing a determined smile. Reynaldo and Trina had come to see what had happened.

"I heard a crash," Trina said. "Are you okay?"

Reynaldo looked into the storeroom, looked back at her, and said, "You owe me another twenty dollars for the rooster cup."

"Put it on my tab," Meghan chuckled. "Between Tommy Richards and my ex-husband, I feel like I'll owe you a million dollars by the time this show is over."

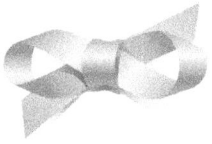

Chapter 7

Meghan

The smell of coffee lured Meghan from sleep.

Good thing I set the timer before bed, she thought groggily.

She groaned, rolling onto her side, blinking against the soft morning light filtering through the curtains. Her body was stiff, her head heavy—not quite a hangover, but definitely the dull ache of too much champagne, too little water.

Rookie mistake.

She stretched, winced, and then caught sight of the dark dress draped over the back of her vanity chair.

The dress that reeked of champagne.

Her eyes narrowed as the night rushed back.

Tommy Richards.

His clumsiness. His damn suit. The way he'd declared "She's with me," like he had some kind of claim.

Meghan sat up with a groan, raking a hand through her hair. "Jesus."

The front door creaked open.

She pushed herself out of bed and headed to the living room.

Trina was trying to sneak in. Hair rumpled, wearing the same dress she had on last night. Meghan smirked. Then smiled. Get it girl.

She stepped into the kitchen just as Trina drifted in—hair wild, dress slightly wrinkled, makeup smudged just enough to confirm a night very well spent.

Trina froze in the doorway.

Meghan crossed her arms, leaning against the counter. "Well, well, well."

Trina pointed a very serious finger at her. "Not a word."

Meghan's smirk widened. "That good, huh?"

Trina made a fatal mistake/ She hesitated. Then a blush formed on her cheeks. She exhaled a long, tortured sigh. "Yeah, wow."

Meghan gasped dramatically. "Oh my God."

"Can we not talk about me?" Trina grumbled, heading straight for the coffee pot.

Meghan grinned, following her. "No, no, let's absolutely talk about this. I thought you didn't like him."

Trina poured herself coffee with the kind of laser focus only reserved for avoiding humiliation. "I don't."

"Really?" Meghan arched a brow.

Trina avoided eye contact. "It was a one time thing. Let it go."

Meghan nearly vibrated with smug delight.

"How was it?" Meghan teased.

Trina closed her eyes, muttered something in Spanish, and took a long sip of coffee like it could wash away her sins. Then, still refusing to look at Meghan, she turned and glided toward her bedroom. "I need a shower," she muttered.

She reached the doorway, then paused.

And just before she shut the door, she added, almost to herself:

"That man is going to get me in a lot of trouble."

Click. The door shut.

Meghan cackled. "Good for you."

She poured and fixed herself coffee, taking a victorious sip before settling into a chair.

Then, she caught sight of her dress again.

The champagne stains. The wrinkles. The lingering scent of Tommy's skin when he got too close.

Her smile faded.

The night came back in waves.

The gallery. The way John just walked in like he still had any claim on her.

Tommy stepping in between them, all broad shoulders and firm words.

The champagne spilling, soaking her dress, soaking her skin.

Meghan sighed, rubbing her temples. She didn't have time for this. Didn't have time to be thinking about Tommy Richards and his damn protective streak.

She stood, taking her coffee with her, and made her way toward the bathroom. Just as she turned on the water, Trina's voice echoed in her head—smooth, knowing, smug as hell.

"He starts out hot, then gets like ice."

Meghan stopped cold. Her grip tightened on her mug.

A part of her didn't want to think about hot men, ice, or anything when it came close to men.

"Dammit," she muttered.

Then she stepped under the spray, letting the heat wash the thought of Tommy away. Or trying to.

And failing.

Chapter 8

Tommy

Tommy pulled into the Wildhorse parking lot Saturday night.

The old honky-tonk sat right off the highway, the kind of place everyone in town knew about—if they liked that sort of thing.

He parked his red King Ranch truck, shutting the door with a satisfying thud. It was still early. A few people were inside, probably unwinding from the week.

George was already here. Probably nursing a beer after a long shift. They had agreed to meet up—he wanted to hear all about last night.

The froufrou food. The art scene. The girl Tommy had his eyes on.

And how the hell he'd managed to spill champagne all over her.

Tommy strode into the place like he owned it. He didn't, but it felt like home.

Here, he could move his body the way he wanted. Let loose. Be free.

At the farm, he had to be solid. Right. Good. Perfect.

Here? He could just be.

Instead of being trapped in his thoughts all day.

Thoughts that always came back to Meghan.

Her soft blonde hair. The way she looked in that tight skirt.

Damn.

He bumped into someone.

Doing it again.

Mabel, built like a bulldog in an AC/DC shirt, looked up at him, arms crossed.

"Watch where you're going, Tommy." She smirked.

"Sorry, Mabel." He rubbed his neck. "Was just... lost in my head."

"Uh-oh."

"What's uh-oh?"

"You're thinking about a girl. I can always tell."

Shit.

Wait till Jolene found out. It'd be all over Newton's Crossing by morning.

He groaned and made his way to the bar, spotting George in his usual seat—gray work shirt, jeans, and a bottle of Bud in hand.

Jolene stood behind the counter, tall, cool, blonde, with a Dolly Parton haircut and a T-shirt that read What Would Dolly Do?

She arched a brow. "What'll it be, farm boy?"

Tommy thought about it.

"Just a Coke." he said, then paused. "Scratch that. Coke with whiskey."

Jolene smirked. "Jack and Coke, coming right up."

As she poured, she leaned in. "How's your sister?"

"Good," Tommy said. "Got a lot on her plate, but she's handling it."

"Still sober?"

"Six months in a few weeks."

Jolene nodded approvingly.

"Good for her." Then she narrowed her eyes.

Tommy said, "And if you ever see her in here trying to buy anything?"

"I'll throw her ass on the curb."

He smirked. "Damn right. Thanks, Jo."

"Anything for you, sonny boy."

She slid the glass in front of him.

Tommy took a sip—then sputtered, coughing.

"Damn, Jo. Is there any Coke in here at all?"

Jolene winked. "A splash."

He sighed. She always over-poured the liquor. One day, it'd probably get her in trouble. He considered what would happen if the alcohol inspector came in. The guy would have his hands full with Mabel for sure.

And no one messed with Mabel if they could help it. Tommy had seen her body-check guys like a pro wrestler before. One time, she threw Harry Wannamaker—three hundred pounds if he was an ounce—straight out the door without breaking a sweat.

An hour later, the place was packed.

The DJ played old Garth Brooks. The air smelled like spilled beer, sweat, and bad decisions.

Tommy had told George about the gallery show. About the champagne disaster.

George kept asking for pictures.

So Tommy pulled up Meghan's gallery website.

There she was. Perfect hair, white blouse, standing in front of her shop like she belonged on the cover of some fancy art magazine.

He scrolled. A Night With Sculptor Reynaldo Cruz.The Wit and Wisdom of Carver, Wine & Discussion With the Portrait Master Himself.

Yeah. He could just imagine the crowd at those things.

Wine snobs and people who think a splatter of paint on a canvas means something deep.

He might go to one. If he wasn't bone tired. And if he wanted to subject himself to being around people who used the word 'avant-garde.'

George leaned over his shoulder.

"That's her?" he whistled. "She's cute."

"Yeah." Tommy went to put his phone away.

Jolene said, "Let me see her."

Tommy reluctantly showed her Meghan's picture.

"Ooh, she's nice. Are you dating her?"

Tommy said, "No." An emphatic no.

Jolene said, "You ought to. She's nice."

"She's not my type. She's a stuffy, upscale city woman," he said.

"You don't give yourself enough credit," Jolene said. "Mabel, tell him how handsome he is."

Mabel looked. Tommy had a bit of a beard, and his hair was a mess. He smelled like the farm.

Jolene smiled. "Ugly as the day is long," she said, before returning to her customer. She gave him a beer and came back. "I wouldn't date him if he was the last man on earth."

Tommy nodded to Jolene. "See, a woman of taste."

Jolene smiled.

"Seriously, though? I'd be a lucky gal if that did it for me."

Jolene just looked at him with a smirk.

George said, "Don't look at me, I'm totally not into that." He pointed to a stage with a few young girls dancing. "But I am into that."

"Dude, they're all old enough to be your daughters," Tommy laughed.

"Old enough being the operative word," he joked. George, all of close to fifty-five, wouldn't know what to do with one of the twenty-somethings bopping on the dance floor to another Garth Brooks song if he had one in his trailer. And George knew it. All innocent flirting.

"What's she doing in town?"

Tommy hesitated for a second, then shrugged. "She divorced some rich, handsome TV actor three years ago."

George whistled. "No shit? Anyone I'd know?"

Tommy answered. "John Masterson."

"The action movie star?" George clapped Tommy on the back. "Stiff competition, buddy."

A thought struck him, hitting harder than he expected. *How the hell can I compare to that?*

John Masterson, wealthy actor. The kind of guy who had people fawning over him. The kind of man who knew which wine went with which overpriced meal. A man who was more at home on a sound stage than a honky tonk stage. And she'd been with him for ten years. She probably knew more about movie galas and red carpet affairs than a place with peanut shells on the floor and country music blaring. Yeah, her scene wasn't his. And it would more than likely stay that way.

That's what she goes for.

And here he was, smelling like farm and horse shit.

Tommy shut his phone and took a long sip of his drink, the burn settling in his chest.

Why would she even consider someone like him?

George didn't seem to notice Tommy's sudden shift in mood. He took another sip of his beer and gestured toward the dance floor.

"Why don't you go up and dance? Take your mind off the girl."

Tommy sighed, finished his drink, and stretched. "Good idea."

He stepped onto the dance floor, moving into the line dance, body finding the rhythm like second nature. He wrapped his hands around a willing partner, a tiny thing with sunshine-blonde hair, saw her blond hair and thought of another ray of sunshine falling through white locks.

And for a second he thought of Meghan. The way her jeans hugged her hips. How much he wanted to be holding her tight instead.

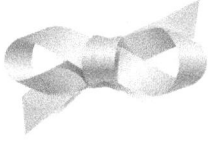

Chapter 9

Meghan

After the weekend, Meghan drove out to Two Bears Farm, the sun light stretching long shadows across the fields. She came to the green and yellow sign marking the lane to a white house and a red barn in the distance. She smiled as she turned, thinking what a difference this vista was from the cities and towns in which she'd lived most of her life.

She parked near the house, stepping out into the crisp air. The scent of earth and hay mixed with the distant smell of woodsmoke, and for a moment, she just stood there, letting it settle in her bones.

Today was a good day.

After everything—the stress, the nerves, the unexpected drama—Arlene's show had been a success. Pieces had sold, buyers had been impressed, and Meghan now had a check in her bag that she couldn't wait to hand over.

Arlene deserved to hear it in person.

Meghan smiled, adjusting her coat before heading up the steps. With a quick knock on the door, she braced herself for Arlene's reaction.

This was going to be fun.

Arlene came to the door, her expression a mix of curiosity and nerves. "Hey, stranger." She pulled the door open wider. "Come on in."

Meghan stepped inside, shrugging off the cool morning air as Arlene led her into the foyer.

"So, what's the good news?" Arlene asked, crossing her arms. "Your text just said, 'Can I come by? I have good news.' And then you didn't reply. I've been on edge all morning."

Meghan smirked. "We need to sit down. Actually, you need to sit down."

Arlene's brow furrowed. "That doesn't sound like good news."

Meghan just smiled, reaching into her bag. "So, some of your pieces sold."

Arlene sucked in a breath. "Wait. Really?"

Meghan nodded. "Not all of them, but a good deal. And your piece of your father? That was the biggest hit." She paused, savoring Arlene's reaction. "The buyer actually said it was like the man stared at her, and she was mesmerized by his beauty and charm."

Arlene blinked, a slow, emotional exhale escaping her lips. "That's exactly what I wanted it to do."

Meghan grinned. "Well, you succeeded."

Arlene fidgeted with the hem of her sweater, hesitant. "So... how much? A couple hundred?"

Meghan laughed, eyes sparkling. "Try a bit more, hon." She pulled an envelope from her bag and placed it in Arlene's hands.

Arlene swallowed, fingers tracing the flap, hesitant and nervous. Then, with a deep breath, she opened it, pulling out the check.

Her eyes scanned the numbers once.

Then again.

Then she looked at Meghan.

Then back at the check.

Her voice came out in a whisper. "Wait. What? No. This is too much."

Meghan's smile widened. "Yep. After my commission, that's the total."

Arlene's lips parted as she barely got the words out. "Twenty-two thousand, eight hundred and forty-one dollars."

She stared at the check like it might vanish. "Meghan, I—this is too much. I can't—"

Meghan shook her head. "You're good, darling. Very good. Welcome to your new career."

A slow, disbelieving breath left Arlene's lips before she reached for Meghan's hand, squeezing tight. "Oh my God." The relief, the gratitude, the sheer disbelief—all of it poured into those three words.

Then, suddenly, she let out a laugh—half a breath, half a sob—and pulled Meghan into a hug.

Meghan chuckled against her shoulder. "Told you it'd be okay."

When they pulled back, Meghan glanced around the cozy home, taking in the little details—soft lighting, handmade decor, the scent of cinnamon lingering in the air.

"Nice place you got here," she said. "Homey. Charming."

Arlene smiled, pride creeping into her voice. "Come on, let me give you the dime tour."

Meghan picked up the wooden cardinal, turning it over in her hands. The craftsmanship was exquisite—delicate yet sturdy, every feather painstakingly carved, the wings outstretched as if frozen mid-flight. The tiny claws gripped a perch, surrounded by leaves so finely painted they looked real. It was beautiful.

"Wow," she murmured. "Where did you get this?"

Arlene, flipping through receipts at the counter, barely glanced up. "That? Tommy made it."

Meghan blinked. "Tommy?" she repeated, startled.

Arlene smirked at her reaction. "Yeah. Since he was a kid. Started with sea captains, actually. We got one at a tourist shop in Wrightsville Beach when we were little. He got inspired, wanted to make one himself."

Meghan's eyes swept the shelf, her fingers still gently cradling the cardinal. "This is pretty far from a sea captain."

"He moved on to birds around twelve."

"Birds?" Meghan's gaze flickered over the room, suddenly noticing them everywhere. A blue jay perched on another shelf, its beady black eyes glinting in the soft kitchen light. Further down, a turtledove fed a pair of chicks in a nest, the eggshells around them painted so precisely they looked fragile enough to crack.

She stepped closer, mesmerized by the intricate carvings.

A voice cut through the moment. "What are you doing?"

She jumped, spinning around too quickly. Tommy was striding toward her, his expression sharp.

"Oh," she stammered, suddenly self-conscious. "I was just—"

In her haste to put the cardinal back, her fingers fumbled. The sculpture tumbled from her grasp.

"Hey!" Tommy lunged for it.

She gasped, reaching down to catch it at the same time. Their heads collided—hard. Stars burst in her vision. A sharp thunk sounded as the cardinal hit the floor. Meghan yelped, landing on her ass. Tommy grunted, dropping to his knees, one hand clutching his forehead.

A terrible cracking noise filled the silence.

The cardinal lay broken in pieces between them.

"Oh no," Meghan breathed, horrified. "Tommy, I—"

"What the hell were you doing touching my stuff?" His voice was harsh, angry.

Meghan's stomach clenched. "You startled me!" she shot back, her voice trembling.

Arlene stepped forward. "Tommy, it was an accident—"

"Stay out of it," he snapped."Get her some ice." Arlene went to the kitchen, knowing better than to question her brother when he was like this.

Meghan barely heard them. Her eyes stayed locked on the shattered cardinal, devastation welling in her chest. She knew what it meant to create something, to spend hours perfecting it, only to see it broken beyond repair.

Her throat tightened. "I'm so sorry," she whispered, tears stinging her eyes. "I'll pay for it—I'll—"

"Hey," Tommy said.

She barely registered his voice, her hands shaking. "Oh my God, I'm so sorry—"

"Hey," he said again, softer this time.

She looked up. He was staring at her, his anger already ebbing away.

She sniffled, swallowing her panic. "Please don't be mad."

He sighed and ran a hand through his hair. "I'm not mad." He reached for her, his large hands gripping her shoulders. "Are you hurt?"

She blinked. "What?"

He brushed his thumb over the side of her forehead, right where they'd collided. His touch was warm, calloused.

"You hit your head pretty hard," he murmured.

She let out a nervous laugh. "I think you took the worst of it." She hesitated, then reached up, her fingers grazing his forehead. "God, what are you made of, rock?"

He chuckled, the tension breaking. "I was about to ask you the same thing."

Arlene returned with an ice pack, handing it to Meghan.She pressed the towel-wrapped ice against her head, then frowned at his forehead. "You need one too."

Tommy smirked. "I've been hurt worse."

She shook her head. "Yeah, but you're still gonna—"

"Don't worry about it," he said easily. He rubbed the back of his neck, exhaling. "Are you sure you're okay?"

She nodded. "I'll live."

His gaze lingered on her for a beat too long. Then he turned, crouching to pick up the broken sculpture. Meghan winced at the sight of it in his hands. "Oh, Tommy, I'm really sorry."

He studied the pieces in his palm for a long moment. Then, to her surprise, he shrugged. "It's fine. I can fix it."

She gaped at him. "But it's in pieces."

He stood, already moving toward the kitchen. "Come on. I'll show you."

She frowned. "Show me what?"

He didn't answer. He just walked to a door near the pantry, opened it, and flicked on a light. A narrow staircase led downward. Meghan hesitated.

"Are you coming or not?" he asked, his voice gruff but teasing.

She rolled her eyes. "Lead the way, farm boy." She followed him down into the basement.

The space was small but neatly arranged. Shelves lined the walls, filled with wooden carvings—some finished, waiting to be painted, others still in progress. A workbench stood against the far wall, scattered with chisels, carving knives, and tiny paintbrushes. A stack of different wood types—oak, pine, and others she didn't recognize—sat in a basket nearby.

Her eyes widened as she took it all in. "Tommy..."

He set the broken cardinal on the worktable, already rummaging through a drawer for glue.

She stepped forward, running her fingers over a partially finished castle—a miniature fortress, its crenelated walls and towers so detailed it looked like it belonged in a fairy tale.

"This is exquisite."

He glanced up. "Thanks."

She wandered further, eyes sweeping over the room. "Look at you," she murmured, spotting a pair of lovebirds perched together, beaks touching in a delicate kiss. "An artist after all."

He scoffed. "It's not art. Just a hobby."

She turned to him. "This is art."

He held her gaze, his usual smirk absent. Picking up a small wooden figure, he turned it over in his hands. "This was my first one," he muttered.

She leaned in. A sea captain. His yellow coat and long gray beard were rudimentary, the strokes rough, but there was something there—the beginnings of talent, of care.

His expression darkened. "Meant to throw it away a long time ago."

She touched his arm. "Good thing you didn't."

His brows furrowed. "Why's that?"

She smiled softly. "Shows how far you've come."

His gaze flicked to the lovebirds, then back to her. "Yeah, I guess I have."

For a moment, neither of them spoke. They were standing too close now, the air between them thick with something unspoken. She could smell the wood, the lacquer, but beneath that—the scent of him. Warm, earthy, familiar.

His voice dropped, softer than she'd ever heard it. "Sorry I startled you."

"It's okay," she murmured.

He reached up, gently touching the side of her head where they'd collided. "You sure you're gonna be alright?"

She smirked, pressing the ice to her temple. "I'll survive."

He turned, leading her up the stairs. Just before they reached the top, she asked, "Why birds?"

His steps paused. Without looking back, he said simply, "Because they can fly away."

Meghan felt something shift inside her. Maybe Tommy Richards wanted to fly away, too.

Chapter 10

Meghan

She drove back to the house. It was a Friday, and more of Arlene's pieces had sold in the last week. The spring sun setting in the fields had her thinking of home for some reason. She didn't know why, but for some reason, she could get used to this simple life. A life with no worries. Rural, bucolic, filled with the sounds and smells of nature. She shook her head, wanting to get those thoughts out. She was here to deliver a check, then she would go home to more paperwork. She needed to think about the business, the gallery, not a guy in a tuxedo, strong arms, heavy-lidded eyes, and a penchant for clumsiness. If she kept running into Tommy Richards, she would have more bruises on her head than hair.

She parked her Mercedes, got out, and went to the door. She smoothed her dress, clutched her purse, and knocked. A few moments of silence went by, and then she heard a strong male voice say, "I'll get it!"

Tommy came to the door wearing tight blue jeans and a white cowboy shirt embroidered with gold and jade swirls along the shoulders, back, and neck. The top two buttons were undone, revealing just enough tanned skin to make Meghan pause.

She did a double take.

He was clean-shaven, smelling of Old Spice that lingered around him in a warm, masculine cloud. His white hat matched the crispness of his shirt, and the clop of his boots across the hardwood floor sent an unexpected shiver down her spine.

"Looking good, bro," Arlene said. "Why all dressed up?"

"Going to the WildHorse, like every Friday night," he replied, adjusting his cuffs. "Going dancing."

Meghan raised an eyebrow. "You dance?"

Tommy's gaze locked onto hers, challenge sparking in his dark eyes. "I do. You look surprised."

Arlene grinned. "He's a damn good dancer, Meg. You should come out and see for yourself."

Meghan crossed her arms, tilting her head. "I just might. It's not every day you see something so... unbelievable."

Tommy smirked. "Why is that so hard to believe? What makes you think I can't dance?"

"Momma told me to keep my mouth shut when I didn't have anything nice to say," Meghan replied sweetly. "So we'll leave it at that."

Arlene laughed. "Why don't you come with us?"

"And watch him fumble around a honky-tonk?" Meghan scoffed. "I'd sooner watch paint dry. Besides, I have paperwork to do."

Tommy rolled his eyes. "I don't need to hear any more insults tonight. I wouldn't want you to suffer through line dancing, anyway."

"Oh," Meghan said mockingly. "Line dancing? That paperwork is looking even more exciting now."

Arlene looped her arm through Meghan's. "No, girl. You're coming with us, even if I have to drag you. Don't make me suffer alone."

Meghan sighed dramatically. "Tell you what, farm boy, buy me a drink. At least make it a little more bearable, especially after all I've had to endure tonight."

"You've got yourself a deal, darlin'."

With the plan agreed, they headed out.

They drove out of town, down the highway, and turned onto the gravel road leading to The WildHorse Saloon. The parking lot was already packed outside the one-story building, a converted gentlemen's club that still bore faint traces of its previous life.

On the way, Arlene kept up a steady stream of chatter about the gallery show—mishaps, unexpected visitors—but Meghan's thoughts kept drifting back to Tommy. How surprisingly he'd defused the John situation. How, beneath all that rough-edged bravado, there was something else there.

And how the initial spark of attraction was starting to flare into something much more intense.

Inside the saloon, the atmosphere buzzed with energy. Tall tables lined one side, a long bar stretched across the other, and a multicolored disco ball cast flickering lights across the crowd. Country music blasted from the speakers—Waylon Jennings, Johnny Cash, and the unmistakable strains of The Devil Went Down to Georgia.

Meghan scanned the room.

Tommy was in his element, shaking hands, dipping his hat, greeting men and women alike. The men respected him.

The women?

They devoured him with their eyes.

Arlene shook her head. "I don't know how he does it. He's shy outside, but in here? He's the life of the party."

"Is he like this every Friday?" Meghan asked, a strange twinge settling in her chest as she watched the women watching him.

She suddenly felt out of place in her black silk shirt and slacks. "I should've worn a hat."

At the bar, two women tended to the patrons—one with a Dolly Parton hairstyle and a sparkly shirt, the other a towering brick house of a woman with a butch cut, tree-trunk arms, and a Guns N' Roses tee with the sleeves ripped off.

The butch-cut woman sauntered over. "What'll it be, ladies?"

Arlene ordered a Pepsi. The woman smirked. "Still on that, huh?"

"You know it," Arlene replied. "Almost six months, so I really shouldn't be here."

"The day I give you a drink, they'll have to kill me first," the woman said.

"You're a doll, Mabel," Arlene said.

Mabel turned to Meghan. "What about you?"

"How's your Long Island Iced Tea?"

"Stronger than a bull in rutting season."

"Perfect," Meghan said. "I'll need something strong if I'm going to watch Tommy dance."

Mabel snorted as she poured the drink. "Tommy's here? Where's my future ex-boyfriend?"

"Probably on the dance floor," Arlene said.

The Dolly Parton lookalike came to them. "She ain't drinking, is she?"

"No, Jolene," Mabel assured her. "Just a Pepsi."

"Good." Jolene nodded firmly. "We catch you slipping, sis, we'll throw you out."

Arlene smirked. "You think I'd waste six months in this dump?"

Jolene softened. "That's what I like to hear, honey." She pulled Arlene into a tight hug. "Proud of you."

"Now let's get you girls some front-row seats."

Jolene muscled them through the crowd—"Move it, Hoss!" and "Get out the way!"—until they were seated at a table overlooking the dance floor.

Meghan's breath hitched.

Tommy was dancing. And not just dancing. He was moving with a confidence and precision she hadn't thought possible, twirling a blonde woman in tight jeans and a tank top, spinning her effortlessly before pulling her back into a smooth two-step. His steps were perfectly in sync, his body fluid, his rhythm undeniable.

When the song ended, he clapped along with the crowd before seamlessly transitioning into line dancing.

Meghan's jaw tightened.

Tommy Richardson was good. Too good.

"You look like you've seen a ghost," Arlene teased.

Meghan snapped her mouth shut. "I should've worn a damn hat."

Tommy spotted them and sauntered over.

"Hey," he grinned. "What took you so long?"

Meghan crossed her arms. "We didn't speed like our lives depended on it."

Tommy tipped his hat. "You should've."

He turned to her, eyes gleaming with mischief. "How 'bout a dance?"

Meghan's stomach twisted. "Me?"

"Yeah, you." He extended a hand. "Come on."

Meghan hesitated, staring at his outstretched palm. The air between them thickened.

She took a sip of her drink. "I don't dance."

Tommy arched an eyebrow. "Don't dance? What kind of artist doesn't dance?"

Meghan smirked. "What kind of farmer does?"

Tommy laughed. "Touché, darlin'." He stepped back. "Suit yourself. But you're missing out."

Meghan watched him return to the floor, clapping along with the song.

Arlene leaned in, whispering, "Just wait. You'll be eating your words soon enough."

Meghan took another sip.

And, against all reason, she couldn't take her eyes off him.

Meghan nursed her drink, the ice clinking softly as she swirled it around. She watched as Tommy joined the dancers again, seamlessly slipping into place, his body moving with an ease that contradicted everything she'd assumed about him.

The song changed—something a little slower, sultrier. The kind of song that made couples pull close and let the music guide them.

Meghan didn't realize she was gripping the edge of the table until Arlene nudged her.

"You alright?"

"I—yeah," Meghan said, clearing her throat. "It's just... I didn't expect that."

Arlene smirked knowingly. "Told you."

Meghan took a deep breath and another sip of her drink. "You did."

The ice-cold liquid did nothing to cool the warmth creeping up her neck as she watched Tommy move, his jeans hugging every step, his shirt shifting over broad shoulders as he twirled his partner effortlessly. He tipped his hat at the blonde in his arms, and she laughed, touching his chest as they moved.

Meghan's stomach tightened.

What was this feeling?

She chalked it up to the Long Island Iced Tea.

Definitely the drink.

The song ended with a final twirl and a dip, and Tommy straightened with an easy smile, clapping along with the others. But then, as if he felt her watching, he turned his head and locked eyes with her.

The world around them seemed to fade for a moment.

Meghan swallowed hard.

Then, with the cocky smirk of a man who knew exactly what he was doing, Tommy touched the brim of his hat and stalked toward their table.

Arlene leaned over. "Oh, girl. You're in trouble now."

Meghan set down her drink, suddenly unsure what to do with her hands. "Shut up."

Tommy stopped in front of her, one hand resting easily on his belt buckle. His cheeks were flushed from dancing, his hair slightly damp at the edges. The Old Spice clung to him, mixing with the scent of warm skin and something unmistakably him.

"So," he drawled, his voice low and teasing. "Still think I don't know what I'm doing?"

Meghan lifted her chin. "You get one point, farm boy."

He grinned. "Oh? Out of how many?"

She crossed her legs, feigning indifference. "Jury's still out."

His smile deepened, and for a moment, she thought he was going to lean in closer. Instead, he tapped the table.

"Well, when the jury makes up its mind, you know where to find me."

He turned and walked back to the bar, tipping his hat to a few people along the way.

Meghan exhaled the breath she hadn't realized she was holding.

Arlene burst into laughter.

"Oh my God, girl," she cackled. "You are so gone."

Meghan shot her a glare. "Shut. Up."

Arlene only grinned wider. "I'm just saying, for someone who claims to hate my brother, you sure do watch him a lot."

Meghan huffed, tossing back the rest of her drink. "It's just surprising, that's all. I didn't peg him for a dancer."

"You didn't peg him for a lot of things," Arlene said, sipping her Pepsi. "Guess you'll have to start reevaluating that little opinion of yours."

Meghan rolled her eyes, but she couldn't deny it.

Tommy Richards wasn't at all what she thought he was.

And that realization was dangerous.

Meghan ended up having two more Long Island Iced Teas.

Which, in hindsight, was probably a mistake.

Because by the time Tommy returned to their table, flushed from another round of dancing, Meghan was feeling very warm, very bold, and very much in the mood to make poor life choices.

"You ready to admit it yet?" Tommy asked, reaching for Arlene's Pepsi again.

Meghan blinked at him. "Admit what?"

"That I'm a damn good dancer."

She tilted her head, pretending to consider it.

"I'll give you a solid seven."

Tommy laughed. "You really are something else, you know that?"

Meghan smirked. "I've been told."

Arlene stood suddenly. "Well, I gotta go. Dana's waiting on me."

Meghan frowned. "You're leaving?"

"Yup," Arlene said, grabbing her purse. "And since I highly doubt you should be driving, looks like my brother's taking you home."

Tommy sighed. "You owe me, Arlene."

Arlene patted his cheek. "I owe you plenty." She winked at Meghan. "Y'all have fun."

Meghan watched her go, then turned back to Tommy. "So."

"So," Tommy echoed, smirking.

She reached out and tapped his chest. "You're real pretty, you know that?"

He arched an eyebrow. "You're drunk."

"Yeah," she admitted. "But it's still true."

Tommy sighed. "Come on, sweetheart. Let's get you home."

The drive back to her place was a blur.

She vaguely remembered leaning against the window, humming to herself as Tommy drove, his hands steady on the wheel, his focus straight ahead. She found herself looking at his forearms, strong, hard, his long fingers tightened around the steering wheel.

"Why so quiet?" she slurred.

"I have a lot on my mind," he said.

"Like what?" she teased. "Me?"

"As if," he fell silent for a few seconds. Then explained. "Arlene, the kids, mom, the farm. A whole lot of stuff you wouldn't want to hear about."

"Try me."

"How about I don't." He stayed silent the rest of the way.

When they reached her apartment, they sat in silence. Her head swam, and she looked over at tommy, seeing two of him. Two handsome faces peering back at her asking if she was okay. She went to kiss him, and he pushed her away.

"Not like this," he said.

She crossed her arms. Pouting she said, "Why not?"

"You're drunk, Meghan," he told her. A red blush of anger passed through her face as she reached for the door. It was locked.

He got out first, coming around to open her door.

"I can do it myself," she muttered, fumbling with the handle.

The door swung open, and she fell into his arms.

Tommy caught her easily, his hands firm around her waist. She looked up at him, blinking in the dim streetlight. She felt the anger go away the second she looked into his eyes.

"God, you're so good-looking," she murmured.

Tommy chuckled. "That's the drink talking."

She reached up, tracing her fingers along his jaw. "You should let me kiss you."

His smile faded. "No."

"You want to," she whispered, her breath warm against his skin. "I know you do."

Tommy swallowed hard.

Then, gently, he pried her hands away.

"Not like this," he said softly.

Meghan frowned. "Why not?"

"Because I don't kiss drunk girls. I don't want to take advantage of you."

She scowled. "What if I want you to take advantage of me?"

His jaw tightened. "Even if you did, I couldn't. It wouldn't be right."

Meghan groaned, stepping back unsteadily. "God, why do you have to be so good?"

Tommy chuckled, shaking his head. "Come on, let's get you inside."

He helped her up the steps, keeping a firm grip on her arm. She fumbled for her keys, finally unlocking the door and stepping inside.

She turned back to him, lips parted. "You sure you don't wanna come in?"

Tommy leaned against the doorframe, looking at her for a long moment.

Then he reached out, cupped her cheek briefly, and whispered, "Another time."

Meghan sighed. "Always so good."

"Goodnight, Meghan."

And with that, he turned and walked away, disappearing into the night.she listened to the rumble of his truck speed off down the street.

Meghan stood there, watching him go, her heart pounding.

Damn him.

Damn that stupid, stupid farm boy.

Because she suddenly realized—

She really wanted to kiss him.

Chapter 11

Tommy

He was twelve again, digging a trench line for the green army men in front of the house. Darkness was creeping in, and the sun hung just above the horizon, that brief moment when the sky burned its brightest before slipping into night.

Sergeant Rock was ordering Ice Cream Soldier to set up an ambush against the gray plastic Germans in the trenches across from them. Yellow and red Legos formed pillboxes and ruins in the no-man's-land between the rival armies.

Maggie Grace, twelve years old—same as him—stepped out of the house, her bike propped against the porch. She watched him for a moment before asking, "Why do boys like playing army so much?"

Her blonde hair caught the last bit of light, a slick of pink gloss on her lips, freckles scattered across her nose like cinnamon. When she smiled, a dimple carved into her cheek, deep and perfect.

Something inside him, an unformed, instinctual whisper, told him he should like her. He just didn't.

Girls were... important, he knew that. But the only female lips he'd ever known belonged to his grandmother, papery and scented of peppermint.

"We should be friends, shouldn't we?" she asked, voice bright.

"I don't know," he mumbled, kicking at a loose pebble. "You're friends with my sister, aren't you? Do you need more?"

"No," she said, a flicker of confusion crossing her face. "I mean, like... boys and girls can be friends."

"I don't have any girl friends," he retorted.

Her smile faltered. "Your mom and dad are friends."

"Yeah, but that's different," he insisted.

"Well, that's how married people start."

"Who wants to get married?" He scoffed. "I don't want to get married."

"So you don't want to be friends? Not with a girl?" The light in her eyes dimmed. "So... you don't want to kiss me?"

Her fingers curled around the banana seat of her bright blue bike, her knuckles white.

"No," he said, the word sharp. Final.

She hesitated, lips pressing together, then whispered, "Your loss." There was something sad in her voice—something he didn't understand.

"Well, see you tomorrow," she said, swinging a leg over her bike. "Maybe then you'll change your mind."

And then she was gone, pedaling fast down the dirt track, a cloud of dust and pebbles swirling in her wake.

He hadn't thought much about it.

Not until the screech of tires tore through the quiet afternoon.

His head snapped up, eyes widening.

A crash. The crunch of metal, a sickening grind.

Then what felt like a longer than normal silence.

For half a second, everything was still.

And then, the screams.

A woman's wail was a raw desolate, and desperate cry. It was a sound that burrowed into his bones and would never leave as long as he lived.

He ran. Feet pounding against the dirt, lungs burning. The road stretched in front of him, too far, too far—

He saw her.

Maggie Grace lay crumpled across the hood of a black Trans Am. The windshield was shattered, caved in where her head had hit.

Her Huffy bike lay twisted on the asphalt, its frame bent in ways it shouldn't be.

A dark-haired teenage girl sat in the passenger seat, gripping her head, her body wracked with sobs—gut-wrenching, broken sobs of shock and anguish.

And the blood.

God.

So much blood.

It bloomed in thick pools around the tires, mixing with the dust, clotting the dirt road beneath it.

The woman's cries—those terrible, heart-shattering cries—echoed in the silence.

Tommy woke with a jolt.

His shirt clung to him, damp with sweat, his chest heaving, heart hammering against his ribs.

His fingers curled into the sheets, shaking. His breath came hard, frantic, like he was still running, still trying to get there in time.

His throat was dry.

His mind ached.

"Why didn't I kiss her?" he whispered into the darkness.

"Why didn't I fucking kiss her?"

The words sat there, heavy and unanswered.

A question without an answer.

A torment that never left.

Then, the thought struck him.

Why hadn't it come to him before?

He would carve her.

Not like his birds, not like anything he'd done before. This wasn't for show, wasn't for sale. It was a memorial, a quiet tribute. A way to remember, to honor, to acknowledge.

A piece of her, set in wood.

Maybe then, the dreams would stop. Maybe then, the weight in his chest would ease.

Maybe then, he could let go.

It was time.

And carving her was the only way he knew how. The only way he could set the nightmares of that day to rest after so many years.

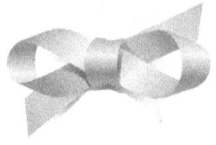

Chapter 12

Tommy

MORNING LIGHT POURED through the kitchen window, stretching long across the farmhouse table. He ate another fork full of eggs, thinking of an almost kiss with a drunken blond. Across from him, Arlene was smirking like she had a secret she couldn't wait to spill.

"So," she said, stirring sugar into her coffee, "you and Meghan."

Tommy shot her a flat look. "What about me and Meghan?"

Arlene leaned her chin on her hand. "You like her."

He snorted. "Yeah, like that'll ever happen. She's way out of my league, so stop trying to make that a thing."

Arlene's smirk deepened. "A thing I could get behind. She's nice. And you didn't see her eye fucking you last night, like a a perfect steak to a starving man."

He scoffed. "She was drunk, sis. Besides, you just want a sister-in-law you can take on girls' trips."

"Yeah, what's wrong with that?" She shrugged. "I need a friend."

Tommy shook his head, shoving another bite of eggs into his mouth. He was not having this conversation. "So be her friend. I've got too much work to do around here without adding a woman to the mix."

Arlene pressed on, undeterred. "You do too. It's been too long since Callie. And bro... you need to get laid."

Tommy nearly choked on his coffee. He wiped his mouth, glaring at her. "Jesus, Arlene, can we not do this at breakfast?" He flicked a glance toward their mother.

Catherine, unfazed, sipped her coffee, her expression unreadable. "Sister's got a point, though."

Tommy groaned and looked at his mother. "Not you too."

Catherine simply raised an eyebrow. "All I'm saying is, you remind me of your father. He was a stoic too, you know."

Arlene grinned. "Oh, here we go."

Catherine ignored her. "Remember how tight-lipped he was about how we met?"

Tommy gave a half-shrug, poking at his eggs. "Yeah. He always played it off like it was no big deal. Told us you were the big city girl he wasn't looking for."

Catherine smirked. "Because he didn't want you kids knowing that I wasn't convinced at first. There was a spark, sure, but he smelled like farm, and I was a city girl. Thought we had nothing in common."

Tommy looked up, mildly curious despite himself. "What changed?"

Catherine set her cup down, meeting his eyes. "I learned to appreciate that smell after a few months. The same way I learned to appreciate your father." A small smile tugged at her lips. "Give the girl a chance, son. You may not be out of her league after all. I'm sure your dad felt the same way about me."

Silence stretched for a moment. He considered his parents for a second. His father, a farm boy, his mother, fresh out of college in DC.

Meghan's soft blue eyes and blond hair in the golden sun pushed into the forefront of his brain.

Tommy shifted in his chair, thinking about their first disastrous meeting. Broken pottery and angry words. Then he thought about how she held his hand, putting the bandage on it, looking him in the eyes. Her soft expression of caring. "Yeah, well... I wouldn't count on it."

Catherine just hummed knowingly, standing to take her mug to the sink. Arlene nudged him under the table.

"Maybe she's right," she said, her voice teasing but thoughtful. "Maybe Meghan's your city girl."

Tommy rolled his eyes, but deep down, the thought lingered.

Was he really that out of her league? Or had he just convinced himself of it before even trying? What would it hurt to try? Worst thing she could say was no. But deep down, hoping maybe she would say yes.

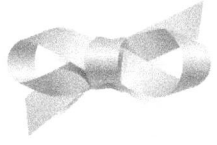

Chapter 13

Tommy

MORNING LIGHT POURED through the kitchen window, stretching long across the farmhouse table. He ate another fork full of eggs, thinking of an almost kiss with a drunken blond. Across from him, Arlene was smirking like she had a secret she couldn't wait to spill.

"So," she said, stirring sugar into her coffee, "you and Meghan."

Tommy shot her a flat look. "What about me and Meghan?"

Arlene leaned her chin on her hand. "You like her."

He snorted. "Yeah, like that'll ever happen. She's way out of my league, so stop trying to make that a thing."

Arlene's smirk deepened. "A thing I could get behind. She's nice. And you didn't see her eye fucking you last night, like a a perfect steak to a starving man."

He scoffed. "She was drunk, sis. Besides, you just want a sister-in-law you can take on girls' trips."

"Yeah, what's wrong with that?" She shrugged. "I need a friend."

Tommy shook his head, shoving another bite of eggs into his mouth. He was not having this conversation. "So be her friend. I've got too much work to do around here without adding a woman to the mix."

Arlene pressed on, undeterred. "You do too. It's been too long since Callie. And bro... you need to get laid."

Tommy nearly choked on his coffee. He wiped his mouth, glaring at her. "Jesus, Arlene, can we not do this at breakfast?" He flicked a glance toward their mother.

Catherine, unfazed, sipped her coffee, her expression unreadable. "Sister's got a point, though."

Tommy groaned and looked at his mother. "Not you too."

Catherine simply raised an eyebrow. "All I'm saying is, you remind me of your father. He was a stoic too, you know."

Arlene grinned. "Oh, here we go."

Catherine ignored her. "Remember how tight-lipped he was about how we met?"

Tommy gave a half-shrug, poking at his eggs. "Yeah. He always played it off like it was no big deal. Told us you were the big city girl he wasn't looking for."

Catherine smirked. "Because he didn't want you kids knowing that I wasn't convinced at first. There was a spark, sure, but he smelled like farm, and I was a city girl. Thought we had nothing in common."

Tommy looked up, mildly curious despite himself. "What changed?"

Catherine set her cup down, meeting his eyes. "I learned to appreciate that smell after a few months. The same way I learned to appreciate your father." A small smile tugged at her lips. "Give the girl a chance, son. You may not be out of her league after all. I'm sure your dad felt the same way about me."

Silence stretched for a moment. He considered his parents for a second. His father, a farm boy, his mother, fresh out of college in DC.

Meghan's soft blue eyes and blond hair in the golden sun pushed into the forefront of his brain.

Tommy shifted in his chair, thinking about their first disastrous meeting. Broken pottery and angry words. Then he thought about how she held his hand, putting the bandage on it, looking him in the eyes. Her soft expression of caring. "Yeah, well... I wouldn't count on it."

Catherine just hummed knowingly, standing to take her mug to the sink. Arlene nudged him under the table.

"Maybe she's right," she said, her voice teasing but thoughtful. "Maybe Meghan's your city girl."

Tommy rolled his eyes, but deep down, the thought lingered.

Was he really that out of her league? Or had he just convinced himself of it before even trying? What would it hurt to try? Worst thing she could say was no. But deep down, hoping maybe she would say yes.

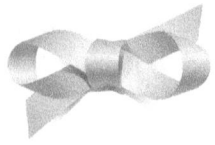

Chapter 14

Meghan

Meghan groaned as she shuffled into the kitchen, her head pounding like a bass drum. She ran a hand through her tangled hair, grimacing at the taste of stale liquor on her tongue. Coffee. Now.

She set the machine to brew, leaning heavily against the counter while she waited. The smell of rich, dark roast filled the air, offering a sliver of salvation. She rubbed her temples, then it hit her.

Oh. Oh, shit.

Her hand froze on the coffee pot, heart thudding in her chest.

Did I almost kiss Tommy last night?

Shit.

What was she thinking?

Her coffee finished brewing, but suddenly, caffeine wasn't going to be enough. She needed answers—confirmation that she hadn't made a complete fool of herself.

Trina bustled into the kitchen, already dressed, "Mmm-hmm," she hummed, giving Meghan a once-over. "I know that look. Somebody's got a hangover."

Meghan winced. "What gave it away?"

"The way you're clutching that coffee like it's holy water." Trina smirked.

She barely had time to recover before Trina started pulling things from the fridge.

"Eggs. Bacon. Toast. Coffee. I'll get you started. Go take a shower and get some water on you. You look like hell warmed over."

Meghan groaned. "I feel like hell warmed over."

"That's what you get for drinking on an empty stomach." Trina shooed her toward the bathroom. "Now go. Before you scare the customers."

Meghan trudged to the bathroom, standing under the cool spray of the shower, trying to piece together the night before.

Tommy had driven her home. He had stopped her from kissing him. Had she really thrown herself at him?

She groaned, pressing her forehead against the tile. There was only one way to find out.

After wrapping herself in a towel, she grabbed her phone off the counter and dialed Tommy.

The phone rang twice before he answered.

"You alive?" He asked, and she heard mirth in his tone. His deep, amused drawl made her stomach flip. Oh god.

"Barely," she muttered, running a hand through her damp hair. "Tell me something, Tommy."

"Uh-oh." He sounded like he was smiling. "This oughta be good."

"Did I...?" She swallowed hard. "Did I try to kiss you last night?"

A beat of silence. Then—

"Try? Yes, but I didn't let you."

Her stomach dropped. "Oh, God."

He chuckled, low and warm. "Relax, city girl. I didn't."

She squeezed her eyes shut. "You didn't?" she exhaled, relieved.

"No," he said earnestly. "we're good."

"Why not, though?." She turned over on the bed, groaning.

"You were drunk." she heard him chuckle warmly. "And I didn't want you to wake up thinking you did anything stupid."

She peeked through her fingers. "So you stopped me."

"Yeah." His voice was quieter now. "You were drunk, Meghan. I'm not that kind of guy."

A pang of something—gratitude, guilt, admiration—hit her square in the chest.

"...Thank you."

"Don't mention it." He said. "That's what friends do."

A pause stretched between them, the weight of the conversation settling in. Meghan exhaled, flipping onto her side and staring at the ceiling.

"So," she said carefully, "we're just... friends?"

Tommy's voice was unreadable. "Isn't that what you want?"

Meghan chewed her lip. Did she?

"No," she admitted quietly. "I don't know."

Another silence. Then he sighed. "Don't know, huh? Well, that complicates things."

Her brows knitted together. "How so?"

"You tell me." He sounded almost... cautious. "Last week, you could barely stand me. Then we go to the honky tonk, and suddenly, I'm the best thing since sliced bread. Then you get wasted and try to crawl into my lap."

"Oh my God," she groaned, shoving a pillow over her face. "I want to die."

He laughed, deep and easy. "No you don't."

She rolled onto her stomach, kicking her feet against the mattress. "So... what now?"

"You tell me."

Meghan hesitated. "I don't know."

Another pause. Then, quieter—

"I do."

She sat up, the playfulness draining from her. "Yeah?"

Tommy's voice was serious now. Steady.

"You're still figuring things out," he said. "I get that. But I'm not some rebound, Meghan. I won't be your way of getting over your ex, and I damn sure won't be some mistake you regret the next morning."

A lump formed in her throat. "Tommy—"

"You don't have to say anything," he cut in. "Just... figure out what you want. And when you do, let me know."

Her stomach twisted. He was giving her space. Giving her time. But for the first time in a long while, she wasn't sure she wanted it.

"...Okay," she whispered.

"Good." His voice softened. "Now go take some Advil. You sound like hell."

She huffed a small laugh. "Gee, thanks."

"You're welcome," he drawled. Then, after a pause, "However, well...are you free on Sunday?"

She blinked. "Sunday?" She paused to think. "Tommy are you asking me out?"

"Yes. No?" he said casually. "I guess I am."

She hesitated, her heart kicking up speed. "And if I say no?"

"Then you say no."

A slow, reluctant smile pulled at her lips. "What if I said yes."

"Then you say yes."

Meghan sighed, shaking her head. What the hell was she getting herself into?

"And where does 'yes' go?" she asked.

"Wherever it goes." He sighed.

"What happened to just friends?" she asked.

"Can 't friends just hang out on a Sunday night? Have dinner?"

"That sounds more than like friends."

"Listen," he said. "I'm no good at this. You're talking to a guy who's had two major relationships his entire life. I just thought—"

"Thought what?"

"Since you're friends with Arlene, we could at least be civil. Hang out, you know, get to know each other."

"And that's all?" she asked, dubious.

"Yes," he answered. "That's all. I promise."

"...Fine," she relented. "Sunday. Where, and what time?" Jesus, what am I getting myself into, she thought. And why am I suddenly nervous?

"Same place as last night."

"Are they open on Sunday?"

"Yes," he replied. "But they'll be open for me and you."

"So we'er breaking and entering."

"Just trust me," he said.

Her mouth parted. "Oh my God, you're impossible."

"See you Sunday," he laughed and hung up.

She stared at the phone, caught somewhere between exasperation and excitement.

Then, pressing the pillow over her face again, she screamed into it.

What the hell was she getting herself into?

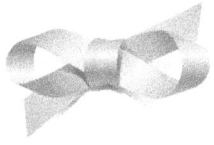

Chapter 15

Tommy

The bells over the door jingled as Tommy stepped into Bennet's Hardware, the scent of sawdust and freshly cut wood filling his lungs. He pulled off his cap, raking a hand through his hair as he scanned the store.

"Welcome to Bennet's! I'm Lizzy! What's your name?"

The sweet, singsong voice came from the young woman standing near the front entrance. Lizzy, Derrick's daughter. Eighteen, but with a youthful, girlish energy that made everyone she met feel instantly at ease.

Tommy smiled, tipping his cap. "Morning, Lizzy."

The bell dinged again from behind him. Lizzy repeated herself to the new customer.

Before he could say more, another voice answered.

"Hi, Lizzy. I'm Meghan."

Tommy's body tensed. His heart stumbled in his chest. He turned toward the sound, toward the light pouring through the window, and there she was.

Jesus Christ.

Meghan stood framed in the golden sunlight, her blond hair catching the glow like spun silk. She wore snug blue jeans and a white blazer over a fitted tank top, and she looked... magical. Like something out of a damn fairytale.

His breath caught.

Derrick snapped his fingers in front of his face. "Earth to Tommy."

Tommy blinked, still caught in the haze of her presence. Meghan moved toward them, her steps slow and unhurried, like she had all the time in the world. Her smile was warm, teasing.

"Tommy?" she asked, eyes sparkling. "Fancy meeting you here."

He cleared his throat, willing himself to function. "Yeah. Real fancy."

Meghan glanced between him and Derrick. "Are you guys talking business?"

Tommy nodded. "Just picking up some wood."

"Sounds about right," she teased. "You always have your hands on something rough."

Derrick snorted a laugh, while Tommy felt his ears heat.

Meghan grinned. "So, about that get-together Sunday... I still can't believe I let you talk me into that."

Tommy smirked. "I can't either, to be honest."

"Yeah, I'll have to have my head examined," she joked. "You know I have two left feet."

"Oh, don't worry," he said, arms crossed. "I'm sure you'll be fine, city girl."

"I hope so," she said with an exaggerated sigh. "Now, about that bookshelf?"

Derrick pointed toward the front of the store. "Gift shop area, up by the registers. Got shelves, books, knickknacks—whatever you need."

"Thanks," Meghan said, giving Tommy one last playful glance before walking away.

Tommy watched her go. Watched the way her hair caught the light, the way she moved with that easy confidence that made his stomach flip in ways he didn't want to acknowledge.

Derrick smirked, watching him. "Nice one you got there."

Tommy exhaled, dragging his gaze away. "I don't have her yet."

Derrick chuckled. "Yeah, you do. You just don't know it."

"Oh, come on," Tommy muttered, shaking his head. "She's no more interested in me than a bull to a filly."

Derrick gave him a flat look. "You really didn't notice she was flirting with you?"

Tommy scoffed. "Oh, bull. She was being nice."

"She was flirting," Derrick said. "I've seen a lot of girls flirt with me, and that was textbook, my guy."

Tommy rolled his eyes. "Yeah, but look at you. You're a handsome guy. Women always flirt."

Derrick arched an eyebrow. "And you're not?"

Tommy glanced down at himself. His baggy jeans. The oversized hoodie with a faint Cheeto dust stain. A smudge of dried ketchup on the sleeve.

"Not in a million years."

Derrick let out a full laugh. "Jesus, man. Still, she agreed to a date."

"It's not a date," Tommy said quickly.

Derrick grinned. "Uh-huh. That's what I said about a girl once, too." He lifted his left hand and wiggled his ring finger.

Tommy groaned.

Derrick clapped him on the back. "I'll grab your wood."

Tommy stayed behind, glancing toward the gift shop area.

Meghan stood near a display of books, running her fingers along the spines, utterly lost in her own world.

His fingers curled into a fist.

Out of your league, farm boy.

Still... he couldn't look away.

Finally, he shook his head, forcing himself to turn. He started after Derrick, who had stepped through the lumberyard doors.

He didn't notice Meghan look back in his direction, scanning the store.

Not seeing him.

Her smile faltered. A small frown flickered across her lips.

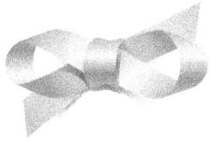

Chapter 16

Tommy

Tommy picked her up right on time, standing tall in his black boots, crisp jeans, and a pearl-button shirt that hugged his shoulders just right. When Meghan opened the door, she practically took his breath away.

Her flirty outfit was a mix of edgy and elegant—a leather miniskirt paired with a low-cut tank top, a denim jacket slung casually over her shoulders, and a wide black belt with a gleaming gold buckle. Everything about her screamed confident, beautiful, and out of his league, but she wore it with effortless charm.

"Where did you and Arlene go shopping?" he asked as he opened the truck door for her.

"Saks, in Raleigh," she said, settling into the passenger seat with a grin.

He shook his head, chuckling. "Fancy."

"You like it?" she teased, adjusting her jacket.

"I like it a lot. Especially the top."

She rolled her eyes but smirked. "You mean you like looking at it."

"Sorry, not sorry," he shot back with a grin.

"It's okay. Happens a lot," she said, brushing him off playfully.

When they arrived at the honky tonk, Meghan was surprised to find it empty except for a pair of older women setting up a spread. Mabel and Jolene Tommy had called them.

"They owed me a favor," Tommy explained as he led her inside. "I asked them to open up tonight, just for us."

"You did all this?" she asked, genuinely impressed.

"Well," he said, rubbing the back of his neck, "I wanted to teach you how to line dance without an audience. Didn't want you to feel embarrassed or anything."

"And what made you think I wanted to line dance?" she teased, raising an eyebrow.

"Just a hunch."

"What if I just want to watch you?"

"Not as fun that way," he said with a lopsided grin. "Besides, there are a couple of dances that work better as duets."

"Ah," she said, smirking. "And you thought of me for the duet?"

"Was hoping."

"You're cute, Tommy Richards."

"Back at ya, Meghan Holloway."

After dinner—Jolene's famous fried chicken and buttermilk biscuits—the two women started packing up.

"You two need anything else before we finish cleaning up and head out?" Jolene asked.

"Nope, we're good. Thanks for the meal. I left you a tip," Tommy said.

"Oh, you didn't have to do that!" Jolene said, smiling.

"Yes, I did," Tommy replied firmly.

"Well, you got a key. Lock up when you're done, and don't do anything we wouldn't do," Jolene teased.

"Not planning on it," Tommy quipped. Then he turned to Meghan with a mischievous grin. "Unless...?"

"Not happening," Meghan said, laughing. "You promised."

"Straight from the horse's mouth," Tommy said to the women.

"Who's the horse?" Meghan asked, raising an eyebrow.

"It's just a saying."

"I know," she said, smirking.

Jolene gave Tommy a quick hug, then whispered in his ear, "Take care of this one. I like her."

He nodded, smiling. "I like her too."

Jolene turned and went back to the kitchen.

Once they were alone, Tommy led her to the small stage. "Follow me," he said, walking to the DJ booth in the corner. A few button presses later, a lively country tune filled the air.

"What are we doing?" Meghan asked.

"I'm teaching you to line dance."

"I know how to dance," she scoffed.

"Not like this."

He demonstrated a few steps, thumbs hooked in his front pockets as he two-stepped smoothly across the floor. Left, right, spin. The rhythm seemed to be in his bones.

Meghan couldn't help but laugh as he tried to coach her through the moves. "You really know what you're doing," she said, breathless after a few attempts.

"It's my happy place," he admitted. "Growing up, Dad used to play all kinds of old records—country, big band jazz. He loved dancing."

She smiled at the image of young Tommy dancing around a living room. "You surprise me," she said, letting her guard down for a moment.

"Oh?" he asked, stepping closer.

"I figured all you farmer guys knew about was tractors and corn."

"There it is," he said, shaking his head with mock disappointment. "Stereotypes."

She giggled. "Okay, you got me."

"You're too easy," he said with a laugh. "you're right, that's all we think about. Tractors and corn futures."

"I'm sure there's something more than that, you think about."

"There is," he winked. "Now, let's see if you can tango, city girl."

Meghan

When he pulled her into the tango stance, Meghan took a sharp breath. His hands—strong, steady—settled against her with ease, one gripping her waist, the other capturing her fingers with a practiced gentleness.

Those hands, she thought. God, those hands.

The first time she met Tommy Richards, she noticed them—rough, calloused, capable. Hands of a man who worked hard, a man who could fix things, break things, shape things. And now, they held her like something delicate, something to be handled carefully.

She looked up, and for the first time, she realized—really realized—how beautiful he was.

Not just handsome in that rugged, farm-boy way, but something deeper. The way his eyes locked onto hers, unwavering. Focused. Like she was the only thing in the room, in the world. A slow breath left his lips, and she swore she felt it against her skin.

"Now follow my lead," he murmured.

Gladly, she thought, fucking gladly.

She let him guide her, her body moving effortlessly with his. When he tightened his grip on her waist just slightly to steer her through the turn, her stomach fluttered, traitorous and wild.

Does this man have any idea what he's doing to me?

She prayed to every saint she didn't believe in, that he wouldn't see the way her pulse was hammering. Wouldn't notice the way her breath kept hitching.

The music swelled, wrapping around them like a spell. The whole damn world narrowed to the space between their bodies, the slide of his fingers against hers, the way his thumb lazily traced the edge of her palm like he wasn't even aware he was doing it.

God, she needed air.

She glanced up, catching the fan of his lashes as his gaze flicked between her eyes, her lips, back to her eyes. He was breathing a little harder now, like her. A muscle in his jaw ticked, like he was holding something back.

The thought sent a fresh rush of heat through her.

What if he wasn't holding back?

What if he wanted to kiss her? Would he? Would she let him?

Hell, at this point, she might kiss him.

The song slowed, the final notes lingering in the air. Their bodies stilled, but neither of them moved away.

His hand was still on her waist. His thumb brushed against the fabric of her skirt. Barely there, but enough.

If he kissed her now—God help her—she wouldn't stop him.

But then the song changed.

Something fast, upbeat, a complete mood-killer.

Meghan exhaled, stepping back. Thank God for terrible DJ timing. Tommy cleared his throat, ran a hand through his hair. His lips twitched, almost a smirk, but not quite.

"Saved by the song change," he muttered.

She raised a brow, folding her arms. "And why exactly did we need saving?"

He hesitated, then shrugged, looking away. "No idea."

Liar. She knew it. She knew he felt it, too. That pull. That slow, impossible gravity between them.

And the worst part? She wasn't sure if she wanted to stop it.

Tommy exhaled slowly, rolling his shoulders back like he was shaking something off.

"Now," he said, drawing in a breath, "let's practice those moves I taught you a few minutes ago."

Meghan nodded, but her body wasn't as confident as her mind. She followed his lead, stepping into the rhythm, but her movements were stiff, too focused on remembering the steps rather than feeling them.

Meanwhile, Tommy moved like he was born for this.

She caught herself watching him more than her own feet—damn, he was good. Effortless, smooth, a natural performer. His body twisted and turned with precision, his footwork quick but controlled. It was like he wasn't even thinking about it, just being in it.

And then, She lost her balance. She felt herself wobbling, then twisted into the start of a fall.

It was just a misstep, her boot catching on the wooden floor as her focus drifted from her steps to him.

Her stomach lurched, her arms flailed.

Before she could even yelp, Tommy's hands were on her, catching her mid-stumble, pulling her upright like it was second nature.

"Whoa there, city girl," he said, voice rich with amusement, his grip firm around her waist.

She exhaled sharply, gripping his arms instinctively. "Thanks for the save, farm boy," she gasped, barely managing a laugh.

His breath was hot on her skin.

The way she liked it.

The way it sent shivers prickling down her arms, making her stomach flutter, her pulse stutter.

His fingers flexed slightly against her waist before he let go, and for a moment, she swore he lingered just a second too long.

She swallowed hard, willing herself to ignore the heat curling through her.

Before she could say something—anything—to break the spell, the door creaked open, and Jolene's voice rang out.

"Hey, you two, we're heading out. Clean up after yourselves, will ya?"

Tommy turned toward the sound, hands sliding into his pockets. "Yeah, well, it's getting late anyway," he said, his voice still thick with whatever had just passed between them. "We'll be right behind you."

Meghan sucked in a breath, forcing herself to nod.

"Yeah," she echoed, then thought—Right behind you. Like right behind me.

And just like that, her mind betrayed her.

Because suddenly, she was thinking about Tommy behind her—his hands on her waist, his chest flush against her back, the way he looked in those damn jeans, how they hugged his hips just right, the curve of muscle there—

Oh, God.

Her face went up in flames. Jesus, Meghan, get a grip.

She coughed—loud, abrupt—trying to mask her completely inappropriate thoughts.

"Uh, yeah, right behind you, ladies," she said quickly.

And then she did not look at Tommy.

Nope. Not even a little.

Because if she did, she was afraid he might see.

Jolene and Mabel said their goodbyes and headed for the door.

Tommy exhaled, rubbing the back of his neck. "Well, that's our cue to leave."

But Meghan didn't want to go.

Not yet.

She wanted to stay here and dance with him all night, keep his hands on her waist, watch the way his body moved so damn effortlessly. If he moves like this in bed...

She swallowed hard, shaking off the thought as Tommy took her hand, leading her from the dance floor.

She curled her fingers around his, and he held her in a tight, warm grip.

Neither of them said a word as they stepped outside. The air was crisp, the stars spread wide and glittering above them. The only sound was the quiet hum of crickets and the distant shuffle of Jolene's car pulling out of the parking lot.

Meghan knew she shouldn't want to kiss him.

They'd agreed—not a date.

But his lips looked so damn good.

And truthfully? She had wanted to the other night. Badly. She wasn't sure what had stopped her then—maybe nerves, maybe the quiet voice in her head reminding her she barely knew this man.

But after tonight?

God, she knew enough.

Tommy opened the truck door for her, the perfect gentleman, and she climbed inside. He shut it gently behind her, walked around to the driver's side, and got in. Still, neither of them spoke.

She felt him, though. The presence of him—big, warm, and quiet, his energy still thick from the dance floor.

Finally, he started the truck, and they pulled out of the lot, heading toward town.

A few minutes passed in silence.

Then Meghan glanced at him and said, "I had a really nice time tonight. You're a really good dancer."

He made a sound—half chuckle, half exhale. "Uh-huh."

And kept driving.

Her brows pulled together. "Was it something I said?"

He didn't answer right away. Then, finally, he glanced at her, his face unreadable.

"Meghan, I'm no good at this," he said, his voice low.

She frowned. "No good at what?"

He exhaled through his nose. "This. Whatever this is. Dating. I'm sure Trina's told you."

Ah. Here it is.

She had felt hot Tommy on the dance floor—now she was getting cold Tommy.

She folded her arms. "So what are you saying?" she asked, tone careful. "We can't date?"

"We agreed this wasn't gonna be a date."

Her pulse kicked up. Deflection.

"Tommy, do you even like me?" she asked.

His hands tightened on the wheel. "Yes," he admitted, coughing slightly. "I do."

She raised a brow. "And that's a problem?"

He sighed. She could almost see him trying to put his thoughts together, to get them into words without saying the wrong thing.

"How do I put this right?" he muttered.

She huffed. "Put what right?"

He hesitated. Then, finally, he spoke.

"Look," he started, "I like you. I think you're great. But you're friends with Arlene. And you've got business stuff going on. I don't wanna get in the middle of that. I think..." He tightened his grip on the wheel again. "I think we need to be friends right now."

Meghan stared at him. "Friends," she repeated flatly.

He nodded. "Besides..." He let out a humorless laugh. "You already made it sound like you wouldn't wanna get involved with someone like me."

Her stomach flipped. "Someone like you?"

"Yeah." He glanced at her briefly, then shook his head. His jaw worked, like he was chewing on words he didn't want to say.

"Tommy," she pressed.

He let out a sharp breath. "A farmer type, Meghan. You're a city girl. And I know I joke about it, but I know your type. You're not from here. You don't have it in you to settle down on a farm, with someone who's gonna be smelling like dirt and cow shit half the time."

You're used to..." He hesitated. "Parties. Movie galas. Premieres. Hell, you married a fucking action star, for God's sake."

Her stomach went ice cold.

John. The comparison to him made her chest tighten. She exhaled, "Wait."

Tommy sensed her cold silence.

"Sorry," he muttered. "I didn't mean—"

She cut him off. "Yes, you did."

His hands curled tighter around the steering wheel.

"What do you think this was, Tommy?" she asked, her voice sharp now. "Why did you think I went out with you tonight?"

"I don't know," he admitted. "I took a shot and you said yes."

"I said yes because I wanted to see you, you dumbass." She let out a bitter laugh, shaking her head. "Don't judge a book by its cover, you ever heard that?"

Tommy didn't say anything.

"Yes," he finally muttered.

"Good, Tommy." She leaned back, exhaling. "Because I had fun tonight."

Silence.

Then, finally—

"I did too," he admitted.

Something passed between them then. Something different.

Meghan looked at him and started to see him.

And God help her, all she saw was a kind-hearted man. A good man. Strong, tall, hopelessly handsome.

But then—her eyes dropped to herself.

The way her stomach folded slightly over her lap, how her thighs pressed together, how her arms weren't small, weren't delicate.

What does he even want with me?

He had dated Trina, for God's sake. Trina, a size-four on her worst day, the kind of woman who looked perfect in anything, the kind of woman men gravitated to without thinking.

Meghan swallowed hard, suddenly feeling small.

Tommy turned to look at her again. "You okay?"

She forced a smile, trying to push the thoughts away. "Yeah. Just tired."

"Me too," he said, voice softer now.

The rest of the ride was quiet.

But for Meghan, her mind screamed the whole way home.

They pulled up in front of her house, the engine humming low before Tommy cut it off.

For a second, neither of them moved.

Then he turned to her, clearing his throat. "Let me walk you up."

He stepped out of the truck, walking around to her side. She opened the door before he could, but he still held out a hand, steadying her as she slid down.

The porch light cast a soft glow over the front steps, white paint catching in the moonlight. His gaze flickered up to her door, then back to her. Why did this feel like a damn high school first date? Like he was some nervous kid walking the best girl in town to her doorstep?

But Meghan just smiled. "Well," she said lightly, "I guess I'll see you later."

She stepped forward, wrapping her arms around him in a warm hug.

He wasn't expecting it.

His body locked up for half a second—before he melted. His arms slid around her, holding her just a bit tighter than he should have. She smelled like vanilla and the lingering hint of warm summer air.

Before he could say anything, she pulled back slightly and pressed her lips against his cheek.

Soft. Warm.

He barely held in a breath.

She pulled away, but his hand instinctively went to his cheek, fingers pressing against the spot where she kissed him.

"I don't think I'll wash this for a few days," he muttered, mostly to himself.

Meghan laughed, shaking her head. "Oh, go on," she teased, but there was a blush creeping into her cheeks.

He smiled.

A pause stretched between them.

"Maybe another time?" he asked, unsure why his voice felt rougher than usual.

Meghan tilted her head, lips twitching. "Let me check my schedule, see if I have time for a next time."

He huffed, smirking. "You can say no, you know. I won't be offended."

"What if I didn't want to say no?"

His stomach flipped.

"That'd be good too," she murmured, adjusting the strap of her purse over her shoulder.

She hesitated, just for a moment.

Then she let out a breath. "Well," she said softly, "I better get in. It's late, and I'm tired."

"Sure," he said. "Go ahead."

But before she could go, he reached out, pressing his hand gently to her shoulder. A quick touch—nothing more—but damn if his palm didn't burn from it.

He swallowed. "See you around, city girl," he drawled.

Her lips parted slightly, something unreadable flickering in her expression.

Then, just as quietly, she whispered, "You too, farm boy."

And with that, she turned and floated up the steps, moving like she was still dancing—the smallest, unconscious two-step as she disappeared inside.

Tommy lingered for just a second longer, staring at the door.

Then, with a long exhale, he finally turned, got into his truck, and drove away—his cheek still warm where she kissed him.

Chapter 17

Tommy

"How was the date last night?" Catherine asked, handing Tommy a cup of hot coffee.

Tommy raised his cup and took a sip. "It wasn't a date."

Arlene raised an eyebrow, a playful smirk tugging at her lips. "Dinner and dancing is a date, bro," said his sister."

She's right, you know," Catherine agreed.

"This was different," Tommy replied, trying to find the right words. "We're just trying to be friends.."

"Did you kiss her?" Catherine teased.

"Friends don't kiss," he let out an exasperated sigh. "Besides, what makes you think a city girl like her wants to kiss me, unless she was drunk?" he thought back to the first time they were at the honky tonk, and Meghan had polished off three of Jolene's long island ice teas.

Catherine paused, her gaze drifting towards the old barn she could see from the kitchen window.. "I was a city girl once, you know."

"Yeah, Dad told me. You guys were oil and water."

"We were," Catherine admitted, a hint of wistful nostalgia in her voice. "But he could dance, I'll give him that. Did I ever tell you about the VFW? My friend Stacy dragged me, kicking and screaming. Your dad was there, trying to be all charm and flirty."

Tommy shook his head, a smile playing on his lips. "Never heard that one."

Catherine launched into the story, recounting the night at the VFW, the reluctant dance, and the unexpected connection she felt with Thomas. As she finished, her eyes met Tommy's, a knowing glint in their depths.

"Give the city girl a chance, Tommy," she said softly. "God knows you need a good woman in your life, and I'm not always going to be around."

Tommy nodded, a warmth spreading through his chest. "Oh, hush, you're only seventy."

Catherine stood and walked to the sink. "It's what the good Lord gives us, son."

"Stop it," he said. "You just need to get yourself a man." He meant it as a joke.

She was quiet for a moment. Then she turned around, her eyes glassy. "I had one once. Best there ever was. You can't replace that."

He went to her. "Oh, come on, Mom," he said, enveloping her in a hug. "I only meant it as a joke."

"I know, son." She held him against her body, breathing in his scent. "You smell like your dad."

Tears started flowing. He held her through them. After a few minutes, she pushed him away. "Look at me, sitting here blubbering."

"It's fine, Ma," he said.

She turned to the refrigerator and took out eggs and bacon. "Want breakfast?"

"Sure," he said. "Arlene is going to help with the books for the month. And boy, do they need it."

"It's the numbers. You were never good with math."

"I was never good at a lot of things." Tommy said, musing at the lack of enthusiasm about the chores around the farm there always seemed to be more of.

He breathed in the scent of sizzling bacon and eggs, wishing this feeling of being served by a mother's love would never go away. Catherine coughed. She coughed again.

"You okay?"

She waved him away. "Spring allergies. Pollen hits me every year like this."

He just nodded, drank his coffee, and pushed away the worry that something bigger was wrong. Just pollen season like this every year, he told himself.

. . ∾ . .

THE CHISEL SCRAPED softly against the wood, the sound rhythmic, steady, the only noise in the workshop.

Tommy sat hunched over the sculpture, his eyes narrowed in focus as he carved the last delicate folds of the t-shirt. It was almost finished. The bike, the girl, the way her hands curled around the handlebars, caught forever in movement.

Maggie Grace.

She was right there, in the wood grain, taking shape beneath his hands. He'd carved her sneakers, the little scuffed-up Converse she used to wear, the laces slightly untied. The bike was almost exactly the one she'd been riding that day, down the old gravel road near the school, wind in her hair, smiling like she didn't have a care in the world.

Like she wasn't about to die.

Tommy swallowed, adjusting his grip on the chisel. He wasn't sure why he'd started this one. Maybe because she kept coming back to him—a flash of color on a bike, a scream that still lived in his bones. Maybe if he carved her, if he got her down in wood and paint, he could finally let her go.

The basement door creaked. "Bro?" Arlene called.

Tommy didn't look up right away. He recognized the sound of Arlene's footsteps, light and slow, pausing just inside like she was debating whether to step farther in.

She always hesitated in his workshop. She had learned a long time ago to make sure he was at a stopping point before coming down and disturbing him.

"You about ready for dinner?" she asked. Her voice was casual—too casual.

He still didn't look up, just kept running his fingers along the wood, smoothing out the rough edges. "Yeah, almost."

Arlene stepped closer, her arms crossed.

She didn't say anything for a long time. Just looked at it.

Finally, her voice came quieter. "That's pretty. What made you do this one?"

Something about the way she said it made Tommy finally lift his head.

She was staring at it with this strange expression—half curiosity, half something else. Something deeper.

He exhaled, rubbing his thumb over the chisel. "I dunno," he admitted. "Something about her keeps coming back to me. Thought maybe putting her in a statue would get it out."

Silence stretched between them.

Then he asked, carefully, "You remember that day?"

She didn't look at him when she answered.

"Yeah," she said softly, her voice barely a breath. "I do."

Something flickered across her face, too fast to catch, and then—just like that—she was moving again, stepping back, clearing her throat like she was shaking something loose.

"Dinner's almost ready," she said. "Did you want cheese on your burger?"

The shift was so abrupt that Tommy blinked.

He looked at her, really looked at her.

What kind of question was that? She knew exactly how he liked his burgers.

He opened his mouth, about to ask, but she was already turning away, already walking toward the stairs.

Then—

She coughed.

It was small, but it was enough to make Tommy pause.

Arlene wiped at her cheek, clearing her throat. "Damn dust," she muttered. "Always kicks up when I come down here."

But Tommy wasn't looking at the dust.

He was looking at her hand.

At the way it trembled, just slightly. At the tear she thought she had wiped away but had missed—a single track down her cheek, catching the dim light of the workshop.

"You sure?" he asked, voice a little rougher.

She didn't turn around.

"Yeah," she said, a little too quickly. "I am."

Then she was gone, heading up the stairs before he could say anything else.

Tommy exhaled, running a hand down his face.

He looked back at the sculpture.

Maggie Grace, frozen in time.

Her hair had been almost white in the sunlight that day.

His fingers brushed over the wood grain at the top of her head, tilting the sculpture slightly. The way he'd carved it, the grain followed the movement of the hair perfectly. It looked natural. Almost like it had been part of the wood all along, and he'd just uncovered it.

Maybe he wouldn't paint that part after all.

Yeah. He'd leave it just like that.

Chapter 18

Tommy

Meghan caught Trina slipping through the front door in the early morning light. They didn't exchange words—just a knowing glance. Trina, looking like she'd had one hell of a night, simply nodded in Meghan's direction, a look that said, Don't say a word, before stalking off to her bedroom.

Meghan smirked into her coffee, taking a slow sip. She didn't need to guess where Trina had been. Reynaldo was practically written all over her face.

A few minutes later, Trina reemerged, fresh from a quick rinse, dressed in her oversized Hello Kitty T-shirt and gray sweatpants.

"How you feeling?" Meghan asked, raising an eyebrow over her mug.

"Good," Trina muttered, heading straight for the coffee maker. She poured herself a cup, scowled at the rooster-printed mug in her hand, and sighed. "You ever gonna throw these fucking rooster cups away?"

"Not as long as you're dancing around with the man," Meghan teased.

"Whatever." Trina rolled her eyes, added creamer, and sat across from her.

A comfortable silence stretched between them as Meghan sifted through her morning emails. One from a town commissioner asking for re-election donations—delete. Another from a local artist inquiring about a gallery showing—she skimmed the attached pictures. Great. Another cubist who thinks he's Rembrandt. She started a polite reply.

Trina drummed her nails on the table. "Well?" she finally said.

Meghan looked up. "What?"

"We haven't talked in a few days," Trina pointed out. "I've been working doubles, and you've been gallivanting all over town with Tommy Boy. So what's the latest?"

Meghan went back to her laptop. "I don't know."

"There it is," Trina said knowingly.

"There what is?"

"The coldness." Trina leaned forward. "Like I told you before—he comes in hot, then goes cold."

Meghan sighed. "Maybe it's me."

Trina frowned. "What do you mean?"

"I feel like if I really wanted something, I'd go for it. Tommy's... nice. He's handsome. He's good. He's everything I should want."

"So what's the problem?"

Meghan hesitated. "Maybe I don't want it enough."

The past few days, she'd been questioning why she was even doing this—entertaining the idea of another relationship. Three years ago, she'd signed divorce papers and vowed to stay focused on herself. Her career. Her life. Hers alone.

And yet—here was this man, pulling her in, making her feel... something.

"You could always back off," Trina suggested.

"What if I don't want to?"

Trina exhaled. "Meg... not him. I've already told you."

Meghan narrowed her eyes. "Why not him?"

Trina hesitated before answering. "Because I know him."

Meghan folded her arms. "So?"

"In the time I've known Tommy Richards," Trina said, "he's seriously dated exactly two women. And you're looking at one of them."

"Why didn't it work out?" Meghan asked. "You've never explained."

"It's a long story."

Meghan glanced at the clock on her laptop. "I've got an hour. Why don't you tell me?"

Trina smirked. "It's a long-ass story."

"Break it down into a soundbite."

Trina took a long sip of coffee before sighing. "Okay. A long time ago, back during Reconstruction, my great-grandfather—something biblical, I forget his name—wanted to buy the Richards farm. Back then, it wasn't Richards land yet. The original owner was killed in the war, no heirs, so the government confiscated the property and sold it at auction."

Meghan arched a brow. "And?"

"The Rittermarks wanted it. But they lost the auction. Some guy named William Richards bought it instead, and that's how the feud started. It wasn't Hatfields and McCoys or anything, but for the last hundred and fifty years, my family has tried to get that land back."

Meghan exhaled. "Jesus. I will never understand Southern life."

Trina snorted. "Right?"

She continued, "Fast-forward a hundred years, and I got pulled into it—after the Penelope debacle."

"The what debacle?"

Trina smirked. "Thomas—Tommy's dad—was supposed to marry my aunt Penelope. But then Catherine swooped in one summer and stole him away."

Meghan's eyes widened. "Wait—his mother?"

"Yep."

"But it wasn't some scandal. Penelope never wanted to marry Thomas. She wanted to do missionary work in Africa. By the time she came back, Thomas and Catherine were already together. It was an arranged engagement, but she told me she never really wanted it."

Trina leaned back. "But my family didn't see it that way. To them, the Richards stole another thing from us."

"And then?" Meghan prompted.

"And then came me. Another Rittermark daughter. And Gideon—my grandpa—noticed me hanging out with Tommy."

Meghan smirked. "I bet that went well."

"Oh, yeah." Trina laughed dryly. "Tommy and I dated for a few months, nothing serious. But then one night, Gideon calls Tommy into his study and asks him—point blank—what his intentions are with me."

Meghan winced. "Oh, no."

"Oh, yes," Trina deadpanned. "And what does Tommy say? 'I don't know. Just having fun, I guess.'"

Meghan groaned.

"Gideon blew up," Trina continued. "Sent Tommy packing. Told me I was forbidden to see him again."

"And did you?"

"Sure. Once or twice. But Tommy... went cold. We broke it off, and that was that."

Meghan hesitated. "Do you still like him?"

"God, no. And I don't think he ever liked me either. I mean, we kissed a few times. Went to prom. But Tommy..." Trina sighed. "He's always been half in, half out. His head's never been in one place. He's always talking about leaving. About never coming back."

Meghan nodded slowly. "Yeah. He does that."

Trina shrugged. "After me, there was Callie—Calliope."

"Who's that?"

"My cousin. Penelope's daughter. Blonde, tiny, waifish—artsy type. They dated for six years."

Meghan's stomach tightened. "And?"

"He grew cold." Trina's voice was flat. "She asked him when they were getting married. He told her, 'I don't want to be tied down to this place.'"

Meghan exhaled. Another red flag. Another reason not to fall for a flannel-wearing farm boy with ridiculously strong hands and dance moves smoother than sin.

Trina snapped her fingers. "Earth to Meghan."

Meghan blinked. "Sorry. Just lost myself for a second."

Trina smirked. "So there you have it. The complicated love life of Tommy Richards. And a ton of town history you probably didn't need to hear."

Meghan laughed. "No, it's fine. Not exactly a ripping yarn, but now I get it."

Trina stretched. "Welp. Gotta go. Scrambles is waiting. And these old guys won't wait on themselves."

Meghan closed her laptop. "Shower first?"

Trina nodded. "Only take a minute. I reek of rooster."

Meghan sipped her coffee. "At least somebody's getting some." After a beat, she wondered aloud. "So, how is he?"

"Reynaldo?"

"No," Meghan blushed. "Tommy."

"Not bad," Trina smirked on her way to the bathroom. "Not bad at all."

Meghan just sat there, smiling to herself. Wondering what not bad really meant.

And wondering if she'd ever find out.

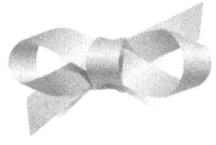

Chapter 19

Tommy

He walked down the steps to the kitchen, where Arlene and Catherine sat hunched over the books for the month.

Tommy heard Arlene say, "Mom, I can give you some of the proceeds from the art show."

Catherine shook her head. "No. That's your money, baby. You need it—to find a place, to take care of the kids."

Tommy barely registered the conversation as he poured himself a cup of coffee, but he kept an ear on it all the same.

The first sip sparked his mind awake. He closed his eyes, savoring the deep, rich taste of the Colombian beans. That first taste of coffee—nothing quite like it.

He turned, mug in hand. "What's going on?"

Arlene glanced up. "Mom and I are going over the books. With the latest harvest, we might make it through the rest of the year, but... at best, we'll break even."

Tommy sighed. Finances exhausted him. Everyone in the Richards household knew he was useless at math, thanks to his number dyslexia. Back when he handled the books, Catherine always had to go back through them, fixing mistakes, balancing the ledgers properly. If she hadn't, they would've been bankrupt years ago.

Then Arlene moved home, took over, and kept things from falling apart. She budgeted, cut costs where she could, helped their mother make sense of it all.

Catherine had often wondered why Tommy hadn't inherited his father's skill for managing money. Tommy agreed. He had no damn clue, either.

"So," Tommy asked, taking another sip, "what do we do?"

Catherine hesitated, then said, "Arlene wants to give us her art money."

Tommy frowned. "No. That's yours."

Arlene waved him off. "It's for the family."

Catherine and Tommy shared a look.

"It's for you," he corrected. "It's for your family. It can't be easy after... everything."

Everything meaning the divorce.

Joe. That son of a bitch.

Arlene sighed. "He's sending child support and alimony payments. He's... being good."

Tommy scoffed. "If he was good, he wouldn't have done what he did."

"Tommy," Arlene said, a quiet warning.

"Don't stick up for that man, sis." Tommy's voice hardened. "Don't ever stick up for him."

"I wasn't—"

He cut her off with a sharp glance.

"No, you weren't," he said. "You didn't do anything wrong."

Arlene sighed but let him think what he wanted. She pushed back from the table and stood. "Well, I gotta go. Dana and I have a meeting in a couple of hours."

Catherine stood, too, using the edge of the table for balance.

Tommy frowned. "You okay, Mom?"

Catherine gave him a tired smile. "Yeah, baby. Just old bones. They don't work like they used to."

Arlene grabbed her keys, then smirked at Tommy. "So... how'd the not-a-date go the other night?"

"It wasn't a date," Tommy grumbled.

Arlene just raised a brow. "You took her to dinner. And dancing."

Catherine smirked. "That's a date, sweetheart."

"Both of you need to stop," Tommy muttered, shaking his head.

The women laughed.

Arlene nudged him. "You like her, though."

He hesitated. Then, finally, admitted, "Yeah. I do."

Arlene's teasing smile softened. "Go easy on her, bro. She's got some baggage."

"At our age, don't we all?"

"Yeah," Arlene said, "but she's got stuff maybe you don't know about."

Tommy frowned. "Like what?"

"You know her ex-husband, right? John Masterton?"

Tommy shrugged. "Yeah. The actor."

"He was kind of a douchebag."

"Then why'd she marry him?"

Arlene's expression darkened. "Because he wasn't always. Then he got famous."

Tommy leaned back. "And?"

"And things went sour."

"How so?"

Arlene hesitated, then finally said, "She had body issues. Take a look."

It started simple. A quick internet search.

Arlene had mentioned Meghan's past—Hollywood, an ex-husband, a marriage that didn't end well. But Tommy hadn't given it much thought.

Until now.

Until Meghan was in his head more than she should be. Until he couldn't stop thinking about the way she laughed at the honky tonk, the way she looked up at him during their dance, eyes dark with something unspoken.

So, he reached for his phone.

Typed her name.

And there she was. Meghan Holloway.

First result? Wikipedia.

Her picture was front and center—a polished headshot, blonde hair pinned back, red lips in a careful smile. The bio listed her as a former socialite, an art curator, and, of course—the ex-wife of actor John Masterton.

Tommy exhaled, scrolling down.

He didn't care about the words, not really. What caught him were the pictures.

Premiere night.

Meghan, dressed in black, standing beside her husband at some movie event.

John, Hollywood-polished, flashing a grin at the cameras.

Meghan is smiling, too—but different. Stiff. Like she's going through the motions.

Tommy scrolls again. More photos.

Another red carpet.

She's in a lemon-yellow, form-fitting gown that hugs her body in a way that makes his breath catch.

She's stunning. Absolutely fucking stunning. He could look at this picture all day.

But it's the expression on her face that stopped him cold.

Her smile is thin. Forced. Her hand rests over her stomach—subtle, almost protective.

He almost didn't see the caption at first. Then what he saw next hit him like a gut punch.

"When life gives you lemons, wear them. 10 Fashion Fails at This Year's Emmys."

His stomach twisted.

Meghan is number one on the list.

He kept scrolling, dreading what was next. The comments.

"Jesus, she looks like she's about to burst out of that dress.", "Who let a whale onto the red carpet?", "Damn, John must really love her money because he sure as hell ain't with her for looks.", "No wonder he's not booking lead roles anymore. No one wants to cast a guy whose wife looks like that."

Tommy stopped reading. His grip on the phone tightened. His chest ached for her.

How many people had said this? How many people had ripped her apart in public, like she wasn't even human?

And worse—had Meghan read this?

He exhaled too sharply.

Arlene glances up. "What?"

He shook his head. "Nothing." But his voice was tight.

Arlene watched him for a moment, then nodded toward his phone. "Looked her up, didn't you?"

He didn't need to answer.

Arlene sighs. "It was bad," she says quietly.

Tommy clenched his jaw. "She ever talk about it?"

"Not much," Arlene admitted. "But I know it messed her up. And John... well, he didn't make it better."

Tommy didn't say anything. He already knows where this is going.

"After that night? After all the press had their say? John turned into a complete asshole," Arlene said. "Blamed her for his career slowing down. Said she made him look bad. That she wasn't trying hard enough to 'keep up appearances.' Told her maybe she should try losing a few pounds."

Tommy's stomach turned.

Arlene shook her head. "She went through hell."

Tommy locked his phone and set it facedown on the table.

Maybe he shouldn't like her. Maybe it's a bad idea. Maybe Meghan Holloway is too far out of his world, too complicated, too much.

But that image of her, standing there in the spotlight while the world ripped her apart?

It lingered.

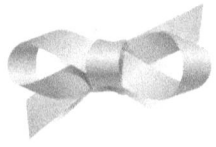

Chapter 20

Tommy

· · ◁⁂▷ · ·

MEGHAN CALLED HIM, her voice bubbling with excitement. "So, I was thinking... Wilmington tonight? There's this club, the New Cotton Club. It's exclusive, but I think I can get us in."

Tommy chuckled, picturing the scene. "Oh yeah? And how do you plan on doing that?"

"I have a few connections," she purred. "And if I smile nice for the bouncer, tell him who my ex was... I think we'll be okay."

"That works?"

"Have you seen what I'm working with?" she teased.

"I have," Tommy admitted, a grin spreading across his face. "Well, the bouncer hasn't. But if I give him the possibility of a shot? I think he'll be okay."

Tommy laughed. "Girls..."

"Hey, gotta use what Mother Nature gave me. I'm not ashamed."

"You shouldn't be," he said, his voice softening. "I'll drive though."

"Deal," she agreed. "Okay, so pick me up at seven? We drive down to Wilmington, doors open at nine."

He blanched. It was later than he thought people went out these days.

"How long are we staying?" he asked, "Because I get up early, remember?"

"Until we dance out our frustrations," she answered.

"Okay, two o'clock then," he joked.

"Sounds about right." He heard her laugh on the other end of the line.

They said their goodbyes, and Tommy sat there, thinking. Nightclub. Shit. That was a different kind of atmosphere than the Honky Tonk. He'd have to get an outfit together. Going to have to talk to Arlene, figure out what to wear.

He went to her room, where she was painting a picture of the barn, all red and old, the Corvette's rear sticking out of the barn doors, white contrasting against the red paint. The sun beamed overhead, and in the distance, corn stalks, green and yellow, stretched into the distance.

"That's awesome, Sis," he said.

She looked up, ear buds in her ears. She pulled them out. "What's that?" she asked.

He admired her painting. "That's awesome. Where do you get your ideas?" he asked.

"They just come to me." She put down the brush she'd been using to whisk some clouds that hung over the landscape.

"Well, keep them coming because I need your creative genius for something."

"What's that?"

"Meghan just asked me to go to the nightclub with her in Wilmington. I don't know what to wear. And I can't go looking like I do when I go to the Wild Horse."

She beamed. "Cool, let's get you dressed then." She stood up, wiped paint on her brown shorts, and said, "Let me get dressed. I'll take you shopping."

"Oh, you don't have to do that."

"Listen, what's the fun of making money off of my art if I can't enjoy spending it?"

"You won't enjoy shopping with me."

"Oh yes, I will, Bro. I've been wanting to get you out of tee shirts and cargo shorts for the longest time."

He looked down; he was wearing a red tee shirt and cargo shorts. He looked back at her. "Noted. Let's go."

Hours later, they had a selection of clothes: nice shirts, a suit coat, tight slacks, and a new pair of shoes to go with the ensemble.

"You sure this is going to look good?" he asked.

"Listen," she said, "if this doesn't make her want to drop her panties on you, then I did something wrong."

He said nervously, "Or I did."

She just smirked. "Yeah, you're probably right."

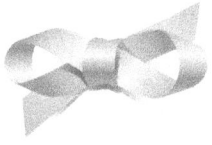

Chapter 21

Meghan

The nightclub was alive with energy, the music pounding so hard it seemed to vibrate in Meghan's chest. She followed Tommy to the bar, where he ordered a whiskey neat, and she opted for a glass of Cabernet. The DJ, a young woman with sleek black hair, commanded the booth, spinning a mix of techno-pop hits. Songs like "Everybody Dance Now" and "Pump Up the Jam" had the crowd moving in sync, their bodies pulsing under the flickering neon lights.

When the DJ transitioned to a slower song, the bassline softened, and Meghan seized her chance. Grinning, she grabbed Tommy's hand and led him onto the dance floor. His surprise melted away as he allowed her to pull him into the crowd, his hands settling instinctively on her hips.

Their bodies moved together to the rhythm, their steps falling into sync. The song's slower tempo didn't diminish its intensity—it thrummed between them, each beat pulling them closer. Meghan tossed her head back to meet Tommy's gaze; their eyes met, mouths lingering with barely a space in between.

Her body pulsed in time with the music, and she felt the heady tension between them. His scent—earthy and raw, like a plowed field—wrapped around her, making her head spin. Kiss me! She willed.

Something familiar caught her eye near the door. A voice from a past she wished would go away.

The moment broke, shattered the moment she spotted him.

John.

He had just walked in, flanked by two women who couldn't have been older than their mid-twenties. Their exaggerated features—plumped lips, enhanced hips, and sculpted curves—made Meghan want to roll her eyes. Her chest tightened as she watched them saunter into the club.

She pressed her face into Tommy's shoulder. "Of all the fucking gin joints," she murmured.

"What?" Tommy looked around.

"We have to go," Meghan pulled back from Tommy.

He frowned. "Why?"

She tilted her head toward John. "Him."

Tommy followed her gaze, his jaw tightening. "Do I need to say something?"

"No," she shook her head. "Let's just leave before he sees us."

Tommy nodded, his hand settling on the small of her back. He guided her toward the exit with quiet determination, his touch steadying her frayed nerves. Meghan allowed herself a moment of gratitude—she could get used to the way he made her feel safe, the way he touched her, warm and protective.

They didn't reach the door.

"Well, look who we have here," John drawled, his voice cutting through the noise of the club. He staggered, the telltale sign of inebriation. The women at his sides giggled, oblivious. "Ladies, let me introduce you to my ex-wife."

Meghan turned, her face schooled into a mask of icy politeness. "John," she said, her eyes blazing hatred into his. "I was just leaving. Nice to meet you, ladies."

John took a step closer, his smirk widening. "No, no, stick around. Let's talk. Catch up."

"I was just leaving," she repeated, pushing past him."And you're drunk."

"Like you care." John pressed, reaching for her. "Come on, what's your hurry?"

Tommy stepped forward, his voice low and measured. "We're late. I've got to be up early. You know, animals and all."

John's laugh was sharp and humorless. "Ah, yes. Farm boy." He looked Tommy up and down with thinly veiled disdain before turning back to Meghan. "Well, it was good seeing you."

"I wish I could say the same." Muttering under her breath, she stepped toward the door. She was already seeing red. The pulse in her temple throbbed, heart beating fast.

"That's right," John smirked. "Go back to where you belong—on the farm with the rest of the piggies."

The insult hit like a slap, and before Meghan could stop herself, her fist was flying. She landed a solid punch to John's face. The crack to his jaw punctuated the nightclub's music. His head snapped back, and he stumbled, clutching his cheek where a red welt was already forming. A trickle of blood dropped from his mouth. Her lips curved in a satisfied smile.

"Holy shit!" he shouted, blinking in shock. He wiped the blood from his mouth. "What the hell was that for?"

One of the women gasped, her eyes wide. "That was uncalled for!"

Meghan glared at her, fist trembling. "Bitch, you don't want the same right now!" The woman shut up.

John's hand twitched as though he might retaliate, but Tommy stepped in front of him.

"I wouldn't," Tommy said, his voice deadly calm, eyes boring into John's in silent warning.

John hesitated, his bravado faltering. Thinking batter of it, he lowered his hand, wrapping it instead around the waist of the brunette at his side.

Meghan, unable to form words, turned and stormed out of the club. She didn't stop until she was a block away, her breath coming in sharp bursts, her hand throbbing from the impact. Tears stung her eyes, a mix of anger and adrenaline threatening to spill over.

"Motherfucker!" she screamed, not caring how loudly or if anyone around her would hear. Her anger ebbed somewhat, but not enough. She breathed in and out through her nose, trying to calm her breath, but unable to do so. Tears streamed down her cheeks. How was it possible that this man could still have such an impact on her after all this time?

Tommy caught up to her, his long strides closing the distance to her.

"You okay?" he asked, his voice gentle.

She nodded but didn't speak, cradling her bruised hand. Tommy reached for it, taking it in his larger, calloused fingers.

"That was quite a punch," he said with a faint smile. "Remind me never to piss you off."

"It felt good," she admitted, flexing her fingers. "But damn, that hurt."

"Here, let me." His touch was so tender as he massaged her hand, his thumbs working soothing circles over her knuckles. He massaged them with tender care. He bent to kiss one, but she pulled away.

Meghan's breath hitched. "What are you doing?"

"My mom always said kissing it makes it better," Tommy said, his lips quirking into a shy smile.

"She was right," Meghan's voice was just above a whisper. He pressed his lips to one knuckle. She left her hand there. Warmth spread through her body.

Tommy glanced at her, his blue eyes searching hers. "You want me to stop?"

"No," she whispered. The rising heat in her neck made her skin blush. "I don't."

They paused, gazing into each other's eyes. The chaos of the nightclub faded into the background. She thought about just kissing him now, but the mood had been ruined. She didn't want to kiss any man, not even the one who held her fingers in a soothing grasp.

"I'm ready to go," she whispered.

"Yeah, let's get out of here," He wiped a tear from her flushed red face and smoothed a blond lock of hair behind her ear.

"Yeah, let's."

During the drive back to town, Meghan sat in her own head, remembering the slight, the insult. Go back to the farm with the rest of the animals. She knew he'd meant it as an insult. Go back to the farm, Miss Piggy. She remembered when he called her that one day, when she'd asked him after some award show, and he'd told her. "I liked the Miss Piggy skit, kind of reminded me of you." And she had shut up, not wanting to know what he actually meant, but knowing all the same.

"You want to talk?" Tommy had tried to break the silence. She had just shaken her head. Sometimes it was okay to be lost in thought, silent, letting your mind work through shit.

"I don't want to talk about it right now," she said. "Just take me home."

All Tommy said was, "Got it." He placed a hand on her thigh, rubbed back and forth to her knee. "You need to talk, let me know."

"I will." She felt the heat of his palm on her leg. She thought, I don't deserve this man.

When they reached her apartment complex, Tommy killed the engine and turned to her.

"Thanks for a fun evening," Meghan said, sitting in the seat, letting the silence in the cab stretch between them.

"You too," Tommy's smile was warm and genuine. "I had a good time."

Meghan hesitated, then smiled shyly. "I like you, Tommy. You're a good guy."

"I like you too, Meghan." His grin widened. "You're a good girl."

Meghan hesitated, fingers gripping the door handle. She stopped.

"Why are you so good to me?" she looked into his brown eyes, safe, trusting.

"It's the only way I can be."

She heard the honesty in his voice.

He paused, reaching out to touch her chin. "Hey. I'm not him."

"I wish I didn't believe it." She looked at him, his honest face, the expression of a man who had nothing to hide from her.

"I saw the pictures." He admitted. She looked away. She knew exactly what pictures he was talking about.

"Not very flattering were they?"

"I thought you looked great," he said. "I thought the media and all those commenters were pieces of shit though."

"So did I." She rested her hand on the door handle to get out.

"Sorry," he said. "You probably don't want to talk about it."

"I don't."

A pause stretched between them. Her heart thumped in her throat. She had to tell Tommy. Had to tell him what was going through her head the entire way home.

"How do I put this, tommy?" she asked finally.

"Put what?"

She let out a long breath, trying to relax her beating heart. "I don't know if I can do this."

He stayed quiet. She looked at him, those brown understanding eyes looked back at her.

"It's complicated. My life is a mess right now. Are you sure you want to be around that?"

"And my life isn't?"

Yes, she had to admit. Both of their lives right now were complicated as hell. "I want to think this is the wrong time. That in another month or two or a dozen we could maybe try to make this work."

"I thought we were friends."

"I don't know about that, farm boy," she chuckled warily. Her mind and body were fast becoming used to the idea of them being more than friends. And 'more than friends' was something she couldn't do right now.

He smiled. "I get it."

"You do?"

"Sure," he said. "How about we call it a night and I walk you to your door?"

"We can call it a night. But I can get there myself. I feel like I need some time alone."

"How much time?"

"I'll keep you posted." She opened the door and got out.

"Hey, You'll be okay. You need anything call me."

"I will." She turned to go, then looked back at him. Before closing the door she said. "Text me when you get home safe."

"I will." He said.

He started the truck and she watched him pull away, drive around a corner and disappear.

Fuck. What a disaster.

A bit later, she received a text, saying simply, "Home."

She didn't text back, as much as she wanted to.

Chapter 22

Tommy

. . ⁓ . .

TOMMY STEPPED OUT OF the truck, the small wooden box tucked under his arm. The gallery door loomed in front of him, a reminder of how much had changed—and how much still felt the same.

Inside, he knew Meghan would be there, surrounded by the clean scent of oil paints and varnish, the quiet hum of a life so different from his. But before he went in, before he handed her the gift, a memory surfaced, sharp and unshakable.

He was sixteen years old, The workshop smelled of sawdust and summer heat. A cardinal, half-finished, perched beneath Tommy's careful hands as he worked the feathers, carving each delicate ridge into the wood.

He barely heard the heavy footsteps behind him before his father's voice cut through the quiet.

"What are you doing?"

Tommy didn't look up, his fingers steady as he shaped the twigs beneath the bird's feet. Almost there. Just a little more detail, then I'll work on the feathers.

"What about the hay bales I asked you to put in the loft?"

"I'll get to it in a few minutes," Tommy said, still focused.

A beat of silence.

"You'll get to it now."

Tommy clenched his jaw, finally turning. His father stood in the doorway, arms crossed, the deep lines of disapproval set into his face. He didn't raise his voice—he never had to. That look alone was enough.

"I just don't understand," Thomas muttered, shaking his head.

Tommy gripped the chisel, forcing himself to breathe. He knew what came next.

"You don't have to," he said, standing and walking past him.

His father didn't move. "You're never gonna get anywhere doing this stuff, you know."

Tommy paused at the foot of the stairs. He should've just kept walking. Should've swallowed it down like always. But this time, the words clawed their way out.

"I know," he said quietly. "But I like to do it."

His father exhaled sharply. "It takes away from your chores. From your schoolwork."

"I'm not like you, Dad."

A sharp silence.

"What's that supposed to mean?"

"Nothing. Forget it. It's getting dark, and I have chores."

He took the steps two at a time, knowing his father was still watching him.

Later that night, when he came back to the workshop, he expected the cardinal to be knocked over, discarded. Instead, it was right where he'd left it—except now, the dust had been wiped from the base, as if someone had run their hand over it.

Three months later, on Christmas morning, a small box sat beneath the tree, his name scrawled across it in his father's unmistakable handwriting. Inside, a brand-new set of carving knives. No note. No words. Just that.

It was the only real acknowledgment he'd ever gotten.

The memory faded as Tommy pushed open the gallery door.

Meghan looked up from behind the counter, tucking a loose strand of hair behind her ear. The smile that crossed her face was instant, easy.

"Farm boy."

"City girl." He smirked, stepping closer. "Brought you something."

He set the box on the counter and slid it toward her.

Meghan arched an eyebrow, then glanced at him. "Should I be worried?"

"Terrified."

She huffed a laugh, lifted the lid—and froze.

Her fingers brushed over the wooden cardinal inside, tracing the ridges of its wings.

"Oh, Tommy..." Her voice was softer now. "You fixed it."

He nodded. "And now it's yours."

"I can't—" She shook her head. "Let me pay you for it."

"It's a gift, Meghan."

"But it's too much." She looked up at him, uncertain. "I have to—"

"Tell you what," he interrupted, leaning against the counter. "Display it. If someone wants something like it, let me know."

She turned the carving over in her hands, studying it. "I can't even tell it was broken."

"Glue, sandpaper, and paint work miracles." He shrugged.

Meghan glanced up at him, something warm in her eyes. "It's wonderful. Thank you."

For a moment, neither of them spoke.

Then she set the bird down and folded her arms, tilting her head. "So, what's next? Are you just gonna disappear back to the farm, or do I get to see more of you today?"

He grinned. "Got some things to pick up from Bennet's. Figured I'd stop by."

"I'm glad you did." Her voice was quieter this time.

He winked. "Me too."

After the nightclub disaster, Meghan had told Tommy she needed time. And he understood.

Now, standing in front of him, holding the wooden cardinal he'd carved just for her, she looked up, something unreadable in her expression.

She ran a finger along the delicate shape. "Thank you for this."

"You don't have to thank me."

A smirk curled at her lips. "Oh, but I do."

A beat. Then— "Got any plans Saturday night?"

Tommy blinked. "No."

"Good." She smiled. "I want to thank you properly."

He raised an eyebrow. "That's not necessary."

"Tommy," she sighed, "I want to spend time with you."

His arms crossed, amusement flickering in his eyes. "And how exactly do you plan to thank me?"

Her grin widened. "By showing you how to eat like rich people?"

His lips twitched. "Why would I need to do that?"

"Just humor me."

He studied her for a second. "I thought you needed time?"

She shrugged. "I took the time. I went to bed. I woke up. And I realized..." She exhaled, tilting her head. "I kinda like you."

His smile was slow, lazy. "Well, I kinda like you too."

Their eyes held—something real settling between them.

"So," she said, breaking the silence, "we go on a proper date. Dinner, dancing, a fine dining experience. The Westchester, downtown. Eight o'clock. My treat."

"Ladies don't pay for dates when I'm around."

"I insist."

His smirk grew. "Insist all you want. You reach for a card, I reach for the door."

She rolled her eyes, waving a hand in surrender. "Got it, Mister Macho."

"When do I pick you up?"

She hesitated. "Let's meet there. I have a bunch of things to do that day, and... I want to make a grand entrance."

He gave her a look. "A guy picks a girl up for a date."

She stepped a little closer, folding her arms. "Tommy," she said, voice light but firm, "you want me to make an entrance."

A slow, knowing grin spread across his face.

He winked. "See you then."

She smirked, shaking her head as he walked away.

And when Tommy got into his truck, he fist-pumped the air. "Yes!"

Chapter 23

Meghan

"I don't know how to dress for this."

Meghan stood in the center of her bedroom, hands on her hips, staring down at the disaster of clothing spread out across her bed—blues, blacks, greens, browns—all tumbling in chaotic piles of indecision.

Trina lay across the edge of the bed, propped on her elbows, watching with an amused smirk.

"I don't even know why you're doing this," Trina said, idly twirling a strand of her sleek dark hair between her fingers.

Meghan sighed, arms flopping to her sides. "I don't either."

Trina snorted. "So why'd you ask him out?"

Meghan hesitated, chewing her bottom lip. "Why did he even say yes?"

Trina rolled her eyes. "Because he likes you, dumbass."

Meghan huffed. "Maybe... maybe I like him too."

Silence.

Trina sat up straight, staring at her like she just said she wanted to become a nun.

"You are not allowed."

Meghan blinked. "Excuse me?"

Trina pointed at her. "You. Are. Not. Allowed. To catch feelings for Tommy Richards."

Meghan folded her arms. "Oh, really? And why's that?"

"Because!" Trina threw up her hands. "He's a farmer, Meghan. You—are you. You used to wear Chanel to Whole Foods. You lived in a high-rise in LA. And now you're telling me you've got heart-eyes for some dirt-covered farm boy who smells like—what was it? Cow shit and fresh hay?"

Meghan fought the urge to laugh. "You do realize I'm standing right here, right?"

Trina ignored her, waving dramatically toward the mess of outfits. "And look at you! You don't even know how to dress for it! That alone should tell you something!"

Meghan sighed, shaking her head. "You know, you sound an awful lot like Tommy right now."

Trina scoffed. "Because he's right! And for once in my life, I hate agreeing with a man!"

Meghan smirked. "I think I'm allowed to like whoever I want."

Trina groaned, flopping back on the bed. "Fine. But don't say I didn't warn you."

Meghan grabbed a deep navy dress from the pile, holding it up against her body.

"What about this?"

Trina glanced up, studying her. She sighed, defeated. "Yeah. That'll work. Now, God help us both."

Tommy

"I don't know how to dress for this."

Tommy stood in front of his closet, arms crossed, staring at the pitiful excuse for 'formal wear' hanging between years' worth of flannels and jeans.

Two suits.

One black. One brown.

Both stiff, rarely worn, gathering dust.

From behind him, Arlene made a noise.

"Is that all you have? A black suit and a brown one?"

Tommy shrugged. "That's all I ever needed. One for funerals, one for church."

Arlene rubbed her temples. "Jesus Christ, Tommy."

"What?" he asked defensively.

She sighed so hard she nearly deflated. "You're meeting Meghan Holloway at the Westchester. Not some dive bar honky tonk. You cannot" she said, pointed at the suit, "show up looking like you're about to either bury someone or praise the Lord."

Tommy frowned. "It's just dinner."

Arlene arched a brow. "With a woman who has literally dated a movie star."

Tommy exhaled. "Fair point."

Arlene smirked, grabbing his arm. "Come on. We're going shopping."

"Shopping?" He nearly recoiled. "No. Absolutely not."

Arlene didn't even humor him with an answer.

She simply dragged him out the door.

Tommy hated this.

The bright lights. The suffocating scent of too much cologne. The goddamn mirrors everywhere, making him feel like a lost farmhand in a funhouse.

"I look ridiculous."

Arlene ignored him, rifling through the racks of expensive sport coats. "You look like a man who's about to take a classy woman to a classy restaurant, which—shockingly—you are."

Tommy grimaced at his reflection. The dressing room mirror mocked him with its truth: he looked unnatural in the slate-gray jacket and crisp white button-down Arlene had thrown at him. The collar felt tight, the fit strange—like the clothes belonged to someone else.

He tugged at the cuffs.

"This ain't me."

Arlene, arms full of more options, snorted. "That's the point, dumbass. You can go back to looking like a grease-stained farmer tomorrow. Tonight, you're going to look like a man who owns a truck instead of someone who just crawled out from underneath one."

Tommy scowled. "Low blow."

She patted his cheek. "Tough love, brother. Now shut up and try on these pants."

Meghan

Meghan hated this.

Her reflection, the way her pulse wouldn't settle, the fact that Trina was right—

God. She wanted Tommy Richards.

She'd spent the last twenty minutes convincing herself she wasn't dressing for him while standing in front of her mirror dressed for him.

The navy dress hugged her in all the right places—elegant but not stuffy, sleek but not too much. She ran her hands down the fabric, smoothing invisible creases, willing the nervous energy away.

Trina, sitting on her bed, smirked.

"You're dressing to ruin him, aren't you?"

Meghan scoffed. "I'm dressing for dinner."

Trina grinned. "Yeah. Sure. And I'm the Virgin Mary."

Meghan threw a hairbrush at her.

Tommy –

Tommy stood stiffly in front of the mirror. Arlene had done the impossible.

He looked good.

The smoky gray blazer fit too well, the crisp white shirt bringing out the sun in his skin, the slacks fit his hips and legs just perfectly. The sleeves hugged his arms, and for once, he didn't look like a guy who spent his days covered in grease and sweat.

He looked—

He swallowed.

He looked like the kind of man Meghan Holloway deserved.

"You're welcome," Arlene said, arms crossed, surveying her work.

Tommy let out a slow breath. "Jesus Christ."

Arlene grinned. "She's gonna die."

After Arlene finished fixing his suit, her phone rang. She glanced at the screen, grumbled under her breath, then waved him off.

"You look great. Now go."

Tommy hesitated. "Who's that?"

She shot him a look. "Who do you think?"

His jaw tightened. "You want me to talk to him?"

"No. I got it, Tommy. Go."

He lingered for a second but knew better than to push. She'd handle it her way.

With a nod, he stepped out, hearing her answer just as the door swung shut.

"Yeah, what's up?" Her voice, muffled by the wood, followed him down the hall.

Catherine looked up as he stepped into the room, her eyes twinkling with amusement.

"Who's that handsome guy, and what have you done with Tommy Richards?"

Tommy rubbed the back of his neck. "Mom."

She grinned. "Go have fun, son. You look handsome."

He shifted uncomfortably. "I feel like I'm itching all over."

"That's what new suits do." She chuckled. "I put your dad in a suit like that once."

A pause. Then, with a small smirk, "Once."

Tommy huffed a quiet laugh. "He grumbled the entire time, didn't he?"

"Oh, nonstop."

His smile faded slightly. "That's Dad."

Catherine's softened gaze met his. "Was Dad."

The weight in her voice hit him square in the chest.

"Mom—" He started, but she cut him off with a small, knowing smile.

"Go." She patted his arm. "Have fun with your girlfriend."

His brow furrowed. "She's not my girlfriend."

Catherine just nodded, her smile lingering. "Yet."

Tommy climbed into his truck, exhaling sharply as he adjusted his cuffs.

What the hell is wrong with me? He grumbled under his breath.

The suit felt tight, unfamiliar, like he was wearing someone else's skin.

But beneath all that?

It wasn't just the suit making him uneasy.

Meghan

Meghan turned one last time in the mirror, tilting her head, running her fingers along her collarbone, brushing back the waves of golden hair.

She looked. Her stomach flipped.

She looked like a woman on a date.

"You're doomed," Trina sing-songed from the bed.

Meghan let out a long breath.

God help her. She was.

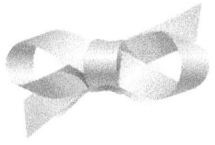

Chapter 24

Tommy

He sat outside the three-story antebellum mansion on Third Street, wondering what he was doing there. He tugged at his collar, wiped the thin sheen of sweat from his brow, and sighed. "What the hell am I doing here?" he thought. He was a guy sitting in a truck that belonged on a farm, surrounded by Mercedes, Saabs, and luxury cars. An older couple, dressed as if they did this every weekend—regal, composed, natural—walked up the large white staircase to the front entrance. Scarlett O'Hara and Rhett Butler going to another cotillion.

What the hell am I doing here?

A girl. Remember? A girl.

She had texted him that she was a few minutes late. "Go inside and wait," the text had said. "I'm on the way."

"Well, here goes nothing," he said to himself. He got out of the truck, smoothed his suit, looked one last time in the side mirror, checked his breath, and went up the steps to the entrance.

He opened the white painted doors with the gold curved handles and went inside.

He heard the violin quartet first. Great. Another indication he was out of his element. Fiddles playing near a stone fireplace? Yeah. Violins playing soft elevator music behind a stand near a grand piano? Definitely not.

A young woman at a stand, dressed in black and white tie, asked, "How many in your party, sir?"

"Two," he said, after a cough. The long hallway to the second floor stretched in front of him. "I have a reservation. Richards? Two?"

She looked. "There's no reservation for a Richards."

"Oh, right," he remembered it was she who set this up. "Meghan Holloway. Try that."

"Oh, yes," she said, giving him a welcoming smile. "Here it is. Follow me."

She led him to a table in the dining room. Chandeliers hung from the ceiling, lit by crystal bulbs. The same type of bulbs sat in wrought iron sconces lining the walls.

Jesus, this place is expensive, I can tell.

She led him to a white tablecloth-covered table, with a tureen of champagne already set up. Tommy looked down. In front of him was a collection of three plates, with a small bowl on top of that. Three forks sat on one side of the plates, and a collection of knives were opposite. Crystal goblets filled with ice water had been set before the plates, and a crystal champagne flute sat next to that.

The whole place screamed "Elegant" in large capital letters, as if mocking this guy who felt like an imposter in a suit.

The young woman pulled out the seat for him, and he sat down.

"This place is nice," he said.

"Thank you," she replied. "Henri hears that all the time."

"I'm sure he does."

He checked his phone to see what time it was. She was five minutes late.

He thought for a minute she was going to stand him up. And there he would be, on the hook for a bottle of hundred-dollar champagne. They'd probably charge for the five minutes he'd sat at the table. What the hell am I doing here? he thought again. I gotta have my head examined.

He put the phone in his pocket, and she walked in.

Jesus, holy fuck.

She glided in on blue high heels, a navy blue cocktail dress that hugged every curve like it was made just for her, gold and silver jewelry, and a hairdo that accentuated her neck. Other men looked in her direction, briefly, so as not to upset the women they were with. How could this woman ever think she was unattractive?

She walked in like she owned the place. This was her grand entrance. He sat there as she walked over, seeing him. He stood up, and banged the table with his knees. The silverware and glasses wobbled slightly.

She smiled, holding back a laugh. Her blue eyes sparkled.

Yeah, he was going to have a hard time keeping his focus tonight. The necklace went down into her cleavage, and he thought again, Yeah, this is going to be hard.

She went to him, put a hand on his shoulder, and kissed his cheek. "You're staring," she whispered.

"Yeah," he stammered. "I guess I am."

"It's good to see you."

"You too." He went to her seat and pulled it out. She sat, he pushed it in. At least I know to do this, he thought.

He went back to his seat.

"I'll assume you like what you see?"

"That was quite an entrance. Yes."

He adjusted his collar again and looked around at the place. Money. I'm smack in the middle of money. And I don't belong here.

Across from him, Meghan watched with barely concealed amusement.

"You've never been to a place this fancy, have you?" she teased, her lips quirking into a grin.

He set the small knife back down carefully, as if afraid it might break something. "No, I haven't," he admitted. "But for a date, Arlene said you'd like it. She said it matches your energy."

Meghan raised an eyebrow. "And what energy is that?"

"She said you'd like a good restaurant instead of something like the Golden Corral."

She laughed softly. "I like your sister. She's smart."

"So... where's the menu?" he asked, looking around as though it might magically appear.

"No menu," she said, a bit of a sly smile tugging at her lips. "You choose vegetarian, chicken, steak, or seafood. Henri takes care of the rest."

"Ah." He leaned back in his chair, looking skeptical. "Do I at least get to pick out my steak? Like at the Roadhouse?"

Meghan chuckled. "No, Tommy. We trust Henri."

At that moment, Gus, the waiter, arrived with a basket of French rolls. Meghan immediately took one, sliced it open with practiced ease, and slathered it with the creamy butter from the ramekin on the table.

Tommy watched her for a moment, then mimicked her movements. Only, when he cut into his roll, he smashed it flat, and crumbs scattered everywhere. "Sorry," he muttered, brushing at the mess. "Just a little nervous."

"You're out of your element, aren't you?" she asked, her eyes sparkling.

"Yeah," he admitted with a sheepish grin. "This is a far cry from where I usually eat."

"Maybe we should've gone there instead," she said, leaning forward slightly.

"No," Tommy said quickly. "I wanted you to have a special night. Besides, we already went to my hangout."

"But this isn't my hangout, Tommy," Meghan said, her voice softening. She toyed with the edge of her napkin. "You have no idea how many of these places I had to go to during my marriage."

Tommy paused, his expression serious for a moment. Then he nodded. "Well, let's just see how it goes. I'm trying to be on my best behavior here."

She smiled warmly. "You're doing great, big guy. Relax."

He leaned forward, resting his elbows on the table despite the elegant surroundings. "So, when do I get to eat this steak I don't get to pick out?"

She burst out laughing, drawing a few looks from a nearby table. For the first time all night, Tommy felt like he was in his element, after all.

Just as Meghan was about to say something else, a man approached the table carrying a large brown wooden bowl filled with romaine lettuce, anchovies, olive oil, parmesan cheese, and various spices.

"Hallo," the man said with a thick accent, bowing slightly. "I am Gus. I vill be making zee salad tonight."

Tommy watched with wide-eyed curiosity as Gus expertly began mixing the Caesar salad, slicing, blending, and tossing with practiced ease.

Tommy frowned at the lettuce. "What's that?" he asked, pointing.

Meghan bit back a chuckle, recognizing this was going to be fun. "That's the lettuce."

"But it's not in a big round ball," Tommy said, his brow furrowed in confusion.

"That's because it's romaine," she explained patiently, her amusement bubbling just beneath the surface.

"I don't like Roman lettuce. They can keep it in Rome," Tommy replied, his voice tinged with suspicion.

"No, Tommy," Meghan laughed now, unable to help herself. "It's just a different kind. There are different types of lettuce."

"There are?" His expression was a mix of bewilderment and embarrassment. He glanced around the room, his eyes scanning for hidden cameras. "You sure I'm not on one of those reality shows? Feels like you're all in on some big joke."

"You're not being watched," she assured him, reaching over to pat his hand. "Relax. Just enjoy the salad."

Gus finished his expert performance with a flourish, placing a perfectly prepared Caesar salad in front of each of them.

Tommy hesitated, looked at the forks, and then back at her. "There's three forks here."

She pointed to the smallest one. He picked it up. "Why are there three forks?"

"You know," she cocked her head, "I don't really know. I think the more forks on the table the fancier the place is?"

"How do you know what fork goes with what?"

"Listen, before I met John, I didn't know either. Try the salad." She stabbed at the romaine and ate. He watched her, wanting to do it right, taking his cues on how to eat at a place like this and wondering what he'd gotten himself into.

He took a bite, crunched thoughtfully, and then nodded. "Oh. That's good."

Gus poured the champagne next, announcing with a flourish, "Champanya!" He filled their glasses and straightened up. "Are you ready to order?"

"I'll have the steak," Tommy said quickly. "Medium rare."

"Ah, zat is zee only vay Henri cooks zee steak," Gus said, nodding approvingly.

"Well, I like the guy already," Tommy said, his tone warming.

Meghan smiled and said,. "I'll have the vegetarian plate."

"Eggzelent," Gus clapped his hands, gave them a gracious bow, and walked away. Tommy thought he caught the subtle shake of the waiter's head as he left the table, likely amused by the farm boy's provincial charm.

Once they were alone again, Meghan tilted her head, studying him. "You clean up nice," she said, her voice soft.

"Oh, Arlene bought this for me," Tommy admitted, tugging at the lapel of his jacket. "She said I needed a better suit than the one I wore to the gallery."

He was dressed in a tailored gray jacket and slacks, a vest, a crisp tuxedo shirt, and a blue-and-yellow tie. His dark hair was neatly combed, and he'd even shaved for the occasion, his jawline strong and smooth.

"You look really handsome," she said.

"Thanks," He met her gaze. "Arlene took me shopping, paid a pretty penny for this. She said I needed more than just a black suit for fancy outings." He looked at her, his dark eyes pouring over her body. "You look beautiful," he said, his voice low.

Meghan was a vision in her black cocktail dress, pearls glinting softly around her neck, and diamond earrings catching the light with every small movement. She carried a matching black purse, and her heels elevated her elegance. A silk shawl draped over her shoulders added a touch of sophistication. The dress was low cut, revealing just enough of her generous cleavage to draw his eye more than he wanted to admit.

Tommy shifted in his chair, fighting the urge to stare, but he couldn't help himself entirely. Meghan noticed and arched a brow, her lips curving in a knowing smile.

"See something you like, cowboy?" she teased, her voice playful.

He flushed, rubbing the back of his neck. "You know I do," he admitted with a boyish grin. "That's a pretty dress." She blushed.

"Maybe if this date goes well, you can see what I look like out of it," she flirted.

"Let's make sure it goes well, then."

She smiled again. Tommy thought he would never stop wanting to see that smile.

They talked companionably about the farm, how Arlene was doing, when the next gallery showing was going to be, and their plans for another date.

"Arlene is really becoming the artist to beat at my shop," she told him. "I've sold three of her pieces this week. She's got real talent."

"She does," Tommy agreed. "There's a ton of pictures and drawings of dad."

"The one she did for the gallery went crazy. I couldn't keep people from trying to outbid each other. There's something about him that she captures, almost giving every picture life. It's really a gift."

"I'll have to tell her you said that," he said. He couldn't keep his eyes off of her. The way their eyes met made his body flutter every time.

"I have to say, your eyes are killing me," he grinned. "Like the pond the other day."

"Aww," she grinned, with a blush on her cheeks. "Tommy Richards, getting all romantic."

"You're making fun of me again," he said, smiling like the football captain that just got the prettiest cheerleader.

"No, you're sweet, that's all."

Gus arrived with the plates, and Tommy sucked in a breath. This was positively the best looking steak he'd seen his entire life. Topped with mushrooms and onions, it sat on a bed of mashed potatoes and asparagus. Her plate was a selection of vegetables, with a collection of red, green, and yellow peppers stuffed with rice and beans. She looked at his plate, and Tommy noticed a bit of drool from her mouth. "That looks good," she said, admiring his dish.

"You want some?" he asked, cutting into the perfectly prepared steak. He offered her a bite.

"Oh, no," she said, patting her stomach. "Have to keep this girlish figure," she giggled.

"You want some, let me know." He put the steak in his mouth and made a soft moaning noise. "Oh, that's good."

Gus smiled, said, "Vill zer be anything else?"

Meghan smiled and said, "No, I think we're okay."

"Eggzelent," he said with a clap of hands, and went to the next table.

"So I assume based on that reaction, the steak is good?"

"I can die now," he said. "My god, this is my new favorite place."

"Well, I wouldn't go that far, Tommy, you haven't tried Kobe beef yet."

"They named beef after a basketball player?" His joke made her smirk.

"No, silly, it's Japanese," she explained. "It's very rare, and the way you have to prepare it is very involved. Suffice to say it's very lean, tender and tasty. We'll have to get some one day, just to see."

"If it's better than this, I'm sold."

"I can assure you, it's better than that."

"I don't know. This is pretty fucking good." He looked around, after hearing a sharp intake of breath from a nearby table. He looked over, and a woman with her grey hair in a bun sitting across from probably the oldest man alive shook her head and mouthed the word "Language."

He said, "Sorry, lady," and looked back and saw Meghan smiling. "Didn't know it was that kind of place I couldn't talk the way I normally do."

"Keep it up, farm boy, it's funny."

"Nah," he looked around at the place, and noticed the chandeliers, the violin players, and the grand piano. "I'll watch my language. Gotta respect the place, you know?"

She giggled. He loved watching her laugh. He could do it for the rest of his life.

They finished the meal, drank the champagne, and had a lovely time. The chocolate truffle desert left Tommy wanting more, and he asked for a to-go box. You would think Gus would have had a stroke for the way he looked shocked. Meghan laughed, "You don't ask for to-go plates here, Tommy."

"Well how was I supposed to know?" Then the bill came, he took out his credit card, slipped it into the card slot on the pad, and noticed the price. Forty dollars for a steak, he thought. Remind me to never come back here again. Sure, he had the money, but daddy didn't raise no fool. Of course, given the nature of the establishment, he begrudgingly understood. He thought maybe he would bring her back one day, after he'd researched how to use that many utensils.

They walked out into the night air, the vibrant scent of spring wafting around them. Meghan pulled her shawl tighter around her shoulders, and Tommy, noticing, shrugged off his jacket.

"Take my coat," he said.

She hesitated, her eyes flickering to his forearms before quickly looking away, a blush creeping up her cheeks.

"Oh, no, I couldn't," she protested, shaking her head.

"I insist."

"Okay," she relented, taking it and wrapping it around her shoulders. She smiled. "Thanks."

They walked toward the parking lot, hands intertwined.

"So," she said, glancing up at him. "How did you like it?"

"Like what? The steak?"

"No, dummy." She nudged him playfully. "The restaurant."

"Oh." He sighed, as if weighing his answer. "A little fru-fru for my taste. And way too expensive. I mean, who charges forty dollars for a ribeye?"

"It's about the experience," she teased. "Once in a lifetime and all that."

"I could do without a guy making salad at the table and listening to our conversation."

"Again," she said, grinning.

"Part of the experience," he finished for her. They laughed together.

"I had a really good time tonight," he admitted. The silence of the night cocooned them. "It was nice getting to know you better. Experience and all."

He twined his arms around her back, face beginning to lower to hers. She looked up hope in her delicate eyes.

Then his phone rang.

Shit.

Tommy pulled it from his pocket, glancing at the screen. Arlene. His jaw tightened.

"Something might be wrong with Mom."

Meghan nodded, stepping back. "Go ahead. Family, you know."

He pressed the call button. "Hello?"

His expression darkened instantly.

"Joey? What's wrong?... Okay, just calm down. Take a breath. Who? Mom? But—" His body went rigid. "oh, your mom...Shit... No, you can't repeat that...I know. I'll be right there, buddy. I'm on my way."

He hung up. "Fuck!"

Meghan's stomach twisted. "Everything okay?"

His eyes met hers, stormy and full of frustration. "No. It's Arlene. She drank again."

Meghan exhaled. "Oh."

"I have to go." He pressed a hurried kiss to her cheek. "Another time?"

She nodded, already shoving him toward his truck. "Go. Take care of her."

"I will. After I give her a piece of my mind."

Meghan tried, "Go easy on her, Tommy."

His fingers clenched around the door handle. "You know, I thought this time... I really thought—"

His breath hitched.

Then, with a frustrated grunt, he yanked the door open and slammed it shut. "Fuck!"

He roared off into the night.

Meghan leaned against her Mercedes, exhaling.

"Shit," she muttered, then got in and drove home.

Chapter 25

Tommy

The flew open as he stepped inside and he slammed it shut behind him. All during the drive he fumed, and before he came in, he tried to calm himself down enough to do this.

Joey sat at the kitchen table, hunched over a plate of cold, leftover mac and cheese, idly stirring it with his fork.

"Where's your grandma?" Tommy asked, shrugging off his jacket.

Joey hesitated. That was another bad sign.

"She's been in bed," he said. "Told Mom to make dinner."

Tommy frowned. "And did she?"

Joey poked at the macaroni again. "Cathy made this for me. But it's microwave, and it sucks."

Tommy's chest tightened. He clenched his fists, frustration mounting. He'd just walked away from a perfect night, a perfect woman, all because his sister couldn't get her shit together. From somewhere in the house he heard music. Janis joplin. Taking a piece of my heart. Fuck.

"Where's your mother?" he asked, voice tight.

"Upstairs," Joey finally answered. "I heard her yelling a few hours ago... then she said she was going to the store. Thought she was getting dinner."

"She didn't?"

Before Joey could answer, Cathy appeared at the top of the stairs, arms crossed tight over her chest. Her expression said it all.

"She got a bottle instead," she muttered."Now she's been in her room, that same song on repeat for a few hours."

Tommy's stomach dropped. He didn't hesitate. Didn't even stop to process. He just moved.

He could hear Arlene crying before he even reached her door. The volume of the song blasted through the door. "Take it! Take another little piece of my heart now baby."

"Arlene?" His voice was firm, but careful.

"Go away. I don't want to talk."

"Open up."

"No. I'm fine. Just help with the kids, will ya?"

That wasn't fine. "Are you okay?"

Silence. Then after a beat. "No."

Tommy exhaled, gripping the doorknob. He wasn't going to do this through the door. It was locked.

"Arlene. Open the damn door."

Arlene didn't answer. Tommy yelled, ""I'll break this fucking thing down right now if I have to."

"Fine. Fuck!"

The lock clicked, and the door swung open. The room smelled like vodka, acrylic paint, and old memories.

The wall had been painted white—stark, fresh, like the way Dad used to do it for her every year after her birthday.

A blank canvas. A blank slate.

In black, she'd painted a mansion—perfect lines, sterile windows. A house just like the one she'd left behind.

In the yard: a stick-figure woman. Two children drawn smaller beside her.

And across the lawn, far away beneath a leafless black tree, a man. Alone. Detached.

Slashes of red paint cut across the entire scene.

Furious, erratic. Like someone had bled over the memory and tried to make it art.

Janis Joplin's voice howled from her phone.

Arlene stood in front of the wall—barefoot, swaying.

A paintbrush dripping crimson in one hand.

A tumbler of cheap vodka pressed to her chest with the other.

Her pajamas—the ones she called her "emotional support jammies"—were streaked with red and black now.

She looked like a war zone.

Tommy's eyes flicked to the bottle on the nightstand.

Half-empty. Rotgut.

He exhaled.

"Nice painting," he said, dry.

"You couldn't afford the good stuff?"

He walked over and picked up her phone, silencing the music.

Arlene blinked, like she'd just realized he was there.

Then he picked up the bottle.

"No, don't—" she gasped, stumbling toward him.

"Arlene." One word. Sharp. Final.

She froze.

Tommy stood at the bathroom sink and turned the bottle upside down.

Clear liquid splashed into the porcelain.

Behind him, he could hear her breathing.Unsteady. Shattered.

She sank onto the bed, defeated.

"Cathy?" Tommy called, eyes still boring into his sister's.

The young girl appeared in the hallway. "Yeah, Uncle Tommy?"

"Find your mother's phone. Call Dana."

Cathy nodded, stepping into the room and grabbing Arlene's phone off the nightstand.

Before she left, she hesitated—just for a second.

"Baby, I'm sorry," Arlene whispered.

Cathy didn't answer right away. She just looked at her mother, then walked away.

There was a tear in her eye—but not sadness.

Disappointment.

This wasn't the first time she'd seen her mother like this. And she hated it.

After a moment, Cathy just shook her head and left the room.

He looked into the mirror and saw his own reflection—the tired version of himself that remembered Arlene like this before. Drunk on paint fumes and rage when she was fifteen. Crying under the porch with a bottle of Boone's Farm when she was seventeen. Screaming at their mother for not understanding her at twenty-one.

And now here she was again. Mascara running. Tears carving down her face. Still trying to find something inside the mess that would let her feel whole again.

He didn't yell.

Didn't comfort.

Just let the last drops of vodka drain away.

And waited.

Tommy stood over Arlene.

She raised a hand. "Tommy, just don't."

"Why?" he asked.

"I don't need your fucking preaching today."

"Oh?" He tilted his head, arms crossed. "Well, you're about to get it. Not from me, though. You already know what I'd say."

Arlene laughed—a bitter, exhausted sound. "I know. It's hard, okay?"

"What's hard?"

She let out a shaky breath.

"All of this. Raising kids alone. Trying to figure out my life. Fucking up. It's all hard." Tears slid down her face. "I don't know what I'm doing, Tommy."

He sat beside her, his frustration subsiding. He could never really stay mad at his sister. He was angry for other reasons. Many tied to that fucking ex husband of hers.

"You don't have to tell me how difficult it's been, sis."

Arlene leaned into him, sobbing quietly.

Tommy didn't speak. Just let her cry. Like she had on numerous occasions before.

"God, I hated the way Cathy looked at me," she whispered.

He squeezed her shoulder.

More silence. More tears.

She pulled away, rubbing her face. "It was Joe. Before you left."

"What did he want?" Tommy clenched his fist. He breathed in an attempt to lower the flood of rising anger. Tommy's body still tensed. "Oh yeah?"

Then she took in his shirt, the tie loosened and awareness flooded her face. "Oh, shit, I fucked up your date. Goddammit! I'm such an asshole. Fuck!"

"Arlene, don't worry about it," he said. "Tell me what Joe said."

"The kids." Arlene stood, grabbing a glass off her dresser, twisting it in her hands. "That's what did it. He wants the kids. For the summer."

Tommy's jaw tightened. "Oh, does he now?"

"Yeah. Said it's unfair he hasn't seen them." She scoffed. "I told him I'm not the one who moved across the fucking country."

Tommy stayed silent, letting her talk.

"Then he started in on his bullshit—how it was his dream, how I never supported him." She clenched the glass tighter. "I told him I was quitting, and you know what he said? 'Yeah, that'll be the day.'"

Tommy's blood boiled. If there was one guy he wanted to kill, it was her ex husband.

"So what did you say?"

"I told him I'd think about it." She paused. "He said it's only fair. It's been six months. He hasn't even talked to them more than a few times."

She snorted. "I said, well, maybe you should call more. And maybe—just maybe—," her breath hitched, trying to retain control. "—you shouldn't have fucked everything that moved while we were married."

Tommy clenched his fists. Joe was lucky he wasn't here. The suit felt tighter on his frame.

"And he had the nerve to say, 'It was only the one time.'"

"'It shouldn't have been any times', I told him, and he said, 'if you were the wife I needed it wouldn't have been'". Her face was red like the paint brush she clung to. "Fuck him!"

Then, she snapped.

She hurled the glass at the painted wall. It shattered, spreading glass shards all over the floor where it had hit. The splattered alcohol made the paint bleed down the wall, black mixing in with scarlet tears.

She collapsed back onto the bed, sobbing harder than before, holding her face. She looked up at him and huffed. "I'm done crying over that man."

He handed her a tissue from the nightstand. "You may want to tell your eyes that."

"I don't know what to do, Tommy." She choked back a laughing sob. "Tell me what to do."

Tommy pulled her into a fierce hug. He sighed. His anger had abated somewhat. He wasn't going to tell her about the almost kiss.

"Talk to Dana," he murmured. "Do what she tells you to do."

Her breath shuddered.

"I need help," she whispered. "I can't do this on my own."

"You don't have to."

She sobbed into his chest.

Apparently she wasn't done crying over that man. After a few minutes, arlene just whispered, "the way she looked at me. And he knew, it wasn't a man. It was her kids. She'd let them down. An she was just now realizing it.

"The way she looked at me," she sobbed again.

Tommy held his sister for the next few minutes until he heard Dana's car stop in the driveway.

"Executioner's here," he joked. She gave him a wan smile.

"Stay with me?" She asked, hope in her voice.

"Nah, this is between you and her."

There was a knock at the door below.

Tommy stood.

He heard Joey say, "Hey, miss Dana."

And Arlene's sponsor's determined voice, "Where is she?"

"Upstairs."

"Thats her,"Tommy said.

Arlene let out a weak laugh. "She's a killer."

"In a good way."

Dana stormed up the stairs like a five-foot-two hurricane of righteous judgment.

Tommy smirked. "The killer's here."

Dana scowled at him. "Where is she?"

He pointed.

"Go easy on her, will ya?"

"Never," Dana said, pushing past him.

Tommy nodded. "Attagirl."

He went downstairs, fixed the kids dinner, and wondered if his sister would be okay.

Tommy sat at the kitchen table, absently pushing around a half-eaten chicken nugget with his fork. Cathy sat across from him, scowling at her plate, arms crossed. Joey, on the other hand, had polished off his food and was now staring at the staircase, waiting.

Tommy could hear voices from upstairs. Sometimes loud, sometimes quiet. Crying at one point. Then laughter, strained but real.

Finally, after an hour, footsteps echoed down the stairs.

Tommy looked up.

Arlene stood there, her hair tied back in a ponytail, wearing jeans and a simple T-shirt instead of her old pajamas. She looked tired—but clearer. Less haunted.

Dana followed right behind her, arms crossed, that no-nonsense grandmotherly look plastered on her face.

Tommy leaned back in his chair. "Well?"

Arlene took a breath. Then she smiled. Not forced. Not broken. Just... small. Hopeful.

"We talked it over," she said, her voice steadier than before. "I'm going to send the kids to see Joe for the summer. It's time. It's fair."

Joey's face lit up. "Yeah?!"

Cathy groaned. "Whatever."

Tommy nodded, studying her. "And what about you?"

Dana answered for her.

"She's going to a group home for a little while." Her voice was firm, but kind. "She's overwhelmed, Tommy. She's drowning in responsibility, and it's too much. Taking a step back is the best thing for her."

Arlene lifted her chin slightly, almost like she expected Tommy to argue.

But he didn't.

"Good," he said simply.

She exhaled, like she'd been holding her breath.

Dana patted Arlene's shoulder. "Go get some clothes together. We'll pick you up in a few days once you've got everything packed."

Arlene nodded, then turned to her kids.

"You okay with this?" she asked softly.

Joey shrugged. "Yeah. I guess."

Cathy didn't answer right away.

Then, finally, she looked up. "I just don't want to get a call that you're dead."

Arlene flinched. But she didn't shy away.

She stepped forward, brushing Cathy's hair behind her ear.

"You won't," she promised. "I swear to you, baby. You won't." Cathy held her mother's gaze for a long moment, searching for something—truth, maybe. Something real.

Finally, she nodded. "Okay."

Arlene cupped her cheek for just a second, then turned back to Tommy. "So. We good?"

Tommy studied her for a beat too long. Not doubting her.

Then, he grabbed a paper plate, loaded it with three chicken tenders, and shoved it at her.

"Dinner?" he asked, a small smirk tugging at his lips.

Arlene let out a breathy laugh, shaking her head as she took it. "Thanks, bro."

He nodded.

Dana clapped her hands together. "Alright, eat up. We've got a meeting to go to."

Arlene groaned. "Can't we get something on the way?"

"No time."

Tommy watched as Dana practically herded Arlene toward the door.

Just before they left, Arlene glanced back—one last look at him. "I'll be okay, Tommy."

"I know," he said. She and Dana walked out.

Tommy leaned back in his chair, staring at the empty plate in front of him. Joey let out a breath. Cathy rubbed her face tiredly.

He pulled his niece and nephew into a strong hug. "She'll be okay," he told them. "I'll make sure of it."

"I hope so," said Joey.

Cathy said, "Me too."

Then he thought about Meghan. The almost kiss. Wondering if tonight had fucked it up between them.

And thought about the broken cardinal waiting for him in the workshop.

Chapter 26

Tommy

• • ✿ • •

IT WAS TUESDAY NIGHT, and everything was shifting.

Arlene had made the arrangements for the Lighthouse women's group home. She'd swallowed her pride, called Joe, and asked him to pay for the kids' flights to Arizona. Tomorrow, he'd take them to the airport in Wilmington after dropping her off at the small house in Castle Hayne, an hour from town. She'd be gone for two months. The kids would be gone just as long. That left Tommy and his mom alone on the farm, with nothing but time, soybeans, and the old Corvette waiting in the barn.

He should have felt relief. Instead, a knot sat in his chest.

They were all sitting at Angelo's. Catherine, Arlene, the kids shared pizza and ice cream, pretending this was just another dinner. But Tommy couldn't fake it. The moment felt heavy, like something had cracked and no one knew how to put it back together. Catherine must've sensed it because she looked across the table and said gently, "We haven't talked about your date, son."

Tommy looked up, startled. "It was fine," he said, his voice neutral.

But it wasn't fine. He was still pissed. At Arlene. At Joe. At himself. Saturday night had been a near-perfect moment, and then it was gone. stolen by his sister's relapse and a phone call from Joey that shattered everything.

He hadn't been able to shake it. The last three days had passed in a fog of work, responsibility, and resentment. He wanted to be a good brother, but the weight of always holding things together was starting to splinter. Arlene had explained—Joe stirred things up, pushed all the wrong buttons. Still, Tommy couldn't let go of the anger. Joe had broken something sacred when he cheated. A wife, a family—it wasn't something you discarded because you couldn't keep it in your pants. Tommy had been raised to believe family came first. Joe didn't. And now they were all paying for it.

Arlene had told him a few months ago, "You weren't there, Tommy. You didn't know what it was like. I learned early on it takes two people to destroy a relationship. Two people to kill a marriage."

Tommy wasn't convinced. Catherine said, "Still with us, big guy?"

He looked up from his ice cream, rocky road, which had started to melt into a puddle, uneaten. He'd lost his appetite. "Yeah, Mom," he said. "Just can't get my head wrapped around things. That's all."

Catherine said, "I know it's hard, son."

He sighed.

Hard was having a girl in your arms, almost getting ready to kiss that girl, and having it ripped away by reality.

"I just don't understand why," he said, his voice low.

Arlene talked to the kids, ignoring him. The family sat in a corner booth. Cathy was being sullen, but Joey was talking animatedly about all the things he was going to do in the desert. About how his dad was going to let him ride horses. And asking if he could get a cowboy hat, like Clint Eastwood. Arlene said, "If your dad wants you to, I'm sure he will." She asked Cathy, "What do you want to do when you get there?"

Cathy just sat and mumbled something like, "Burn the place to the ground."

"Come on, dear, you don't mean that." Cathy just looked at her with a 'see if I don't' expression. Arlene backed off.

Catherine said to Tommy, "I know how it goes, son." But Tommy wouldn't have it.

"I don't think you do," he said. Then shoved a bit of ice cream in his mouth.

Catherine said, "Call her tomorrow. She's probably giving you and the family some space."

"Yeah, all the space in the world. She's had three days and all he got in that time was a 'how's Arlene' text, which he answered 'fine, she's going to rehab. The kids are going to Arizona with their dad.'" He'd thought about asking her if they could get together again. But deep down, he knew the time had passed.

If she wanted to get together, they'd still be talking. She was busy. He was busy. Time hadn't given them any chance to even talk. He'd had to help the kids pack, spend days in the field, and she'd been busy with gallery stuff. Maybe it was for the best. Maybe it shouldn't happen.

Catherine said, "Call her tomorrow, after you get back."

"I might," he said. It felt like the rails they had been on had derailed. Any chance he'd had of even getting with her had gone into the ditch. The bridge had collapsed, all because of a phone call. Fucking Joe. You couldn't wait one more day, you son of a bitch, he thought.

"I don't think there's going to be any more tomorrows between us, Mom."

The door opened and let in a swish of wind. Catherine smiled. "You sure about that?" she asked.

"What do you mean?" He shoveled another bite into his mouth.

She nodded toward the door. "Tomorrow just might be tonight," she said.

He looked up, and there she was. A yellow rain slicker pulled tight against the weather, phone in her hand. Meghan.

She hadn't noticed them. She was on the phone. "I'm here," she said. "Let me go so I can pay for this," she said. "I know, Trina, yes, I'll get the extra marinara."

She headed to the counter. Angelo sat behind the register, counting the day's inventory. The sandy-haired gent looked up at her.

"Two for Holloway?" she said, after he'd asked what he could help her with.

"Ah yes," he said, "Chicken Parm. The best."

Meghan said, "Yeah, let me go. I'll be home in a bit." She hung up. "My roommate thinks so, How much?" Angelo pulled a couple of to-go boxes from the heat rack.

"It's paid for, the girl on the phone used her card."

"Oh, I'm going to kill her," Meghan said. "I told her I was going to pay."

Angelo smiled, "Nope, all taken care of."

Tommy was on his feet, heading straight for her.

She turned at the movement and saw him. Her face blushed. She smiled. "Hey," she said. "Fancy meeting you here."

"Yeah," he said. "Small town, you know. Bound to meet at one point or another."

"How's Arlene?"

"I'm taking her tomorrow."

Angelo put the to-go boxes in a bag. She left five dollars in the tip jar.

"Call you tomorrow?" he asked. "After I take the kids to the airport?"

"I don't know, Tommy," she said. "I might be busy."

"Yeah, I got it. I've just been thinking about you. Sorry. It's been a whirlwind at the house."

"I'm sure." She stepped away from him. "Well, I gotta go, this is best hot, you know."

"Sure," he said. He stood there, watching her go.

Then she turned. "Yeah," she smiled. "Call me tomorrow. Let's talk."

"Sure," he said. And she started out the door from the foyer.

No. He shook his head. He watched her open an umbrella she'd left in the foyer area. He went to her. But she was already out the door, umbrella blowing in the wind, the to-go boxes waving with the breeze.

He watched a blond girl ride away on a bike. A blond girl that could have been saved. A blond girl who said tomorrow.

Fuck that.

She was already at her car, parked under a light post in the gravel parking lot. He started out the door.

He had to. For weeks, the rubber band had grown between them, tighter and tighter, drawing them together.

This was the moment it snapped back. If he didn't do this now, he never would. It would break from the tension.

His body carried him forward, out into the breeze and the pelting rain.

She put the to-go boxes in the front seat and went to close the umbrella.

Her hair beat in the wind.

His t-shirt clung to his body. Rain slapped his face. He didn't feel it. His feet splashed in the puddles in the parking lot. And then he was there.

She looked up.

"Tommy?" she started.

He grabbed her face in both hands and pushed his mouth down to hers. The warmth hit his lips. She stopped, stunned. Seconds seemed like hours.

She moaned.

Her lips parted.

He felt her body melt. Her hands pulled him in, wrapping around his back.

Their tongues danced. He let out a low growl.

Rain fell around them.

Their bodies were tight against each other.

A spectral amber spotlight above them, cocooning them in light.

He drew back. Her face blushed red. Their eyes met.

She looked at him with blazing hunger.

Then kissed him back. Her hand went around the back of his neck. Her fingers fisted in his wet shirt.

His hands went around her waist, then lower. Their bodies pressed close, tight, warm. Hot. Blazing.

Rain fell on them, but they didn't feel it. Wind whipped around them, they ignored it.

He pulled back, they took a breath.

"Hi," she said.

"Hi," he said.

She breathed a breathless sigh. They were speechless. He couldn't form words. She said, "We're getting wet."

"I don't care," he said.

She grinned, larger than he'd ever seen her smile. "I don't either." They kissed again, warmer, longingly. And then she pulled back. "I have to get home."

"I know."

He opened her door for her. "Call me tomorrow?" he said.

"Yes," she answered. And he knew she had meant it. "Let me know when you get home safe," he said.

"I will." He breathed in her scent, jasmine and honey. He kissed her again, quickly, wanting to press into her swollen lips again. But he had to let her go.

"Food's getting cold," she reminded him.

He couldn't take his eyes off of her.

"Sure, take it easy."

He was a gibbering idiot now.

She got into the car, closed the door, and started it. He watched her leave. She gave him a small wave and pulled away. He waved back.

He looked back at the store. He saw five faces pressed to the main window, watching him. Catherine, seeing her son happy, Arlene seeing her brother finally get the girl. The kids, open-mouthed, and Angelo, hands on his heart, smiling, like he had just watched an Italian love movie from the fifties.

Tommy drifted back to the comforting warmth and dry atmosphere of the restaurant. He didn't care that the rain spilled over him. He didn't give a damn about the wind whipping through his hair. All he cared about was here.

When he reached the door to the restaurant, he shook himself off. Catherine beamed.

"Not a word, Ma," he said. "Not a word."

Chapter 27

Tommy

• • ✿ • •

HE DROVE DOWN THE HIGHWAY, the late morning sun stretching long shadows over the road. Tommy tapped his fingers against the steering wheel, half-listening to Joey talking about some video game, while Cathy sat in the passenger seat, scrolling on her phone, pretending not to care.

Arlene sat in the back, staring out the window, her overnight bag tucked at her feet.

No one spoke about where they were going. But they all knew.

The Lighthouse Home sat just outside of Wilmington—a small place, quiet, tucked into the countryside. Peaceful. The kind of place where, if someone really wanted to turn their life around, they could.

When they finally pulled up, Arlene exhaled deeply and muttered, "Well, shit."

The building was nice. Too nice. White wraparound porch, flowerbeds full of pink azaleas, and a calmness that felt unnatural to someone used to the chaos of raising two kids alone.

"Guess this is it," she said, grabbing her bag and stepping out of the truck.

Tommy followed, hands in his pockets, watching as Cathy and Joey climbed out, too.

Arlene turned to her kids, dropping her bag at her feet. They'd talked in the past few days. Tommy could see it in the way Cathy stood closer than before, in the way Joey actually leaned into her hug instead of pulling away.

"Alright, listen up," Arlene said, gripping Joey's shoulders first. "You guys will be with your dad for two months. If you need anything, call Uncle Tommy. He'll take care of it."

Joey nodded. Cathy didn't.

"Be good for him," Arlene added.

Cathy snorted. "Fuck that. I'm gonna be a living nightmare."

Arlene barked out a laugh. "Attagirl."

Tommy shook his head, but there was relief in his chest. At least they were joking again.

The front door of the home swung open, and a young woman in a nurse's uniform stepped out. Michelle.

Long black hair, tied into a neat bun.

"You must be Arlene," she said, offering a warm smile.

Arlene picked up her bag. "That's me."

Tommy stepped forward, his voice even, steady.

"Take good care of her."

Michelle met his gaze. "She has to want to take care of herself."

Arlene gripped the strap of her bag tighter. "I want to."

That was all Tommy needed to hear.

She turned back to the kids. One last hug.

"Two months," she reminded them. "It'll go by fast. And God forbid your dad calls me with any complaints, because I swear to Jesus—"

"—he won't," Cathy said, rolling her eyes. "I got it."

Joey squeezed her tight. "Love you, Mom."

"Love you too, baby."

Then she turned to Tommy.

For a second, it was like they were kids again. Like she was fifteen, asking for a ride home after sneaking out. Like she was eighteen, leaving for college she'd never finish. Like a few years ago, coming back with two kids and a broken marriage.

He pulled her into a hug.

"You'll be alright," he murmured.

She exhaled. "Yeah."

Then she turned, stepping onto the porch. She paused at the door, looking back one last time.

Joey waved wildly. Cathy just nodded once.

And then—she was gone.

The drive to the airport was quiet. No music. No talking. Just the hum of tires on the pavement.

Tommy pulled into the drop-off lane, parked, and walked the kids inside.

The airport felt too big, too bright. Cathy was cool and collected, but Joey stayed close to Tommy's side.

They reached the gate.

"Alright," Tommy said, kneeling in front of Joey. "You remember what I told you?"

"Yeah," Joey nodded. "Look out for Cathy, don't talk to weirdos, and don't eat anything Dad cooks unless I want food poisoning."

Tommy smirked. "Good man."

He stood, turning to Cathy. "You got this?"

"Yeah, yeah," she said, shoving her phone in her pocket.

A stewardess walked over, offering a kind smile.

"Are you two flying as unaccompanied minors?" she asked.

"Yeah," Cathy said. "Dad's meeting us in tuscon."

Tommy nodded, handing her their documents.

The stewardess looked them over, then gestured toward the gate.

"Alright, kids. You're in good hands."

Joey hesitated. Then, suddenly, he threw his arms around Tommy.

Tommy stilled for a second—then hugged him back.

"Love you, Uncle Tommy."

"Love you too, kiddo."

Cathy didn't do hugs. But she paused before heading toward the gate, eyes flicking up to meet his.

"See you later, Uncle Tommy."

"See you later, kid."

Then—they were gone.

Tommy watched the plane taxi down the runway.

Then he exhaled, turned, and headed back to his truck.

There was a picnic to plan.

And a woman waiting for him on Saturday.

Chapter 28

Meghan

The afternoon sun streamed through the gallery windows, catching on the glass cases and warming the polished wood floors. A customer walked out, hands full of handmade plates, and Meghan smiled. Another sale for Reynaldo.

Before she could return to her desk, the bell over the door jingled again.

Derrick Bennet stepped inside, tall and broad, his blonde hair catching the light. He had the simple confidence of a man who knew what he wanted.

"Afternoon, Meghan," he greeted, his eyes scanning the room.

"Afternoon, Derrick. Looking for something in particular?"

"Yeah," he nodded. "Carrie's birthday is coming up, and I want to get her something one of a kind. Something you can't find in a store."

"Good man," Meghan said with a grin. She walked him through a few options—paintings, handwoven blankets, pottery. But nothing seemed to catch his interest.

Then his gaze landed on the cardinal sitting on the glass counter.

"Now that," Derrick said, stepping closer. "That's great."

Meghan followed his line of sight. "Oh, yeah, a local guy makes these, Tommy Richards. You know him, right?" she said, smoothing a hand over the glass. "I'm trying to get him to see he could make some real money off his work, but he's stubborn as hell."

Derrick chuckled. "That so?" He leaned in, studying the intricate details. " I've only seen a few of his things. Jamie at the store asked him to display them, but he said no. How much?"

Meghan hesitated. "It's not for sale, but I'm sure he could make you one."

Derrick frowned. "Carrie's birthday is in two weeks. This looks like it took a lot longer than that."

"Yeah," Meghan admitted. "It does. I've seen his workshop—some of his pieces look like they took years to make. You should see his Eiffel Tower."

Derrick exhaled, nodding in understanding. "So what would it take to get this one?"

Meghan bit her lip, thinking. Tommy had told her, If someone wants something like it, let me know. He'd said it so casually, like it wasn't a big deal. But there was no way he could finish another one in two weeks. Derrick wanted this one, now.

Would Tommy really mind?

She took another look at the carving. It had been broken, once. Tommy had restored it. And if he wanted to, he could make another.

"It's not really for sale," she said again, hesitant. Then she added, "But... I guess I could let it go."

"How much?" Derrick asked.

"Oh, I wouldn't even know what to charge," she said.

Derrick tapped his fingers against the counter. "I have a budget of three hundred. That work?"

She blinked. Three hundred? That was more than Tommy ever expected to make on one of his carvings. More than he ever let himself believe he could earn.

"Sure," she said, pushing aside the tiny flicker of doubt in her chest. "That's great."

Derrick grinned. "Worth every penny."

Meghan forced a smile. "Sold."

She turned, heading toward the back to find a box. Tommy won't care, she assured herself. It's just a piece of wood.

Meghan stepped back into the showroom, the cardinal in her hands, just as the bell over the door jingled again.

She looked up—and her stomach dropped.

Tommy stood in the doorway, his blue eyes flicking to the carving in her hands. His expression didn't change, but something in the air shifted.

Derrick, oblivious to the sudden tension, greeted him with a firm handshake. "Hey, Tommy. Hell of a piece you made here."

Tommy's gaze lingered on Meghan for half a second longer before he turned to Derrick, his face unreadable. "Derrick."

Meghan cleared her throat. "Derrick offered to buy the cardinal," she said with a nervous smile, trying to play it casual.

Tommy's jaw tensed, but his voice stayed level. Too level. "Oh? I didn't realize it was up for sale."

Meghan flushed. "Well, you said if someone wanted one—"

"Yeah," he said, cutting her off. "I did say that."

Derrick, sensing the undercurrent of tension, hesitated. "Listen, if it's not for sale—"

Tommy shook his head, his lips curling into a tight, forced smile. "No, it's fine. If she wanted to sell it, it's hers to sell."

The words landed like a slap.

Meghan opened her mouth to say something, anything, but Derrick shifted the conversation before she could.

"Actually," he said, rubbing the back of his neck, "I was wondering if you could do another piece for me. My daughter Lizzy's obsessed with Strawberry Shortcake. Think you could carve one for her?"

Tommy's eyes didn't leave Meghan. "When do you need it?"

"Oh, not until August. Doesn't have to be perfect."

"It'll be perfect," Tommy said, still staring at Meghan. His voice was even, controlled.

Derrick grinned. "Appreciate it. And thanks again, Meghan." He took the boxed carving from her hands and tipped his hat before heading out the door.

The bell jingled behind him.

Tommy just stared at her.

Meghan swallowed. "Tommy, before you say anything—"

"It's okay," he said, cutting her off again. But it wasn't. Though his voice remained steady, a simmering anger flickered in his gaze.

"Tommy—"

"No, really," he said, shaking his head. "If you wanted to sell it, it's yours to sell." He turned to leave.

Meghan felt panic rise in her chest. No, this isn't how this was supposed to go.

"But he gave you three hundred dollars," she said, stepping forward, offering the cash. "Here. Take it."

Tommy didn't even glance at it. "It's not about the money, Meghan." He exhaled, shaking his head, running a hand over his face. Then, quieter, "It was for you. You, Meghan. As a gift."

The words hit like a punch to the stomach.

"Tommy, I—"

"Keep the money," he said, already turning away. Before she could say anything else—before either of them could say something they'd regret—he pushed open the door.

She swallowed. "What made you come by today?"

Tommy stopped, hand on the door frame. He didn't turn around.

"I wanted to see how you were doing," he said, voice quieter now. "After the other night. With John."

Meghan's throat tightened.

"I'm okay," she murmured. Then, softer, "But now, I don't know."

Tommy nodded once, just a quick, sharp movement. "Good to know you're alright."

Then he stepped outside, letting the door swing shut behind him.

A second later, she heard his truck door slam. The engine roared to life. Then he was gone.

Meghan stood there, the gallery bathed in golden light, three hundred dollars burning in her palm like blood money.

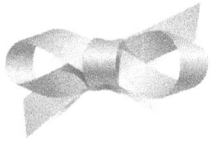

Chapter 29

Meghan

. . ✤ . .

SHE TURNED ONTO THE dirt road, the tires of her Mercedes kicking up a trail of dust as she made her way toward the farmhouse. It was her first time visiting, and equal parts trepidation and excitement churned in her stomach.

She'd chosen a blue-and-white floral sundress, light and airy, brushing mid-thigh. Maybe it would make Tommy pause. Maybe it would soften the tension still lingering between them.

First things first: apologize.

She still had the three hundred dollars in her purse. If he wanted it, she'd give it to him. If he didn't... well, she still didn't know what to do with it.

The two-story farmhouse stood at the end of the road, its white siding gleaming in the late spring sun. The barn, though sturdy, showed its age—faded red clapboard siding, sagging boards, a tin roof that had seen better days. Tommy had mentioned it needed repairs.

She put the car in park and exhaled. "Here goes nothing," she muttered, gripping the steering wheel for a second before reaching for her purse and stepping out.

The front door creaked open.

Tommy stepped onto the porch, his face lighting up when he saw her.

Her heart fluttered. That had to count for something.

He waved, descending the steps as she approached. Before she could second-guess herself, he pulled her into a hug. His arms wrapped around her, warm and strong, and she let out a muted sigh, leaning into him just a little longer than necessary.

"Hey," he murmured.

"Tommy, before you say anything—" she started, pulling back, wanting to explain.

He paused, waiting.

"I'm sorry."

He studied her for a moment, then pressed a soft kiss to her forehead. A simple gesture, but it sent a shiver through her, prickling her skin in goosebumps.

"Hey," he said. "I'm sorry too."

Meghan frowned. "What do you have to be sorry about? I messed up. I should have talked to you first."

"Meghan," Tommy murmured, a teasing glint in his eyes. "You're babbling again."

She let out a breath, smiling despite herself.

His fingers traced along her jaw, tilting her chin just slightly.

"I was mad at first," he admitted. "But I had some time to think about it. It's over now."

"You're sure?"

Tommy huffed a small laugh, shaking his head. "You worry too much, city girl."

She sighed, relieved, the tension in her chest unwinding.

Then he kissed her. Not rushed. Not desperate. Just slow, steady, a kiss meant for solace and reconciliation.

She melted into him, her hands resting lightly against his chest.

"You're sure you're not mad?" she murmured against his lips.

"I can't stay mad at you," he said. Then, with a grin, he stepped back. "Come on in. Mom made iced tea."

Meghan hesitated. Now was the time "I still have the money, you know." She felt him bristle, even though he kept his voice casual.

She reached into her purse, pulling out the three hundred dollars. He took it, but hesitated.

For a second, she thought he might change his mind.

But then he tucked it into his pocket, rolling his shoulders like he was shrugging off whatever weight still lingered. Thanks. But here."

To her surprise, he pulled out a hundred-dollar bill and handed it back to her.

"Your commission," he said.

She laughed. "No, Tommy. You keep it. It's all yours."

"You sure?"

"Yeah." She pushed the money back into his hands, firm this time.

He studied her for a moment, then nodded. "If you insist."

"I insist."

She smiled, this time without hesitation. "Now, about that iced tea?"

Tommy chuckled, stepping toward the house and pushing open the front door. "Come on in."

As they entered the home, he said, "Let me show you around."

She had fallen in love with the place, ever since Arlene had shown her around. It was full of rustic charm. The entry led into a large open living room with a comfortable looking gray couch and antique love seat of wood and gold cushions. Art pieces from several generations of Richard's family life hung on the walls. Portraits of the men and women who lived her adorned almost every surface.

"This is pretty," she said. "How many generations have lived here?"

Tommy, surprised at her reaction, answered, "Since the late eighteen hundreds. My great grandfather bought the farm after the civil war when the Reconstruction era started. He wasn't well liked because he was a carpetbagger, but over the years we've been accepted into the community. Some people still call us come heres."

"You know your history," she said. "That's funny."

"Why is it funny?" he gave her a quizzical look.

"Its heartwarming," she explained. "That you have a sense of place, a legacy. Hell, I don't even know where my own family came from, and when I was a kid since dad was in the military we moved every three or four years." She thought back on her childhood, all the states she lived in. "It must be nice to have a home that generations have grown up in and lived lives."

"You didn't?"

"I had to make new friends every few years, I can't think of anyone from school I remember. You probably grew up going to the same schools every year."

"Yeah, I did." She noticed the look of contemplation on his face, the way his brow furrowed when he said it.

"Did I strike a nerve?"

"No. Just thinking about what you said, moving every few years. You must have seen a lot of the country."

"And the world. One year we had to live in Germany. Then France, and a few years in England."

"See now you're making me jealous," he said, his eyes seeming far off.

"You've never been out of the country, have you?"

"No," He said, walking her through the living room, through a white painted arch to the dining room and kitchen area.

Catherine was at the sink, finishing dishes. A sky blue bathrobe tugged tight against her delicate frame. She turned when the two entered. "Hello," Catherine's warm eyes beamed as she came to Meghan. "You must be Meghan, I've heard so much about you. Its a shame we've never met up to now."

"Yeah, funny how we keep missing each other," Meghan said. She gave Tommy a sideways glance. "All good, I hope,"

Catherine answered, "Of course, hon, of course. You should see the way he looks when he talks about you. Like the sun and stars are dancing around his head."

"Mom..." Tommy said, giving her a pointed look. "You promised."

"I did no such thing."

"You should have, then."

"Oh hush," she swatted her son. "Come in, honey, welcome to the farm. She grabbed Meghan by the arm and led her to the large dining room table. Megan saw the age in the round mahogany table's dark wood and its ornately carved pedestal, a testament to years of work.

"So tell me," Catherine started, "How did you two meet?"

The next hour, Meghan and Tommy explained to his mother about their fateful meeting, the gallery show, the honey tonk, and how Meghan was surprised he could dance.

"My son learned that a long time ago," she said, patting her son's forearm. "Would you be surprised, his father taught him?"

"Yes, I would be," Meghan answered. "I've heard nothing but good things about his dad. That just makes him more endearing."

She noticed Catherine's eyes get a little glassy at that comment as the woman dabbed at her eyes with the tissue she had been using to stifle coughs during their conversation.

Tommy said, "Yeah, that was the same year he taught me and Arlene square dance."

"No!" Meghan said, shocked. "He didn't. Don't tell me you can Allemande left and Allemande right, cowboy."

"Right up there with the best of them, I'm afraid." He chuckled.

"Oh, I have to see that," she teased. Tommy blushed, embarrassed. He stood up.

"I don't have to suffer this abuse from you two," he said, smirking. "I'm going outside." He made for the door. Meghan stood up and went to him, chuckling.

"Oh, don't be so butthurt, big guy. We're just teasing."

"I know," he laughed, then whispered. "Just was getting tired of this jawing with mom. Wanted to show you the rest of the farm."

"Well lead on, farmboy," she said, turning back to Catherine. "It was nice meeting you."

"You too, dear," Catherine stood up, held on to the table for a moment to catch her balance and said, "You two go have fun. I've got work to do."

"You gonna be okay here?" he asked. "By yourself?"

"Oh, I'll be fine," she said. "Gonna go out and talk to your dad."

"I'll get to restoring the car one day," he promised. "One of these days soon."

She waved him off. "Oh, go on, you've been saying that for years."

"The car?" Meghan said.

Tommy told her, "It's mom and dad's old corvette, been out in the barn for over two decades, gathering dust and bugs."

"It's as beautiful as the day it was made," Catherine said, nostalgia showing on her face. "But you two go on. I set the picnic stuff on the back porch."

"Picnic?" Meghan's eyes lit up.

"Pretty day for it, but we got to ride the horses to get to the spot I have in mind."

"A horse ride and a picnic?" she melted against him as he put his arm behind her to lead her out the back door. "Why Tommy Richards, you old romantic." She mocked a southern accent, sounding like Scarlett O'Hara.

"And maybe when we get there, I'll kiss you like someone who knows how." he mocked a Rhett Butler accent right back to her.

She shook her head, thinking, god, this guy is cuter than he thinks.

Chapter 29

Meghan

He took her to the barn, where she saw the white convertible Corvette, and realized Tommy was right. It was rusty, a headlight was gone, and nests for critters of all types had made a home in the seats and rusted holes in the cracked, white-painted hood. Two horses had been saddled and made ready, with bit and bridle. He patted one on the head and said to it, "Hey, Sadie, you're a good girl."

Meghan's body went tight, and her face blushed. She wondered where that particular emotional response had come from. She took a deep breath. "Horses," she said, her voice slightly hoarse. "Such pretty horses."

"This one's Sadie," he said, leading the white and brown spotted mare out of the stable. The other was a deep brown, with a dark black mane. "That's Hank."

"Hank and Sadie," she said. "Why those names?"

"Ask Mom," he answered. "She's always named the horses, as long as I can remember. And we just accept it. She never tells us how she comes up with the names. But once she does, they answer to them. It's like she knows them on some level, and they love her. I don't know how she does it."

"They sense her energy," Meghan said. "It's kind, welcoming. They know they can trust her."

"I guess that's it."

"Like with you," she said. "Like you're a part of the farm, but I get the sense that you aren't a part of it either."

"What do you mean by that?" he asked, raising an eyebrow.

"Let's ride," she said, getting on Hank. "I'll tell you when we get to the picnic spot."

He shrugged, got on Sadie, and they trotted out of the barn and toward the treeline at the far north boundary of the farm, over half a mile away.

When they got there, Tommy led them through a small dirt track, and the canopy overhead cooled them as they went through sun-dappled shadows. The air was cooler here, and she shivered. I should have worn something more than a sundress, she thought. Here he is in jeans, a tee shirt, and a white and blue checked flannel. He must be roasting.

He looked at her, noticed her silence, and said, "Do you want my shirt?" He took it off and handed it to her.

"Sure," she said. She took the shirt, smelled it, and took in his scent. Not manure, she thought. That's good. A woman's touch infused his earthy scent, subtly overlaid with laundry soap. She wrapped it comfortably around her shoulders. He radiated warmth.

"Why did you do that?" he smirked.

"It's nothing," she chided. "Just wanted to make sure it didn't smell like cow dung."

He stopped. "What do you mean by that?"

She sighed. "It was a joke, Tommy," she said. He eyed her, stone-faced, arms crossed over his chest. She went to him, put a palm on his chest, and kissed his chin. "I was playing around."

"Sure," he said, obviously hurt. He stared down at her, and she blushed.

"I'm sorry," she said again. "I won't make jokes about manure anymore."

He broke into a smile and guffawed. "Got you," he said, still chuckling.

She hit him playfully. "Stinker!"

"At least I don't stink like cow shit, huh?" He wrapped his hands around her back and pulled her in for a kiss. Their bodies melted together, and she felt at home in his embrace.

He stepped back and said, "Come on, we're almost there." He led the horses through the woods to a clearing that seemed manifested out of a storybook. The sun rippled on a pond of clear blue water. Butterflies danced in the trees and bushes surrounding it, while dragonflies bounced and sped along the water's surface. A large oak tree stood near the pond, old and resolute. He took her reins and walked the horses into the clearing, letting them graze on the green grass.

"Tommy, this is beautiful," she said, awestruck. "Wow."

He took the blanket off of Sadie's saddle and spread it out under the boughs of the oak tree, then set the picnic basket down in the center.

"Yeah," he said, looking around at the space. "Dad showed me this place when I was five. I come out here all the time, just to relax and daydream."

"That's what I was talking about before," she said. She sat down on the blanket, and he joined her, putting a strong arm around her shoulder. They took in the sounds of nature for a minute, basking in the sun poking through the large, green oak leaves above them.

"When you said there was a part of me that didn't belong on the farm?" he asked, sparking the conversation back up. He reached into the basket and pulled out drinks, handing her a can of diet soda. "You like this, right? I think I remember you drinking it at the gallery." He opened a can of iced tea and took a swig.

She popped her own can and took a drink. "Yes, you're very observant."

"Only when I like a girl," he smirked.

"It's good to know you like me," she smiled back at him. He kissed her on the forehead. She blushed again.

"So about that," he started. "Not being a part of the farm, there's a reason."

She didn't expect him to open up about it and said, "You don't have to talk about it if you don't want to."

"Oh, no," he went on. "Everyone knows. I try really hard to like it. I mean, it's my home, you know? But there's just something about it I don't want to do."

"And what's that?"

"Everything."

She looked shocked. "What do you mean?"

"Everything is a chore. It's been a chore my whole life. Get up at the crack of dawn, do this, do that. Work, work, work. And I'm not lazy, trust me. It's just not what I want to do with the rest of my life. I watched my dad work his ass to the bone. My grandpa? The same thing."

"There's an honorable quality about that, though," she said.

"I know." He took another swig of tea. "And I respect that, don't get me wrong. It's just not something I want to do the rest of my life. You know my grandad never left Newton's Crossing? Never went past Raleigh. You've got some people in this town who've never gone out of state. Never left North Carolina. Never went to the mountains, never saw the Eiffel Tower, except in a book or a TV show. I want to see it, though, to touch it, put my hands on something that old."

"Wow," she said admiringly. "Farm boy waxing poetic. I like it."

"You're joking," he said. "I'll shut up."

She laid a hand on his arm. "No," she kissed his cheek. "It's charming. Go on." She wanted him to keep talking, and she enjoyed this boyish man who yearned for things outside of his small-town world.

"Every year, Mom and Dad would go on a vacation, you know, by themselves. It was one of Mom's things, and she dragged Dad along with her. She told me one time that they'd made an agreement. Well, she told him, and he went along more like it. They would go somewhere exotic around the world and enjoy new places. She was always the one with wanderlust, wanting to find new places to see and experience. He told me one time that he went along with her because he loved her, not because he liked the places they went. He did it for her. But if he had his druthers, they'd have gone to a motel or something in Wilmington."

"Not the wanderlust kind of guy, sounds like."

"Not at all," he chuckled. "But she loved him for it. Even though he complained to me after they got back. About fru-fru food, little sandwiches he couldn't eat, bread tough as shoe leather, and weird toilets in Japan. But he did it for her. He would never have gone for himself."

"But you want to," she nestled into his chest, and he put an arm around her.

"Yeah," he said, with a faraway look in his eyes. "I want to try the little sandwiches, the oceans of Tahiti, eat the shoe leather bread, and see the weird toilets. Well, maybe not that, but you get the idea."

"I do, Tommy," she said. "I do."

"That's what made me like you at first," he said after a pause. "I saw that boat captain and literally felt the salt air on my face, the sun overhead, the birds screeching in the ocean breeze

That's what was going on in my brain when I ran into the shelf. I wasn't paying attention to anything around me, it's like I was there. On that deck, fishing in that sea."

"You need to stop, mister man," she said. Her hand went to his thigh, inching up as he talked. "I don't know if I can take any more of this sweet talk."

He smirked. "I could go on, if you want."

She stopped him with a kiss, scorching, deep, as hungry as she had been for him a few nights ago. He sighed, returning the kiss. After a few minutes of making out, they broke apart.

"What was that for?" he asked.

"You're so adorable," she said. "I couldn't take it, I had to. I wish I didn't, but there's something about you I find irresistible."

"Why don't you tell me, then."

"I can't." she pulled away. "What did you bring to eat?"

"Arlene said you were vegetarian," he said. "So I brought some stuff to eat on a cutting board. Grapes, spinach chips, crackers, oranges, you know, fru-fru food."

She smiled. It was hard getting over this man and his attention to her. Most men wouldn't be doing stuff like this, but it's almost like he wanted every chance they could get together to be special for her. It was endearing, and if it kept up, she could see herself falling for him. In ways she didn't want to.

"That's sweet," she told him. "But I'm not vegetarian, I'm just on a constant diet."

"Diet?" he asked, a puzzled look on his face. "Why?"

She paused, trying to think of something to say. "Because I'm a little overweight," she said after a beat. "I have to get rid of this." She put a hand on her thigh and pinched.

"Shut up," he said. "I like this." He bent down and kissed the spot she'd just pinched. "You're fucking gorgeous, Meghan."

"You don't need to flatter me," she said. "I've lost a lot of weight since the divorce."

"I'm not trying to flatter you, I'm telling the truth. I thought you were hot the first time I met you."

"Same for me, but you're handsome, you've got muscles for days, and I'm still a little flabby after stress-eating for years during a marriage. John always complained. I felt like I could never live up to his insane beauty standards. I even got these for him, hoping it would change things between us." She pushed her breasts up, and Tommy blushed, watching her. She smiled as his face turned beet red. He looked back up at her face.

"It's okay," she joked. "You can look. Everyone else does. It's kinda fun, actually."

"So, they're fake, then."

"Yes," she answered. She pushed toward him. "Maybe if you keep being nice and poetic, I might let you see them in person."

"Don't make promises you can't keep," he joked.

"I can keep a promise to you," she said. She brought her hand up to the back of his neck and kissed him, pushing him back on the blanket, then straddled him, still with mouths and tongues entwined.

"Whoa, there, cowgirl," he said, between scorching kisses. Her breath was hot on his skin, and he put his arms around her back. She sighed, melding on top of his body.

"What am I going to do with you?" she asked. She went down to his hardness and swallowed him into her mouth. He gasped as her lips found rigid girth. She hummed, savoring the taste of it.

"You can keep this up," he answered with a slight smile. His hands wove into her hair, a soft tug as he shuddered under her touch. She smiled at the way his breath hitched, at the quiet groan that escaped him. He tried to pull her up to him, but she stilled his hand, meeting his gaze.

"Let me," she whispered, wanting to feel him come undone. She went back down on him, fervent and in charge. By the sound of his ragged breathing, she could sense his building climax.

When he did, his voice broke on her name, his head falling back, body tense and trembling. She kissed her way back up his chest, the rise and fall of his breath slowing as she curled into him.

"You okay there, farm boy?" she teased.

"Jesus," he muttered, still catching his breath.

He turned to look at her, a lazy smile spreading across his face. "Thought I wouldn't reciprocate, did you?"

Before she could protest, he flipped her gently onto her back, pinning her beneath him. She let out a breathless laugh. "Oh, listen to you, using big words."

"Cacophony," he murmured against her skin, kissing the dip of her collarbone. "Alliteration." His mouth traveled lower, teasing, tasting. "Supercalifragilisticexpialidocious."

She gasped as warmth flooded through her, her fingers curling into his hair.

"You're teasing me," she managed, her breath uneven.

"That's the idea."

His lips brushed lower, slow and knowing, and when he finally tasted her, she arched beneath him, a sharp cry breaking free. His name tumbled from her lips as his hands gripped her thighs, holding her to him. His touch sent her spiraling, falling into bliss caused by his too-warm lips and tongue.

When he finally moved back over her, she was breathless, her body humming with warmth.

"Do you have something?" she whispered against his lips.

His lazy, satisfied grin made her heart race. "Boy Scout motto," he murmured, reaching into his pocket. He opened the wrapper and put it on.

She laughed softly as he settled between her thighs, but the sound faded when he paused, his gaze searching hers. He brushed a stray curl from her cheek.

"I don't think I'll be able to stop unless you tell me," he said, his voice rough, restrained. "If you want me to keep going, just nod."

She exhaled, her pulse thrumming in her ears. Then, without hesitation, she nodded.

His eyes darkened as he pushed into her, slow, careful, watching her face as she gasped and arched into him. His head dropped to her shoulder, a shudder running through his body as he buried himself deep.

"You don't have to go slow," she whispered, her fingers tightening around his arms.

His restraint snapped.

He filled her in a single, aching thrust, and she let go, let herself drown in the feel of him. They moved together, the rhythm slow at first, teasing, torturous, until her nails dug into his back and she gasped, "Tommy—please."

And then he gave her what she needed.

The world narrowed down to the press of his body, the warmth of his breath, the way his name spilled from her lips in broken, desperate syllables. She shattered, clinging to him, and he followed with a hoarse groan, his body trembling as he found his own release.

For a long moment, they stayed like that, tangled together, their breathing uneven, bodies still humming with aftershocks. One heel pressed to the small of his back.

Tommy finally lifted his head, his forehead resting against hers. His lips brushed her temple, his voice low and raw.

"Holy shit."

Meghan let out a breathless laugh, still dazed. "Yeah."

And when he kissed her again, slow and lingering, she knew neither of them would ever be the same.

"You keep doing that, you're going to need more condoms, farm boy." she cooed.

"Guess I'll have to keep doing it then." He nipped her lip again. Then went down and tickled her cleavage with his stubble. As if in reflex, her arms went up around his shoulders, pulling him closer. The brush of his beard made her giggle. He pulled up. "Ticklish, huh?" he smirked.

"No," she lied. He did it again, and she let out a blushing smile. He came back up, he ebbed out of her, she frowned.

"Who'd a thunk it, right?" she gasped as he left her.

"What do you mean?"

"Nothing," she said, looking at him. His square jaw smiled broadly, and his eyes appeared brighter in the sun under his thick eyelashes. "God, you're a beautiful man," she sighed.

"You're a beautiful woman." He kissed her again, resting on top of her.

"You don't have any more of those, by chance?" she asked.

"I got one more, so we'll have to make it count."

"Let's make it count, then."

Then he kissed her like he knew how.

Two hours later, they rode out of the picnic spot and back to the farm.

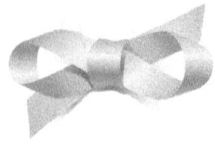

Chapter 30

Tommy

After the picnic, she and Tommy got together any time they could. He turned out to be fun. After all their back and forth, longing looks, friendly talks, and head-butting, they developed a rhythm that didn't feel forced or rushed. Both of them agreed to take things slow.

Meghan helped out around the farm while Arlene and the kids were gone. She got to talk to Catherine about life with Thomas, and she really started liking the woman.

Like turned into genuine love.

At times, when Trina was off gallivanting with the Spanish pottery maker, Meghan and Tommy snuck kisses in her apartment—and on one long weekend, they pretty much christened the entire place.

Those were the days of slow, lingering kisses in the daylight, fast-charging love at night, and at one point, knocking bowls of cereal off the kitchen table in their rush to get to each other.

Weeks turned into a couple of months.

And in the meantime, Tommy started fixing the Corvette.

He called George on a misty gray morning, a few days after Arlene left for the Lighthouse.

"What's up, buddy?" George asked.

"Starting on Dad's car," Tommy answered. "Think Larry would want to help?"

Larry was the chief of the Newton's Crossing Volunteer Fire Department and worked at Bennett's Lumberyard. He was a whiz with cars and loved fixing up the engines of old ones.

Larry's pride and joy—a blue '57 Chevy—still sat in his garage, waiting to be a gift for his son one day. He also owned a small garage on Reynolds Avenue.

That afternoon, the two men came to the farm, rolled the Corvette out of the barn, put it on a flatbed trailer, and hauled it away to work their magic.

"I thought you'd never get to this," George said.

Tommy shrugged. "Well, I need to do something with it instead of letting it gather dust and bugs."

Larry ran a hand over the body of the car. "It'll cost a bit. Looks like it's gonna be a big job. But I can fix the motor, get new tires. She'll drive."

"That's all I need," Tommy said. "I'm ordering the seats and body stuff, and it should be here soon."

George smirked. "Well, if you need help with all that, let me know."

Tommy chuckled. "I think I can manage."

George raised a brow. "Does this helper happen to look like Marilyn Monroe?"

Tommy grinned but said nothing. His silence was answer enough.

George slapped him on the shoulder. "Thought so. Good for you."

The two men drove off with the car.

Tommy exhaled, running a hand through his hair.

Yeah. Good for me.

He checked in with Arlene a couple of times. She was doing well. There were nightly meetings, group activities, and a relaxing jacuzzi and sauna at the rehab center—and she was using every chance she got.

"They give us stuff on addiction to read, but I found a basket of romance and fantasy novels here too, so that takes up more time," she told him over the phone. "Did you know girls around here like guys with masks and tattoos?"

Tommy snorted. "Maybe that's what you ought to go for next time. A bad boy with tattoos and a mask fetish."

Arlene groaned. "No mask. Just the tattoos. Big, broad-shouldered guy who'll chase everyone away that looks at me."

"Keep dreaming, sis."

Arlene sighed. "Yeah, I know. It'll never happen. I think the best I got was a guy who ran off with a redhead to Arizona."

"Speaking of which," Tommy said.

"have you heard from the kids?" Arlene asked.

"I have. Joey loves riding the horses. They have four now. And Cathy is helping Maxine making bead jewelry with jade and stuff to sell at local fairs."

"Don't tell me they're doing better and having more fun than you."

Arlene scoffed. "Who, the kids?"

"No. Joe and her," he joked.

"Tommy."

"Yeah?"

"Shut up. Please."

"Okay, sorry."

A beat.

"So the kids are doing alright," she exhaled.

"Sounds like it. There's a lot of activities on the farm, and I think they've gotten to a point with Joe where they can at least stand him."

"Good. I was hoping." She paused. "Now if I could just get to that same place."

Tommy sighed. "I don't think I ever will."

"Yeah, but I have to," she admitted. "For me, if nothing else."

"Good for you."

Arlene exhaled. "You could too, bro. If not for anyone else. Do it for yourself."

His jaw tightened. "He hurt my little sister. He doesn't get a pass."

"Maybe one day?" she asked.

Tommy exhaled. "We'll see."

They said their goodbyes with love, and Tommy went back to carving a new cardinal while spring turned into summer.

And the humidity of Central North Carolina became thick enough to cut with a knife.

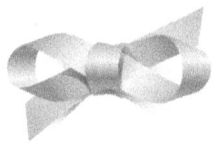

Chapter 31

Tommy

The sun was warm but not unbearable, casting golden light over the old barn where the Corvette sat, waiting for the new parts to be added. Tommy leaned against the workbench, rubbing his shoulder absently. Without Arlene and the kids there, he'd been doing double duty, and there were days his body couldn't keep up with the strain of farm work.

Larry and George had done a number on the engine, replaced the tires, and got the car to a point where it would drive. Larry had had to pay for a brand new axle because the old one was rusted, but he didn't charge Tommy for it, saying it was a gift for Catherine. He looked down at the boxes of goods he'd found to restore the interior. New seats, dashboard components, fuses, light covers, the works. This was going to be a job.

"Hey," he said, glancing at Meghan. "Wanna be my helper?"

Meghan arched an eyebrow. "Helper for what?"

He gestured at the car. "Figured I'd start cleaning her up. Thought maybe you'd want in."

Meghan tilted her head, considering. "You asking for my help, farm boy?"

He smirked. "Don't make a big deal out of it, city girl."

She rolled her eyes but grabbed a rag and a bucket of soapy water. "Alright. What's the first step?"

"Clean it up really good so I can fix the holes and get it ready for anew coat of paint."

She grabbed a sponge from a soapy pail of water. "Let's get to it then."

They worked in comfortable silence for a few minutes, the sounds of water sloshing and rags scrubbing filling the air. Eventually, Meghan broke the quiet.

"You ever restore a car before?"

Tommy shook his head. "Nah. Fixed tractors. Took apart my old truck a few times. But this...this is different."

"How so?"

He hesitated, then shrugged. "I dunno. It's...art, in a way. Taking something broken, worn down, and bringing it back to life."

She studied him, sensing something deeper behind his words. "You ever do any other kind of art?"

His hand stilled on the car's hood. He swallowed, his throat tight.

"Yeah," he admitted. "My carvings. I'm working on a few things I think you'll like."

"You should bring some to the shop. Let me sell it." She said while wiping the soapy sponge over the hood. "I think it would go over big."

"Nah," he said. "It's not for sale. Just a hobby. I couldn't."

Meghan frowned. "Why not?"

He let out a dry chuckle, shaking his head. "You really want to hear a stupid story?"

She leaned against the car, arms crossed. "Try me."

Tommy exhaled, rubbing the back of his neck.

"When I was a kid—eight, maybe nine—we went to the beach. Wrightsville. Mom loved it, so she dragged Dad along even though he hated the sand. Complained the whole way there, but she just gave him this look—you know, the kind that could shut him up without a word. Their marriage wasn't one of those lopsided things.

They were fifty-fifty. But man, when she wanted something, he didn't stand a chance."

Meghan smiled. "She sounds like a force of nature."

Tommy smirked. "Yeah. She was."

He dipped the sponge into the bucket, watching the dirt swirl away. "Anyway, there was this little tourist shop on the pier—Johnny Mercer's. I saw this wooden carving of a sea captain. You know the kind—long beard, yellow rain slicker, looked like he'd been carved right out of a storm."

Meghan nodded.

"I was obsessed with it. Ran my fingers over every little detail. I didn't know back then that they were mass-produced, factory-made. To me, it was the most incredible thing I'd ever seen. Mom bought it for me—seventy-five cents."

He smiled at the memory. "Took it home, studied it, ran my hands over it like it was some kind of totem. And I got this idea—I could do that. I could make something like it. Grandpa—Old Tom—gave me a whittling knife, taught me how to carve. Showed me how to shave off bits, smooth out the edges, take my time. It took a few tries, but I made my own little sea captain."

Meghan could see it in her head—young Tommy, sitting on a porch with an old man, carving with careful, clumsy hands.

"Grandpa thought it was the grandest thing," Tommy continued, voice softening. "And coming from him? That meant something. He never said much—hell, not even about his own family—but he meant it when he did."

His jaw tightened slightly. "So, I painted it. Took it to school for show-and-tell. Thought, Hey, maybe someone else will think it's special too."

Meghan already knew where this was going.

"There was this kid, Danny Wannamaker. Sixth grade. Bigger than me, meaner than me. Dumb as a sack of hammers, but he had more friends, so that made him dangerous."

She swallowed. "What did he do?"

Tommy exhaled sharply, scrubbing at a stubborn spot on the fender. "Laughed. Loud enough for the whole class to hear. Said it looked like a turd. 'Tommy made a turd! Look, it's Tommy Turdmaker!'"

Meghan's stomach twisted. "Jesus."

"Yeah," Tommy muttered. "He wasn't exactly a genius. Heard he went to college, got blackout drunk, and jumped off a dorm roof trying to land in a pool. Missed by a couple feet. Now he eats through a straw."

Meghan blinked. "Holy shit."

Tommy shrugged. "Karma's got a hell of a sense of humor."

A beat of silence. He let out a rough chuckle, shaking his head. "Anyway, point is—it stuck with me. I kept carving, kept getting better, but there was always this doubt. What if this is a turd? What if someone laughs again? What if no one likes it? I've thought about doing craft fairs, flea markets, selling my stuff, but every time I get close...I chicken out."

His voice got quieter. "What if no one likes it? What if no one likes me?"

The last words barely made it past his lips.

Meghan's heart clenched.

She set down her rag, walked over to him, and placed a hand on his forearm. His skin was warm under her touch, the muscle beneath tense.

"Tommy," she said, voice steady. "As an artist? I know art when I see it. And yours? It's beautiful."

He swallowed hard, his Adam's apple bobbing.

Meghan squeezed his arm. "You don't have to prove anything to anyone. Not that kid, not the world. But if it makes you happy? Then you should do it. And screw anyone who says otherwise."

Tommy let out a shaky breath, giving her a half-smile. "Look at me. Big caveman, six-foot-four beefcake getting emotional over a stupid wood-carved sea captain."

She smirked. "I mean, it was a damn good sea captain."

He chuckled, rubbing his face. "Yeah. It was."

A comfortable silence settled between them, the weight of old wounds lifting just a little.

Meghan picked up a rag and handed it to him. "Alright, caveman. Let's get back to work."

He took it with a smirk, nudging her playfully with his elbow. "Yes, ma'am."

And together, they cleaned.

. . ∞ . .

THE CHICKENS WERE OUT, scratching at the dirt, and that old red-headed rooster his mother had bought a few years back came pecking around the Corvette. Tommy shooed it away with a flick of his hand.

The rooster squawked, unimpressed, then fluffed up and advanced.

"Oh, you wee devil," Tommy muttered, kicking at the dirt near it.

The bird hesitated, shot him a beady glare, then turned and strutted off to find a hen to harass.

Meghan, watching with barely contained laughter, finally caved. "Wee devil?" she echoed, smirking. "What are you, a Highlander now?"

Tommy snorted. "Nah, that's just what Old Tom used to call the roosters. Stuck with me."

She caught the shift in his expression—a flicker of something distant, a memory pulling him away.

"Here comes another story," she teased, arms crossed, eyes alight with amusement.

He shook his head. "Nah, it ain't that good."

"Oh, now I have to hear it."

Tommy exhaled, leaning against the workbench. "Alright. You know I don't like farm chores, right? Well, part of that? Is because of roosters."

She raised a brow. "Oh, this should be good."

"When I was five or six, one of my jobs was to go out to the chicken pen and feed the damn birds. Problem was, I was too short to get my hand over the fence properly, so Dad made me get inside the pen with them."

Meghan already saw where this was going.

"This was the Summer of the Rhode Island Red," Tommy continued, deadpan. "Wee Devil—the meanest, nastiest, most ill-tempered bastard of a rooster you ever saw. Every time I stepped foot in that pen, that thing would come running for me, full speed, feathers puffed, ready to end my whole existence."

Meghan clamped a hand over her mouth, stifling a laugh.

Tommy gestured dramatically. "And me? Five years old? Scrawny, slow, defenseless? I ran for my life. Every damn morning. But one day, the gate wouldn't open."

Meghan gasped. "No."

"Oh, yeah," Tommy nodded, eyes wide with faux-trauma. "There I was, scrambling up the gate, screaming for my life, while Wee Devil is pecking me to death. Thought I was done for."

Her laughter finally broke free. "What happened?!"

"Mom," Tommy grinned, shaking his head. "Came storming out of the house like an avenging angel, big broom in hand, swinging it like a damn warrior. She started whacking that rooster, yelling, calling it names I'd never even heard before—scared the hell out of me and the chickens."

Meghan was laughing so hard she had to wipe a tear from her eye.

Tommy smirked. "After that, she patched me up, put Band-Aids on my battle wounds, and when Dad got home? He didn't say a word. Just grabbed his axe, went outside, and..."

Her jaw dropped. "Oh my God, no."

Tommy nodded solemnly. "That night? We ate Wee Devil for dinner."

Meghan gasped, clutching her stomach from laughing too hard. "Are you serious?"

"Gamiest son of a bitch I ever tasted," Tommy mused, shaking his head. "Tough as hell, but man... poetic justice."

Meghan wheezed. "If the wood carving thing doesn't work out, you could be a comedian."

Tommy grinned. "Why's that?"

"Because I've been laughing this entire time."

She looked at him then—not just amused, but admiring. Tommy Richards, rough-edged, awkward, self-deprecating, had a way of telling stories that made you feel them.

And together, for the rest of the afternoon, they worked on the Corvette.

They scrubbed the dirt from the frame, buffed out scratches, and prepped it for a new coat of paint. The hours stretched on, the sun moving in slow arcs above them, but neither of them minded. By the time the final clear coat gleamed in the fading light, their clothes were damp with sweat, their hands stained with grease, their cheeks streaked with smudges.

They stepped back, admiring the Corvette in all her restored glory.

"She's not done yet," Tommy admitted. "Still gotta take her to Larry, get her running. But there she is." He wiped his forehead, exhaling. "In all her damn glory."

Meghan whistled low, impressed. "She looks good, farm boy."

He grinned, eyes shining with pride. "Yeah. She does."

By the time they stumbled inside, exhausted and starving, Catherine was already at the kitchen table, going over the books. She looked up, taking them both in—the dirt, the sweat, the satisfied grins.

"You two look like you've had too much fun," she observed, standing up.

Tommy leaned against the door frame, still catching his breath. "We might have."

She wiped her hands on a dish towel, stepping toward the back door. Meghan followed as Catherine glanced out the window—her eyes landing on the Corvette.

The sunlight hit the white paint just right, making it glow.

Catherine inhaled sharply.

Tommy watched her, rubbing the back of his neck. "Still gotta do a lot to get her on the road.," he said. "But once she's good to go... how about I take you for a ride?"

Catherine's throat bobbed, her eyes suspiciously glassy.

"That'd be wonderful, son."

She touched his arm lightly, voice soft with something deep and unreadable. "You did good."

Tommy swallowed. "Thanks, Mom."

Then, shaking off the emotion, she clapped her hands together. "Alright. You two need to eat."

Meghan flopped onto a chair, groaning. "We were just going to order takeout."

"Nonsense," Catherine scoffed. "I've got a chicken in the fridge."

Meghan's lips twitched. "You sure it's not a rooster?"

Catherine looked at her, unamused.

Tommy shot Meghan a glare.

Meghan grinned.

Tommy shook his head, defeated, and sighed. "Chicken will be fine, Ma."

Meghan winked.

He winked back.

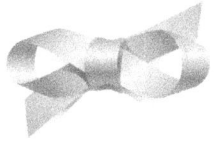

Chapter 32

Meghan

The summer heat pulsed overhead, trapped in the lofty rafters of the barn. The roof creaked and popped under the relentless August sun, the air thick with humidity. Sweat trickled in rivulets down Meghan's back, soaking into the thin cotton of her T-shirt. Her bra clung uncomfortably to her skin, itchy with perspiration.

"I need to take this off," she muttered.

"Then why don't you?" Tommy's voice rumbled from beneath the car, where he was working under the hood.

She glanced over, watching the way his legs flexed in those well-worn jeans as he shifted. Then he slid out from under the Corvette, and she had to bite her lip to keep from gasping.

His T-shirt was a mess of grease and sweat, clinging to his torso like a second skin. The fabric had soaked through in places, outlining every muscle.

Ought to be a law, she whispered to herself.

He chuckled. "I heard that."

Her eyes darted to his. He had that knowing grin on his face, smug and teasing.

"Ought to be a law for what?"

"Nothing," she said quickly, her cheeks burning.

He grunted, reaching a hand out. "Hand me that screwdriver?"

She hesitated, still staring. The moisture between her legs—whether from sweat or something else—was impossible to ignore.

"Meghan?" His voice snapped her out of it. "The screwdriver?"

"Oh. Right." She turned to the workbench, gripping the tool a little too tightly. What the hell is happening to me? She handed it to him.

"Thanks." He slid back under the car, but not before his gaze flicked over her sweat-drenched body.

He cleared his throat. "Damn thing won't come off. Hand me the spray lubricant?"

She barely registered his words. Something about a man, sweaty and dirty, working on a car had always done things to her.

"Don't need that," she murmured. "I'm wet enough already."

His movement stilled. Then his voice, filled with humor: "What was that?"

She blinked. "What was what?"

"What you just said." She could hear the grin in his voice. "About not needing it."

Her stomach clenched. Oh God. Had she said that out loud?

"The lubricant," he clarified. "Blue can, yellow letters."

Meghan spotted it on the workbench and grabbed it, willing herself to keep her cool. When she bent down to hand it to him, their fingers brushed, sending a jolt up her spine.

"Here you go."

"Thanks." He took it, but his eyes weren't on the can. They were on her.

"Nice view," he muttered.

She frowned, then followed his gaze—straight to the deep V of her shirt, now hanging open from where she'd leaned over. Her breasts, damp with sweat, were perfectly on display.

She gasped, straightening in a hurry, yanking her shirt closed around her neck.

He laughed. "Not like I haven't seen them before."

"Fix the damn car," she shot back, flustered.

"I am," he said, amused, before spraying the lubricant. The sound filled the barn, followed by another grunt of effort.

"There you go, baby," he muttered under his breath. "Come on... yes."

She smirked. "Are you having fun?"

"Got the screw out."

She almost responded with something she'd regret. Instead, she asked, "You want some water?"

"Could use some, yeah."

She grabbed a half-empty bottle from the workbench and bent down again—this time deliberately.

"Here you go," she said sweetly.

Tommy reached for the bottle, but his focus lingered on her again, his grip tightening around the plastic. His throat bobbed as he swallowed.

"Thanks."

She licked her lips. "So, what was that about the screw?"

"I was able to get it out of the hole," he said, holding her gaze. "With the lubricant."

Her breath hitched. "Do you flirt like this with all your helpers?"

He took a long drink of water, wiped a droplet from his mouth with the back of his hand. "Only the pretty ones."

She pressed her thighs together.

"It's hot in here," she murmured. "I need some air."

"Yeah, same," he said. "Let me finish up, then I'll—"

She tuned him out. Her eyes drifted to the car, to his long legs stretched out from under the hood. An idea formed.

"So, your mom..." she asked casually, reaching for the hem of her shirt. "She's napping, right?"

"You know she is."

"She's not coming out here?" She peeled her damp T-shirt over her head.

"Why would she?"

Her bra followed.

Tommy kept grumbling under the car, distracted by his work. "Almost done—just a couple more tight ones to—"

She toed off her sneakers. Then, slowly, deliberately, she popped the button of her white shorts.

"No reason," she said.

Her zipper came down.

Tommy grunted. "Damn, this one's tight."

She stepped out of her shorts, her breath quickening.

"Got you, bitch," he muttered triumphantly. "Damn, those were in there tight."

A slow, wicked smile spread across her lips.

"So... you're done then?" she asked.

"Yep." He started inching out from under the car. "Coming out now."

She waited until the moment his head emerged from beneath the Corvette. Then—

"Surprise!"

Tommy's breath hitched. He froze, eyes dragging over every bare inch of her body.

She saw the exact moment it hit him. His pupils dilated. His lips parted.

"City girl," he rasped.

She smirked. "Farm boy."

He swallowed hard. "Seems I'm overdressed."

She stepped toward him. "Seems you are."

He didn't hesitate. He grabbed her hips, pulling her to him.

"I'm all dirty," he murmured, his breath ghosting over the soft curve of her inner thigh. She parted her legs slightly, inviting his exploration.

"I don't mind," she whispered, her fingers threading through his hair, anchoring him to her warmth. She couldn't help but press herself into the intoxicating heat of his mouth, a low moan escaping her lips.

"Mmmm," he hummed against her, his hands sliding around her hips, pulling her closer.

"Keep doing that and I'll lose my balance," she warned, her voice husky with desire.

"Nothing wrong with that," he chuckled, his tongue tracing the delicate folds of her femininity, the hardness of it brushing against her clit. She shuddered, a wave of pleasure washing over her.

Seriously, Tommy, she thought, her mind melting into a haze of sensation. Something about his touch—the rough calluses against her delicate skin, the hot puffs of breath mingling with soft, teasing kisses—undid her completely. She surrendered to the moment, her body a vessel for his exploration.

He knelt before her, his lips and tongue worshipping her heated flesh as he slowly rose, inch by agonizing inch.

"I'm all sweaty," she confessed, her breath hitching as he found that spot that made her whimper with delight. He kneaded her ass, his strong hands shaping her curves as he rose to stand before her, a towering figure in the dim light.

God, this man is huge, she thought, her eyes tracing the lines of his broad shoulders and powerful chest. She reached for his shirt, tugging it over his head.

"Like I said, you're overdressed."

"Let's remedy that, then." He fumbled with the button and zipper of his jeans, shucking them to the ground. She reached out, her fingers closing around his burgeoning manhood. Her palm was slick with sweat and arousal, her grip tightening as she felt him pulse with pleasure.

"How about now?" he smirked, his eyes gleaming with mischief.

"Perfect," she breathed, her gaze locked with his.

He pulled her into a tight embrace, their sweaty, grimy bodies slick against one another. He lifted her, her legs instinctively wrapping around his waist, and turned to place her on the hood of the car. The metal was warm beneath her, but it was nothing compared to the inferno raging within her as he thrust inside.

"Jesus, Tommy," she gasped, her body arching into his.

"Sorry," he murmured, his voice husky with desire. "You have that effect on me."

He slowed, allowing her to adjust to his size, his weight pressing her into the heated metal. Her legs tightened around his torso, pulling him deeper, closer.

He began a slow rhythm, his thrusts deliberate and controlled. She moaned, unable to contain the sounds of her pleasure—the sharp gasps, the guttural cries that echoed through the barn.

"Jesus, Tommy," she cried, her voice raw with passion. "Fuck!"

Birds screeched overhead, their cries a wild counterpoint to the symphony of their lovemaking. The sounds carried on the breeze, drifting toward the open window of the farmhouse.

Catherine sat in her bed, a magazine lying forgotten in her lap. She heard the sounds, faint but unmistakable, and a smile touched her lips. That car gets a lot of action, she thought, her mind drifting back to a hot summer night in '77, two bodies entwined on the hood of that same car, the rain a welcome balm against their heated flesh. The fire between her and Thomas Senior that couldn't be extinguished by a summer storm.

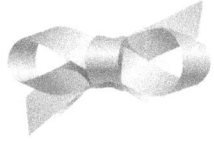

Chapter 33

Tommy

He picked the kids up at the airport in Wilmington.
Cathy looked sunburned, her pale skin now red and peeling in patches, bits of it turning tan while she absentmindedly rubbed at the flaking skin.

As they waited for their baggage, she picked flecks of flesh off her arm, scowling at it like it had personally betrayed her.

Joey, meanwhile, stood proudly beside their luggage, wearing a new cowboy hat—a white, wide-brimmed dome that made him look like a miniature John Wayne.

Tommy smirked as he grabbed a suitcase.

"You know about the rule of no hats in the house, buddy?" he asked, glancing at his nephew in the rearview mirror once they got into the truck.

Joey nodded solemnly. "Yeah. No hats in the house."

Tommy simply nodded back.

He would be a father to the kid, even though he'd just come from being with his real father.

Every time Tommy thought of Joe, a knot of anger bloomed in his chest, but he smiled despite it.

Arlene had told him he'd have to forgive Joe someday—but that would be a long time coming, if ever.

The kids had come back with gifts from their father and stepmother. Jade jewelry for Cathy—bracelets and rings she'd helped Maxine make to sell at summer fairs in Tucson.

"Did you like Maxine?" Tommy asked, watching Cathy from the corner of his eye.

She shrugged. "She's alright," her voice flat, noncommittal.

She turned toward the window, her fingers tracing absent patterns on the glass.

"Did you enjoy the trip?" he asked, keeping the conversation light.

"It was okay."

She blinked quickly, and he caught a single tear slipping down her cheek before she wiped it away.

She swallowed hard. "It's greener here." Her voice was quiet. "I missed it."

Joey piped up from the backseat. "Yeah, there's only brown. But the cactuses have pretty flowers on them."

"It's cacti," Tommy glanced at him. "So, you liked Arizona?"

Joey nodded. "Yeah. But it's not home."

Tommy's grip on the steering wheel loosened slightly.

Glad to hear it, buddy. Glad to hear it.

As they neared home, Tommy passed the ever-present white cross on the side of the road.

Without thinking, he knocked his knuckles against the steering wheel, like he always did.

Then he turned onto the drive, heading home.

Chapter 34

Tommy

He was upstairs when he heard the crash.

A sharp thud, followed by the clatter of something breaking.

Then—

"Uncle Tommy?"

Joey's panicked voice yanked Tommy into motion.

He flew down the stairs, his boots barely hitting the steps before he hit the kitchen doorway.

Catherine lay on the floor, her coffee mug shattered beside her, the dark liquid pooling around her. Joey stood frozen, his face pale.

"Call 911!" Tommy barked, already dropping to his knees beside her.

Her chest rose and fell—shallow, but moving. A pulse. Weak, but there.

"Mom," he said, shaking her lightly. "Hey, Mom, can you hear me?"

Her eyelids fluttered.

Joey fumbled with the phone, his voice unsteady as he gave their address to the dispatcher. Tommy pressed his palm to her forehead—cool and clammy. Not good.

Catherine stirred slightly. "Tommy..."

"I'm here, Mom. Just stay with me, okay?" He squeezed her hand.

She tried to speak again, but the effort drained her.

Sirens wailed in the distance. Relief hit him like a punch to the gut, but his grip on her hand tightened.

"Ambulance is coming, Grandma," Joey said, voice shaking.

Tommy swallowed hard, his heart pounding.

The waiting room felt like a prison.

Tommy paced, jaw clenched, arms crossed so tight his muscles ached. Joey sat with his elbows on his knees, head bowed. Arlene hadn't made it back from the home she was visiting yet. It was a good thing she could check herself out of the Grace house, but given the circumstances, he didn't think even the hulk could keep Arlene there.

It had been an hour. No updates. No doctor.

"Why the hell isn't anyone telling us anything?" Tommy snapped.

A young nurse with blond hair looked up from the desk. "They're running tests. I promise, as soon as we know, you'll know."

He exhaled sharply, nodding.

The doors swung open, and Dr. Paulson entered, followed by another man, much younger. Almost too young to be a doctor. With a black crew cut, and looking barely out of puberty..

Tommy's stomach knotted. He took one step forward, "Doc, what's going on?"

Paulson sighed. "Your mother had a fainting episode—her blood pressure dropped, causing her to collapse. It wasn't a heart attack, but it was a close call."

Arlene rushed through the emergency room doors, out of breath, like she had run from Castle Hayne to newton's crossing. "How is she!" she demanded as she sped toward tommy.

Tommy's shoulders slumped in relief. "Hey, sis."

"Where's mom?" Arlene snapped.

"It's ok. Tommy said. Doctor Paulson nodded. "She's alive, she's going to be alright.

"So she's okay?" Arlene pressed again.

Paulson hesitated.

"She's stable," he confirmed. "But there's something we need to discuss. Now the both of you are here."

The weight in Tommy's chest returned. "What?"

Paulson exhaled. "Your mom has been dealing with congestive heart failure for years."

Silence.

Tommy's jaw tightened.

"Excuse me?" Arlene asked in disbelief.

Paulson continued, "She's been on medication, but her heart is weakening. Today was a warning sign—it's something we need to manage carefully from here on out. With the right treatment, she can keep going strong, but... she should have been upfront about this earlier."

Tommy clenched his fists. "She knew?"

Paulson nodded. "For a while."

Tommy turned away, dragging a hand through his hair. Anger warred with relief. She was okay, but she had hid this from them.

Paulson nodded. "She's awake now. Go easy on her."

Arlene headed for the door, letting tommy talk to the doctors.

Paulson introduced him as "Ray Givens, he's a cardiologist. He'll give you more information."

The cardiologist, Ray Givens, looked barely old enough to shave, let alone hold his mother's life in his hands.

"How old are they making doctors these days?" Tommy muttered, rubbing his temples.

Ray ignored the comment, flipping through the chart. "There's a lot of obstructions around her heart. We could place a stent in a few spots, which would open up some of the arteries in the lower right quadrant. It might buy her a few more years—five, maybe. But her aorta is nearly eighty percent blocked."

Tommy's stomach twisted. "So what you're saying is... there's not much we can do."

Ray hesitated. "Not unless she agrees to the surgery. And from what she told me, she doesn't want, and I quote, 'some kid barely out of high school poking around inside me for nothing.'"

Tommy huffed out a humorless laugh. "Yeah. That sounds like Mom."

Ray's expression turned grim. "Look, Tommy... if she makes it another year, I'd be surprised. She hasn't been taking her blood pressure medication. When I asked how long, she just shrugged and said a month."

Tommy's jaw clenched. "A month?"

Ray nodded. "Said she forgot. That she was busy taking care of everyone else."

Tommy swallowed the sharp words on his tongue. Losing his temper wouldn't fix this. But it damn sure wasn't going to stop him from having a talk with her.

"Thanks, Doc," he said, already heading for the door.

Inside the hospital room, Catherine lay in bed, her silver hair pinned back, her eyes sharper than they had any right to be for a woman in her condition. Tubes and wires were plugged into her body at various points, nose, arms, and chest.

"Why the hell haven't you been taking your medicine?" Tommy snapped, stepping into the room.

Catherine's brows shot up. "And who are you now?"

"Your son," he bit out, turning to Arlene. "She stopped taking her blood pressure meds."

"Mom!" Arlene's head jerked up, magazine forgotten.

Catherine exhaled heavily. "Now you two calm down before I lose my temper."

"But—" Tommy started.

"But nothing." She lifted her chin, eyes sharp. "I have lived too long and changed too many of your damn diapers to let you talk to me like I'm some invalid."

"We just want you healthy," Arlene said, voice softer but no less urgent.

"I am healthy." Catherine crossed her arms. "And I plan on staying that way until I'm not. I am not some fragile old lady you need to fuss over like I'm Miss Daisy."

Tommy took a breath, forcing himself to dial it back. "Mom, we just want to take care of you."

"And you think I want that?" Catherine shot back, her voice steady but fierce. "It's not your job."

"We're family," Arlene said gently. "It's all our job."

Catherine's mouth tightened. "And can you even take care of yourself, girl?"

Arlene flushed.

Catherine sighed, softening. She reached for her daughter's hand, squeezing it. "Oh, baby, I didn't mean that. I'm sorry."

Tommy ran a hand through his hair, his heart pounding. "It's okay. We're all just... upset." He met his mother's gaze. "But, Mom, you didn't tell us any of this. Why?"

Catherine hesitated, then spoke, her voice low and firm. "Because I don't need you taking care of me. The better part of forty years, I've been taking care of you. And it was the best job I ever had. But when I go, I go. And you move on. That's life." She looked between them. "And I'll be damned if I go out as some mewling old hag in a nursing home. I'll be making coffee and sweet tea right up to the point you have to shove me in the dirt."

Tommy swallowed past the lump in his throat. "We would take care of you, you know."

"The hell you will." Catherine's eyes glinted with steel. "You try spoon-feeding me applesauce, and I'll spit it right back at you."

Tommy huffed a small laugh. "Amen to that."

Arlene wiped at her eyes. "So... what now?"

Tommy rubbed at his face. "Well... there's the surgery. It could buy you time. If we don't do it, you've got a year or two at best."

Catherine waved a hand. "Good. I'm already tired of this place."

Tommy stiffened. "So you don't want the operation?"

Catherine shook her head. "No."

Arlene's voice cracked. "Why not?"

Catherine turned to her, her gaze softening. She lifted a weathered hand to Arlene's cheek. "Because, baby... I miss your dad. You two are grown. You can take care of yourselves. I'm just an old relic hanging around. Let me go when it's my time."

Tommy's throat felt tight. "What about the grandkids? Joey? Cathy?"

"They'll get along just fine," Catherine murmured. "I got time with them. And I got time with you two, here at the end. That's enough." She studied them both, her smile small but certain. "You'll take care of each other. I know you will."

Arlene's lip trembled. "We miss Dad too... but isn't there something you still want to do with your life?"

Catherine exhaled. "I did it. I loved the best man I could with all my heart. I brought two wonderful kids into this world, and they brought two more." She squeezed their hands. "I got lucky."

Tommy clenched his jaw. "There's no talking you into the surgery?"

Catherine shook her head. "No, baby." She squeezed his hand again, firmer this time. "I've already put my wishes in my will. When I get out of here, I'll sign some more papers, a DNR, and then we let God sort the rest."

Arlene sniffled, tears rolling down her cheeks. "But, Mom... you have to—"

"No," Catherine said, cutting her off gently. "I don't."

Silence filled the room.

Tommy swallowed hard, then cleared his throat. "They're keeping you overnight. More tests. But then... you're coming home."

Catherine gave a small smile. "Good. Then I'll get to see you married off to that fine girl you've got."

Tommy snorted. "She hasn't said yes yet."

Catherine smirked, a knowing look in her eyes. "She will, baby." She glanced out the window, her voice quieter but sure. "She will."

Chapter 35

Tommy

Tommy pulled up to the house on Sycamore Drive, deep in the exclusive White Pines community of Newton's Crossing. Once he had made the plan to buy the cardinal back from Derrick, everything had fallen into place.

He knew most folks in town, and Derrick Bennett was no exception. They'd crossed paths plenty of times at the hardware store, and now Derrick and his new wife had just moved into the neighborhood, fresh off their wedding a few months back.

Tommy parked, stepped out of his truck, and walked up to the front door. He knocked twice.

A quick shuffle of footsteps came from inside, and a moment later, the door swung open.

"Hi!" said a little blond girl with bright blue eyes. "I'm Lizzy! What's your name?" She spoke so fast it all blended together. She wore a flowery shirt with a Strawberry Shortcake motif and blue jean suspenders, her hand already extended in greeting.

Tommy grinned. "Hey, Lizzy. I'm Tommy." He shook her small hand, amused by her enthusiasm.

From inside the house, a deeper voice called, "Lizzy? How many times have I told you to wait for me before opening the door?"

"Sorry, Daddy," Lizzy said sheepishly, stepping aside. "There's a man here named Tommy."

A tall, blond-haired man appeared in the doorway. Familiar blue eyes flickered with recognition before Derrick broke into a smile. "Hey, man. What brings you by?"

"I need a favor," Tommy said.

Derrick pushed the door open wider. "Come on in."

Tommy stepped inside as Lizzy shut the door behind them.

"I'm gonna watch my show again, okay, Dad?" she announced.

"Sure, sweetheart," Derrick said.

Tommy wasted no time. "It's about that cardinal—the one you bought at the gallery. I need it back."

Lizzy, still within earshot, turned around. "I like that bird. It's really pretty."

"Carrie loves it too," Derrick said, folding his arms. "But I get the feeling we're about to do a handoff." He nodded toward the box in Tommy's hands. "Lizzy, can you go get Carrie for me?"

Lizzy nodded and ran toward the hallway, shouting, "Carriemom! Daddy wants you!"—a little louder than necessary.

Tommy chuckled. "So, Carrie liked the cardinal, huh?"

"Loved it," Derrick said. "Want something to drink?"

"Nah, I won't keep you long. Just figured I'd drop by and ask."

A few seconds later, a tall, dark-haired woman appeared from the hallway, Lizzy trailing behind her. Carrie Bennett was striking—Derrick had finally lucked out after years of fumbling relationships.

"Hey, what's up, hon?" Carrie asked, wiping her hands on a dish towel.

"Tommy came by. He's got a favor to ask," Derrick told her.

Tommy met Carrie's gaze and pulled the lid off the box, revealing a brand-new cardinal, perched on a delicate twig, its feathers and leaves painted with breathtaking realism. The colors shone under the warm glow of the house lights, and every tiny detail had been carved with precision.

"I need the cardinal Derrick gave you," Tommy said. "This one's better."

Carrie blinked, looking between Tommy and Derrick. Then, as if something clicked, a knowing smile spread across her face.

"There's a girl involved, isn't there?" she teased.

Tommy chuckled. "Nailed it."

She reached for the sculpture, turning it in her hands, running her fingertips over the intricate details. "This is really beautiful, Tommy," she said, admiration in her voice. Then, without hesitation, she went to the shelf where the original sculpture sat, picked it up, and handed it to him.

"Thanks a lot," he said, carefully placing the original cardinal back in the box. "If y'all ever need anything, let me know—it's on me."

"No problem," Carrie said.

Derrick, however, rubbed his chin. "Free, huh?"

Tommy raised a brow. "Sure, what do you have in mind?"

Derrick smirked. "We talked about the Strawberry Shortcake. We still on for that?"

Tommy thought of Lizzy's shirt and grinned. "Give me a couple of weeks."

Derrick clapped him on the shoulder. "Appreciate it, man."

Tommy tucked the box under his arm and said his goodbyes.

As he walked back to his truck, he glanced down at the familiar carving in his hands. He knew exactly what he was going to do with it.

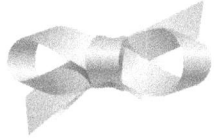

Chapter 36

Meghan

She came to the farm to help one day, feeding Sadie and Hank. One afternoon, she started feeling sick while smelling the hay. She wrinkled her nose and went inside to get something to drink.

Catherine studied her, frowning.

"You okay?"

Meghan nodded slowly. "Yeah. Just... something about the hay smelled off."

Catherine tilted her head. "Did Tommy get a different batch somewhere?"

"No clue." Meghan swallowed hard. "It smelled weird—like mold and vinegar."

Catherine's expression shifted. "I'll have to ask him." Then she paused, watching Meghan closely. "Why don't you go home, take a rest, get off your feet? See how you feel."

Meghan exhaled. "Yeah. I'll do that."

She told Tommy on her way out, and he frowned.

"Stay safe," he said. "Let me know when you get home, okay?"

She nodded and left.

The nausea still clung to her.

Maybe it was the manure, she thought.

She started thinking back, trying to rationalize it.

Yeah, that was it. Sadie had just let out a big one, and she had been right there in the stall, brushing her coat.

That was it.

It had to be it.

Had to be.

Right?

Meghan had been feeling off since yesterday.

She had blamed it on the hay at the farm, the smell of the manure, maybe something she ate. But after a full night's rest, the queasiness hadn't gone away.

Now, sitting in her office, trying and failing to focus on paperwork, she nibbled on celery sticks, crackers, and cheese, hoping it would settle whatever was going on with her stomach.

It didn't. With a sigh, she stood, pushing away from the desk. She needed to keep busy.

She stepped into the back room to catalog the new acquisitions, hoping distraction would help.

The gallery door chimed. Good. Maybe we'll sell something big today.

As she reached for her clipboard, her stomach twisted sharply at the sight of a bag of snack chips on her desk.

She pressed a hand to her belly. What the hell?

Her phone buzzed.

Tommy: Feeling any better today?

Meghan stared at the screen for a second.

Meghan: Yeah, must've been bad shellfish or something. I'll be fine.

A few seconds later—

Tommy: You sure? You were looking kinda pale yesterday.

She rolled her eyes but smirked.

Meghan: I'm fine, farm boy. Go wrangle some chickens or something.

A pause.

Tommy: Lol Alright. But let me know if you need anything.

She set the phone down and took a deep breath.

She had spent all day ignoring how bad she actually felt. But now, with the weight of the conversation settling in, her stomach clenched painfully.

No. Her heart thumped a bit to fast. She swallowed hard. Fresh air. Maybe she just needed some fresh air.

She turned toward the door, but the second she moved, a violent wave of nausea hit her.

Her stomach revolted. She ran to the bathroom.

She barely made it to the toilet before everything came up—her knees slamming onto the cold tile as she heaved.

The first wave. Then another.

She gasped, chest heaving, her forehead pressed against her arm as she struggled to catch her breath.

She blinked through bleary eyes at the toilet bowl.

Her fingers curled into her lap. Her mind flashed back—uninvited—to the last time she had to think about buying tampons.

A week ago? No... longer. Maybe she just had to go to the doctor.

Her stomach lurched with the thought. Something in her brain said, "You'll need a doctor, but this? A doctor can't fix."

Fuck.

She tipped her head back against the wall, her breathing shallow. Her hands trembled.

No. No, no, no.

She squeezed her eyes shut. And then, she cried.

Chapter 37

Meghan

Waiting was always the hardest part of these tests. She sat on the edge of the toilet, looking at the Clear Blue test strip that she'd bought a few hours earlier. Her period was five days late. With a nervous shaky breath, she looked down on the small pink and white test strip, willing it to be anything but what she thought.

I can't be pregnant, she thought. "I got on the pill."

She shook it, like that was going to alter the results. The box said it took five minutes, but it seemed to be taking an hour. That's what happens when you're waiting on bad news, time just goes slower.

Two thin lines materialized in the small window. She looked at the instructions. Two lines equals baby.

She couldn't breathe.

Her eyes went wide and she took in a sharp intake of breath. She put her hand over her mouth, that had formed into an O.

"Fuck," she said. Her hand shook and the test kit fell out of her grip and clattered on the tile floor. "What the fuck. No no no no no!"

Her face went red with anger and surprise. She couldn't breathe. "This can't be happening."

But it is, though, a voice in the back of her head told her. And you know who's it is. There's no doubt.

I'm thirty nine, that's too old to have a baby. She picked the test strip up again and looked at it. Yep, two lines.

"God damn it!" she cried, throwing it across the bathroom where it hit the interior of the shower surround and smacked on the tub.

She heard footsteps outside the door and then a voice said, "Meghan dear, are you okay?"

Between sobs, she said, "Yeah, sweetie, I'm fine!"

"I heard some sounds, I thought you'd fallen. Do you need help?"

"No," she said through the door. Unless you can reverse a pregnancy, that is. "I'm okay, really."

"Okay," she heard Trina stalk back down the hall to watch her daytime shows.

"Fuck, what am I going to do?" she asked the empty room.

She knew if she told Tommy he would instantly fall on his knee and propose. But she didn't want to marry him.

"I was on the pill, god dammit!" she buried her face in her hands and sobbed. "I don't want to get married."

The phone rang, it was Tommy, and she sent it to voice mail. Then she texted him right after and wrote, "Sorry, can't talk now, in the middle of a transaction. Talk later?"

A few minutes passed. Al he said was "Ok." with a thumbs up emoji.

She picked up the test strip again, got nauseous looking at it, and threw it in the trash.

She went out to the living room, where Trina was sitting on the couch, watching a daytime soap opera. The man on the screen was saying to a blond woman in his arms that he didn't want to go to jail, that he'd been framed, and he knew who the killer was. The woman, with a husky voice, said,"It was my brother, I know. And together we'll bring him down."

"You okay?" Trina asked.

"Yes," Meghan answered, hating to lie to her. "I have to go out, I have an errand to run, but I'll be back for dinner. Text me what you want, I'm going to the store."

"Okay," Trina said, turning back to the show where the man was confronting an older sandy haired gentleman about an accident at the hospital, and how it wasn't really and accident after all.

Meghan left the apartment and headed to her car. She needed air, she needed space. She didn't know what she needed beyond that. She couldn't eat, her stomach betrayed her. She couldn't have a drink now, obviously, and she didn't know about caffeine either.

She stepped into her Mercedes, got out her phone and called the one person she could that knew about these things. Arlene.

"Hey," Arlene answered after the first two rings. "What's up?"

"Arlene," Meghan said. "I need to talk, but I have to ask, is your brother around?"

"Yeah, he's in the other room, what's up?"

"Can you come talk with me? I need someone right now, and I don't want him asking questions."

"Not going to lie sweetie, but you have me worried."

"I'll explain in person. Can you just meet me at the coffee place? La Perk?"

"Be right there, I'm getting my purse."

"Thank you."

Meghan drove downtown to the main crossroads where most of the small business were built in an effort to revitalize the downtown area of the town. She parked in front of the coffee shop, with cartoony letters that said, "La Perk" and went in. She ordered a chai tea from the girl and as she did, she asked, "Does it have caffeine?"

"We have a decaf if you want that, ma'am," the young dark haired girl said.

"Sure," Meghan answered. "That'll be fine."

Minutes later, ensconced in a small table in the back, she saw Arlene come in and make a bee line for the table.

Arlene sat down. "Ok, what's up? You look terrified."

"I am," Meghan said. "I have a huge problem."

"Is it your ex?" Arlene asked, a worried look on her face. "He's not violent is he?"

"No," Meghan started. She took a sip of tea. "It's not that. It's something else. It's bigger than that."

"Go on."

Meghan sighed. "There's no other way to put it, I guess. I don't know what to say."

"Try me," Arlene said. "I've seen quite a bit."

"Well, you know how Tommy and I have been getting along lately, I mean, you probably know."

"I do," Arlene smirked. "But—" She stopped, the implication dawning on her face.

Meghan smiled, and a tear broke from her eye. She felt her throat close up again, and she couldn't breathe.

Arlene reached over and held her hand. "Relax," she told her friend. "Are you sure?"

"Yeah, I took a test an hour ago."

"But they can be wrong. I thought you guys were being responsible."

"I was on the pill. I'd just started taking it a few weeks ago. And we used condoms before that."

"Shit," Arlene said. "You have to tell him."

"I can't, you know how he is."

"i do. That's why you have to tell him."

"Arlene, you know your brother. He'll ask me to marry him on the spot, do not pass go, do not collect two hundred dollars, go directly to the altar."

"Yes," Arlene laughed wryly. "That's my brother. Honorable to the end."

"I don't want him to ask me because of this. I don't even know if I want to be married."

Arlene sighed. "Hon, I don't have an answer. You're talking to a woman who got married because of an unwanted pregnancy to a guy that ran off with some red headed bimbo because I complained and drank too much. Im not the one to ask."

"I guess I was just looking for advice on how to tell him. It's going to break his heart, knowing I don't want to marry him."

"It's going to destroy him," Arlene said.

"Great, that's all I needed to hear."

"Sorry to be the bearer of bad news."

Meghan sipped on her tea, she sat back. "So what do I do now?"

"Tell you what, don't get married because of a baby. I did that and you see how it turned out. Do you love him?"

"Sort of," Meghan had to be truthful. "There's a lot about him I like. But I've been down the marriage road before and it was a disaster."

"Then be honest with my brother. Tell him what's going on, let him make his own decision, and make sure he respects yours. I'm sure with enough communication, you two can come to an arrangement. Just don't get married because of a baby. It's worse. Trust me, I know."

"You think he'll take no for an answer?"

"With you and a baby in the picture? Not likely."

"Shit," Meghan said, "Now what?"

"Tell you what, think about it for a few days. I'll run interference, tell him you've got another show coming up and you need to put him on the back burner. Besides, he's got the car he'd been dealing with, he's recovering nicely, and it'll give you time to decide what to do."

"Thanks," Meghan said. "I really appreciate it."

Arlene got grave then, "Do you want the baby?"

"Yes," Meghan said. "Of course."

"Good," Arlene said.

The two women talked for a few more minutes and then Arlene left. Meghan finished her tea, sitting in the corner, patting her stomach, wondering what she was going to do and having too many questions to answer.

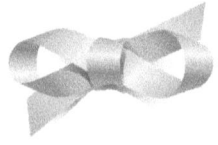

Chapter 38

Tommy

It had been a good day. Summer was coming quickly, and the soybeans in the fields promised a strong harvest. Tommy would finally be able to afford that new tractor.

He pushed the back door open with his elbow, balancing a small bag of tools in one hand. The familiar smell of coffee and something frying hit him as he stepped inside. Catherine stood at the stove, her back to him, while Meghan sat at the kitchen table, fingers tracing absentmindedly along the rim of her coffee cup. The air in the room felt... off. Still.

"Hey, baby," he said, crossing the room to Meghan. He leaned down, pressing a kiss to the top of her head. Her hair smelled faintly of lavender, a scent that usually calmed his nerves. But today, something bristled beneath the surface.

"Hey," she replied, quiet, flat. She didn't look up.

Tommy straightened, frowning. "You okay?" he asked, cautious.

"No," Meghan said simply.

Catherine turned then, drying her hands on a dishtowel. Her gaze flicked between them before she said, "Seems like you two have something to talk about."

Before Tommy could ask what the hell was going on, Arlene clattered down the stairs, her usual lively energy cutting through the tension like a knife. "Hey, bro," she greeted, wrapping her arms around him in a quick hug.

He barely reacted. His eyes stayed on Meghan. Something wasn't right.

"What's going on?" he asked, his grip tightening around the bag in his hand.

Meghan exhaled, then motioned toward the chair across from her. "Sit down."

He hesitated, glancing at Catherine and Arlene. Both of them looked like they knew what was coming. That only made his chest tighten.

Catherine set a steaming mug of black coffee in front of him as he lowered himself into the chair. He took a sip automatically, the heat scalding his tongue. "Alright," he said, forcing a light tone. "What'd I do?"

Meghan didn't answer right away. Instead, she slid something across the table. A small, white plastic stick.

It stopped in front of him with a faint scrape.

Tommy stared at it. Two red lines.

His heart slammed against his ribs.

When he finally managed to look up at Meghan, his voice barely worked. "Really?"

She nodded, her hands clasped tightly in front of her.

For a moment, he forgot how to breathe. Then, slow and wide, a grin broke across his face. "Well, that's great!" he said, full of wonder. He glanced at her again, expecting her to share in his excitement. But instead of joy, her face was clouded.

His smile faltered. "Isn't it?"

Silence in the kitchen stretched.

Catherine and Arlene exchanged a glance, one of those wordless conversations women always seemed to have.

"We'll leave you two alone," Catherine said, pushing off the counter.

"No," Meghan said quickly. "I want you both to stay. Please."

Tommy's stomach sank.

Catherine and Arlene hesitated but stayed. He suddenly felt like a defendant on trial.

"So... what happens now?" he asked, his voice steady. "We're keeping it, right?"

"Yes," Meghan said, so softly he almost missed it. "I am."

The wording struck him. I am. Not we are.

His grin returned, but it was hesitant now, careful. "Good," he said slowly. "Okay... So... what's next?"

Meghan exhaled, fingers twisting together in her lap. "I don't know."

"Well," Tommy said, sitting up straighter, "obviously, we'll have to get married."

"Bro," Arlene said quickly, a warning in her tone.

Meghan looked him right in the eyes. "I can't marry you, Tommy."

Her words hit like a hammer to his chest. He blinked, uncomprehending.

"I'm sorry, what?"

"I don't want to get married," she repeated, steady but vulnerable.

Tommy glanced at his mother, as if she could explain this insanity. "But... we don't have a choice."

"We do have a choice," she said, a touch of anger and fear in her voice. "I do, at least."

"Goddammit, would you just listen to me for a second?" His voice came out too sharp, and Catherine and Arlene both tensed.

Meghan froze, breathing hard.

He forced himself to calm down. "Can we just talk about this?"

Meghan hesitated, then slowly sat back down. Arms crossed, guarded. "So talk."

Tommy swallowed. "I just don't understand. Why don't you want to get married."

Meghan sighed. "Because I need to think this through. We barely know each other."

"Call me old-fashioned," he said, voice firm, "but the baby needs a dad. You need a husband."

Catherine's voice cut in, gentle but pointed. "That's an outmoded idea."

"I'm not leaving this baby," Tommy shot back, ignoring her. His eyes were locked on Meghan. "If that's what you're afraid of."

"I know that," Meghan said, softer now. "I just... I need more time."

"More time," Tommy echoed, leaning back in his chair, staring at the ceiling.

Meghan's voice was steady. "I'm not saying no, Tommy. I'm just... not saying yes."

He looked at her, unable to say anything. This was a hell of a thing, he thought. He clenched and unclenched his fist, not knowing what to do.

Arlene, never one to hold back, broke the silence. "She doesn't want to end up like me," she said bitterly. "Resentful of a man who never loved me and married me for a child and nothing else."

Tommy's jaw clenched. He turned back to Meghan, his voice quieter. "You know I'm not like Joe, right?"

Meghan smiled faintly. "No. You were raised right."

He exhaled sharply through his nose. "Then what the hell are we even arguing about?"

Meghan stared down at the coffee cup, swirling the liquid inside. "I need to know we're doing this for the right reasons. Not just because it's 'What you do.'"

Tommy looked at her, this woman carrying his baby, the woman he thought, and hoped, felt the same way about him that he did about her.

And for the first time since she slid that test across the table, the excitement in his chest flickered into something closer to fear. She didn't. And he didn't know how to fix this.

So instead, he leaned forward, resting his elbows on the table. "Take your time," he said, voice rough. "Take as long as you need."

But the way he gripped his coffee cup like a lifeline, the way his jaw stayed tight, and his shoulders locked stiff, everyone in the room could tell he wasn't happy. He had expected joy. Instead, he felt like the ground had been pulled out from under him.

After a long silence, Tommy pushed his chair back, the legs scraping against the hardwood. He didn't want to say anything that would get anyone more upset than they were.

He stood, rubbing a hand over his face like he could physically wipe away the weight pressing down on him. "I need some air."

Meghan's shoulders tensed, and for a second, he thought she might reach for him. But she didn't. Instead, she just nodded, looking down at her coffee again.

Catherine stepped forward, always the peacemaker. "Tommy—"

But he shook his head. "I'm not mad," he said, voice rough. "I just—" He exhaled sharply and turned toward the back door.

Without another word, he walked out onto the porch, the screen door slamming shut behind him.

The night air hit his skin, thick and warm, but it did nothing to cool the knot twisting in his chest.

He wasn't leaving.

But he didn't know how to stay, either.

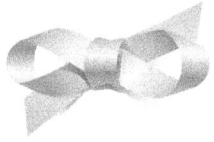

Chapter 39

Meghan

S he pushed open the door to the apartment, shoulders heavy from the weight of the day. She wanted nothing more than to collapse on the couch and let her thoughts settle.

But the moment she stepped inside, she knew something was off.

Trina was sitting on the kitchen counter, arms crossed, one leg swinging idly while the other braced against the cabinets. Her expression was unreadable—somewhere between curiosity and mild exasperation.

And then Meghan saw it.

Sitting on the kitchen table.

The pregnancy test.

Her stomach dropped.

"Uh... I was gonna tell you," Meghan started, hesitating near the door.

Trina arched a brow and picked up the test, holding it between two fingers. "Yeah? When? Before or after I had to find this little surprise while emptying the trash?"

Meghan exhaled, running a hand through her hair. "I needed to process first."

Trina hopped off the counter, landing lightly on her feet. "So... it's Tommy's, right?"

Meghan gave her a deadpan look. "Of course it's Tommy's. Who the hell else would it be?"

Trina shrugged, smirking. "Hey, girl, I don't know your life."

Meghan groaned and moved toward the table, sinking into a chair. Trina followed, dropping into the seat across from her.

There was a beat of silence.

"So," Trina finally said, drawing out the word. "What are you gonna do?"

Meghan exhaled slowly, shaking her head. "I don't know."

Trina studied her for a long moment, then tilted her head. "You tell him yet?"

Meghan nodded. "Yeah. Took the other one to show him."

"And?"

Meghan hesitated. "He... proposed."

Trina snorted. "Of course he did. That's Tommy Richards. No in-between with that man. It's either all in or completely checked out."

Meghan swallowed, fingers tracing the edge of the table. "I don't know if I want to get married."

Trina leaned back, folding her arms. "Look, I get it. You've been through the wringer with men. First with John, now this. But let's be real—you've never had a man fight for you the way Tommy has."

Meghan looked up at her.

Trina sighed. "You know I love you, and I don't want to see you get hurt. But Tommy? He's not like John. He's not like any guy you've been with. He's a good man, Meg. A little thick-skulled, but good."

Meghan let out a humorless chuckle. "Yeah, I've noticed the thick-skulled part."

Trina grinned. "Runs in the family." Then, more seriously, "But I have seen this before. He falls fast, he falls hard, and then..." She shrugged. "Sometimes, he gets cold feet."

Meghan looked down, the words stinging more than she wanted to admit.

Trina's voice softened. "I just don't want you to be the next girl left picking up the pieces."

Meghan swallowed past the lump in her throat. "He's different with me."

Trina nodded slowly. "I think so too. But just... make sure, okay?"

Meghan hesitated, then nodded.

Trina reached across the table and squeezed her hand. "Whatever you decide, I got you. And hey, if that man doesn't know how to change a diaper, Aunt Trina will be here to teach him."

Meghan's lips trembled into a small, grateful smile. "Thanks, Trina."

Trina smirked. "Now, let's get some drinks—oh wait, you can't."

Meghan groaned. "I hate you."

Trina cackled, standing up and heading toward the fridge. "You love me."

Meghan sighed, watching her best friend grab a soda and pop the tab. No matter what happened next, at least she wasn't alone.

Chapter 40

Meghan

The gallery was quiet.

Meghan stood near a display of pottery, pretending to adjust a price tag, but her thoughts were elsewhere. She had barely slept. Everything felt like too much—John, the baby, Tommy, the goddamn future.

The door swung open, and she knew before turning around who it was.

Tommy.

He stepped inside, his boots heavy on the hardwood. He looked tired, like he hadn't slept much either. His hat was in his hands, fingers gripping the brim. She braced herself.

"We need to talk," he said.

Meghan exhaled. "Yeah."

A long pause.

"I'm scared, Tommy," she admitted, her voice quieter than she intended.

"Of what?" His brow furrowed. "Marriage?"

She hesitated, then shook her head. "Everything. You. John. The baby. The gallery. Life."

He took a step closer. "So don't be scared." His voice was steady, warm. "I'm with you."

She let out a sharp, bitter laugh. "That's the worst part."

Tommy looked confused. "I don't understand."

Meghan clenched her fists. "Because you being here makes it real! I didn't want this, Tommy. I didn't want to be a mother, or a wife. I wanted to be on my own. I wanted to see the world, build something that was mine. And then you came along and took it all away!"

His jaw tightened. "How the hell did I do that?"

"Because," she nearly shouted, her voice breaking. "You made me fall in love with you, goddammit!"

Silence.

Meghan's breath hitched. Her heart pounded.

Shit.

Her eyes went wide, like she wanted to snatch the words back.

"Fuck," she whispered, then turned sharply, storming toward the back room.

"Wait."

His voice stopped her.

She didn't turn around.

"Did you just say—"

"No," she blurted.

"Yes, you did."

She squeezed her eyes shut, her breath shaky. A tear slipped down her cheek.

Tommy stepped closer. "Meghan." His voice was softer now. "Did you mean it?"

She turned then, meeting his gaze. Her bottom lip trembled. "I guess I did."

Something shifted in his face.

"So what if I feel the same way?" he asked.

She swallowed hard. "I didn't want any of this." Her voice wavered. "I just wanted a fling. Something fun. But you..." She exhaled shakily, running a hand through her hair. "You just wormed your way in. And now here we are."

A beat of silence.

Then he took another step forward, closing the distance between them.

"Come here," he murmured.

She didn't resist. She let herself fall into his embrace, his arms strong and warm around her.

Tommy rested his chin on the top of her head, breathing her in. She smelled like lemons and paint—like her.

"Listen," he said, his voice steady. "I get it. You're afraid. And to be honest? So am I."

She closed her eyes.

"But I don't want to put pressure on you," he continued. "You don't want to get married? Fine. I get it."

Meghan pulled back just enough to look at him. "I'm sorry," she whispered.

"Don't apologize." His voice was gentle, but there was sadness there, too. His rough hand came up, tilting her chin so she couldn't look away. "But I will say this—whatever we are, whatever this turns into... I want to be in this baby's life. I will be a father."

A small, wobbly smile pulled at her lips.

He kissed her forehead.

"You got it?" he said, voice firm. "That kid will know a dad."

She nodded. "I appreciate that."

"So you're not mad?" she asked, hesitant.

He shrugged. "How could I be mad at you?" He inhaled deeply, then admitted, "I love you, Meghan."

Her breath hitched. She pressed her face against his chest, the scent of farm and earth grounding her.

"You too, big guy," she murmured. Then she looked up at him, a soft sadness in her eyes. "But love isn't enough for a marriage."

He nodded. "It's a start."

She exhaled slowly. "Yeah," she admitted. "Maybe it is."

Tommy cupped her cheek. "Wherever this goes, I'm here."

Meghan smiled faintly. "So am I."

"Good." He laced his fingers through hers, squeezing lightly.

There was a beat of silence between them—something lighter, easier than before.

Tommy smirked. "So... we're good?"

She chuckled. "Yeah. We are."

His grin widened. Then he hesitated. "Hey... I have to go see Mom at the hospital. Any chance I could convince you to join me?"

Meghan bit her lip, considering.

Then she nodded. "Sure. Let's go."

Tommy gave her hand another squeeze before leading her toward the door.

And as they stepped outside, she felt the warmth of his touch linger.

Maybe—just maybe—she wasn't so sure she wanted to fight this anymore.

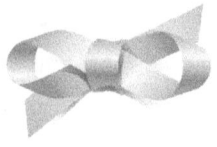

Chapter 41

Tommy

It was a bright and shining morning, a beautiful day for a drive with the top down. Tommy backed the newly restored Corvette out of the barn and stopped for one last inspection before he left. He had done what he could. Meghan and he had painted it white, with the red racing stripe. It wasn't professional, but it would do. There's only so much one can do with spray paint and tape. But it looked as good as the original, and it drove, so that's all he needed.

Even if it just drove in the city, they'd gotten it running. He'd replaced the seats, cleaned the dashboard, and got the engine running after having to replace most of it. But she purred just like she did when she came off the factory floor, so there was that.

Larry had helped, and George, of course. Here it was, cleaned, polished, tape deck working, and ready for love, as they say. He honked the horn, beckoning his mother. A few minutes went by, and she came out, wearing a white housedress, with a blue shawl.

She looked stunned when she saw it, the white metal gleaming in the summer sun. Bright and beautiful.

"Tommy," she said. "What in the world? You got it running."

"All for you, Mom. Happy birthday."

"But it's not my birthday yet."

"Well, call it an early Christmas present. Wanna go for a spin?"

"Look at you," she said. "Thinking I would say no."

She walked down, and he opened the passenger door for her. She slipped in, putting a hand on the dashboard, reliving memories in her mind, Tommy saw.

"Cleaned up nice," she said, her voice hitching with emotion.

She looked at him as he sat in the driver's seat. "You outdid yourself."

"It's not a hundred percent, but it's a start."

"It's perfect to me, son."

"So," he said, settling into the driver seat. "Where to?"

"Let's have breakfast. The diner—Scrambles, it's called now. I think back in my day, the owner was Gus, and it was just called The Crossing. Down on Main and Front Street."

"Your wish is my command." He revved the engine and sped off down the highway toward the city center of Newton's Crossing.

When they got to the diner, she told him about the first time she and his father were there, arguing over the farm. Over eggs, grits, and the best bacon she'd ever had, Catherine told him about arguing over stupid stuff like two people who hated each other. But the spark was there, nonetheless, she said.

"He had this cute way of smiling. These dimples. You have those same ones. God, it's uncanny how much you look like him."

"I still have a lot of you, though," he said.

"More than you know," she said. "You have my wanderlust, which is good."

"How do you mean?" he asked.

She just smiled at him and ate her bacon. "Nothing, just an observation I've had about you. For a while now."

"Like I want to leave town?"

"Something like that."

They paid their tab and left. Tommy put in a tape of seventies hits, and Wild Cherry started singing about funky music.

"Where to now?" he asked.

"Rogers and Third," she answered, settling into the newly reupholstered leather seats.

They drove in silence for several blocks and then pulled up in front of an old VFW hall—a tan facade with a big VFW sign over a set of glass double doors.

The parking lot had weeds growing out from cracks in the asphalt, and a few pieces of detritus—an empty beer can, a fast-food wrapper—jangled and flew in the morning breeze.

"It didn't used to be here," she said. "The VFW."

"Where was it?"

"Downtown on Hooker Street. But that's a lawyer's office now. Your dad used to come here for Friday poker nights with the guys. But over the years, the poker nights got few and far between, and his veteran buddies did, too."

"But we had a lot of fun dances here, too. The first time, I didn't want to be here. I was half out the door when your dad brought me back in for a dance. I was amazed at how good a dancer he was."

"You are too, from what I hear."

"All because he taught me. I can still remember those stupid square dance lessons, having to dance with my sister. Ugh," he said, exasperated.

"Oh, stop it, you had fun."

He paused in thought, remembering those nights at the house, in the living room, furniture pulled aside, dancing with his sister, his father marking the beat in time with the radio, fiddle music playing from the Victrola. Mom looking on in awe at the man she married.

"Yeah, I had fun," he said.

"I knew it."

She sat glassy-eyed for a few minutes. Then, she looked over at him, a tear streaking down her cheek. "Want to go roller skating?" she said, her mouth lifting in a smile that took up her whole face.

"Lead the way. I am your willing and obedient servant for the day."

Three blocks later, near the highway, was a large brown brick building. The sign, Cardinal Skate, hung lopsided from rusty bolts.

They parked in the lot, overgrown with weeds, choked in places with trash. Long abandoned.

Tommy listened as his mother reminisced about their early days, her voice filled with a mixture of love and longing.

"We used to come here when we were dating," she told him.

"It's been closed down quite a while," Tommy said. "Kids don't rollerskate anymore."

"Always on their phones," she scoffed.

Tommy nodded in agreement.

"He used to kiss me," Catherine continued, her gaze drifting into the past. "All the time. And I couldn't stop kissing him. I told you about it once, didn't I?"

"Yeah," Tommy said. "In the barn. You were watching him do something with a horse, and he had his shirt off."

"He looked so pretty, sweaty, with that sun hitting his muscles," Catherine sighed dreamily.

"Okay, going somewhere I don't want to hear, Mom," Tommy said, a blush creeping up his neck.

The Bee Gees started crooning about staying alive on the car stereo.

Catherine chuckled. "Oh, hush. You think I don't hear what you do with that girl of yours?"

Tommy's blush deepened. "You heard that?"

"You hadn't fixed the shocks yet." She choked back a laugh.

"Keep your window closed next time," he grumbled.

"And deprive myself of memories? I think not," she said, mocking a shocked tone.

"Whatever," he laughed.

"But getting back to that kiss," Catherine said, her voice softening again. "It was our first. There in that barn. Lips so soft, the way he smelled—like sweat and oak. And manure. I got used to it that summer, staying at the farm. Didn't like it at first, but soon it started smelling like home."

"I never liked it," Tommy admitted.

"I know," she said with a smile.

"So that was the start of it?" he asked.

"Yep. Your father kissed me and lit a fire in my belly I could never put out. That's when I knew. He was the one."

"That's how I felt the first time I kissed Meghan," Tommy confessed.

"She's the one, son. May not feel like it now, with you two going through difficulties. But she is. You'll see."

"I don't know. She's got a lot going on. Doesn't need me in the mix."

"When she's got a lot going on, she'll see she needs you most of all."

He shook his head. "Nah."

"Yeah."

Catherine looked with nostalgia at the roller rink building, with its faded yellow sign, the roller skates gone gray, and the word "Skating" hanging from rusted bolts.

"One more place," she said.

"Where to?"

"The drive-in."

. . ⚓ . .

THE DRIVE-IN WAS JUST an empty lot, surrounded by trees. Looters and souvenir collectors had long since taken all the metal posts that held the stereos you had to put in your windows. A few remained, sitting like skeletons in the weed-choked lot. Rusty, unmoving chains barred the entrance. In the distance, the old screen lay battered by weather, the uprights holding it long since disintegrated and bent by age.

Catherine sat for a long moment, silent, hearing the breeze whispering through the trees. "We had a fight. A big one. Your dad and me."

"He told me once. Penelope, right?"

"Never told me about her."

"Did he tell you why?"

She didn't answer. Her face flushed red.

"Said he loved me too much to tell me the truth. That was your dad. Kept things close to the chest to keep me happy. Ahh, the sin of omission."

"He had a good reason, though."

"There's never a good reason not to tell the truth, son."

"Still and all, you guys got together in the end anyway."

"Because he chased me down."

"That was the Greyhound night, huh?"

"Yeah, rain coming down to beat the band. Here he was, in this car, chasing that grey bus, fighting traffic on a two-lane road just to catch up and stop it."

"He said you called him an idiot."

"Yeah, but he was my idiot."

"What happened to Penelope?"

"She went back to doing mission work. He broke it off that night. He was doing that when I walked in and saw them hugging. Here I was, a kid in love, finding my man in the arms of some floozy. Didn't stick around for an explanation."

She paused in thought. Tommy let her have her silent thoughts.

"He explained. Me standing at the threshold of that bus. Rain whipping my hair all over. And there he was, on his knees in the road. Cars honking. Telling me he loved me. Asking if I loved him."

"Grand gestures, Dad was famous for those."

"That was his most famous," she said.

"And you agreed, or else we wouldn't be here, Arlene and me."

"You wouldn't, for sure."

She got out of the car and went to the front of the Corvette, laying down to look up at the sky.

Tommy didn't get out. He watched as his mother crossed her arms on the hood of the car, reliving a time decades ago, summer rain splashing on bodies, creating the son that drove the car she was on now.

The afternoon sun beamed bright overhead.

His mother sat up and came back to the passenger side of the car, tears in her eyes.

The wind moved through the empty lot, rustling weeds that had long since claimed the cracks in the pavement. The old drive-in screen stood in front of them, its tattered remains fluttering like ghostly ribbons in the breeze. The once-sturdy wooden frame sagged, the decay of time breaking it apart, piece by piece.

Catherine looked up at it, quiet for a long moment. Then, in that no-nonsense way of hers, she said, "You don't like the farm."

Tommy felt the words hit him like a slow-moving freight train. Not because they were a surprise—hell, he'd been carrying that truth in his gut for years—but because she was saying it out loud.

Matter-of-fact. Plainspoken. Straight to the point.

He hesitated, feeling the weight of what he was about to say. He knew that's why she brought him here—not for nostalgia, not just for a drive. She wanted the truth. Needed him to admit it. And the thing was... she already knew.

She'd always known.

Still, she waited. Giving him space. Letting him get there on his own.

Tommy swallowed, staring at the ruined screen, at the pieces of a once-beloved past breaking apart. And finally, for the first time in his life, he said it.

"No," he murmured. "Dad had his heart in it. I don't. Never really did."

The words hung in the air, raw and real.

Catherine exhaled softly, the corner of her lips twitching into something like a smile. Not because she was happy—but because she was relieved.

"I knew it," she said. Her voice was light, but there was something deep behind it. A kind of knowing that only mothers have. "Just wanted to hear you say it."

Tommy let out a shaky breath, the weight of it all finally slipping from his shoulders. The truth had been buried for so long, it almost felt strange to say it out loud. He coughed, clearing the tightness in his throat.

"Sorry," he said, rolling his shoulders like he could physically shake off the years of expectation. But he wasn't. Not really. If he was being honest with himself, the farm had always been a burden—a chore he was ready to be free of.

She turned to him then, her eyes softer than he'd seen them in a long time. She sighed, reached up, and cupped his cheek, her palm warm against his skin.

"Oh, baby," she whispered. "You don't have to keep it."

Tommy's breath caught.

"One of these days, I'm gonna be gone," she continued, her thumb brushing absently over his cheekbone. "Your name's on the deed. Dad left it to you in the will. But you don't have to keep it. Not for me. Not for him."

The relief hit him so hard, he almost felt weightless. Like he'd been carrying something too heavy for too long, and only now realized he could finally let go.

Like he'd been carrying something heavy on his back his whole life without realizing it—and now, finally, he was allowed to set it down.

He exhaled, a long, shaky breath. "Are you sure?"

Catherine nodded, her smile small, but steady. "Sure as grass is green."

She turned back to the wreckage of the old drive-in, watching as the wind tugged at the torn remnants of the screen. "Sometimes, it's okay to let things go, baby," she murmured. "Even the big things. Even if it makes you sad to see it go. Sometimes, you have to."

Tommy stared at her, taking it in. Letting it sink into his bones.

The farm wasn't his. It never was.

And for the first time, he realized... he was ready to let it go.

"So you're not mad?" he asked.

"I could never be mad at you, son." she smiled proudly, and Tommy sighed with relief. He'd finally admitted it to the one woman he loved more than anyone in his life.

Thanks mom." he said, he tightened his grip on her hand.

A long understanding silence stretched between them. Nothing more needed to be said.

"where to next? He asked.

"Take me home," she said. "Done enough reminiscing. It's time for lunch."

As they drove back to the farm, Tommy sat with his thoughts, his mother's words echoing in his head.

"He chased me down. That's why we got together in the end. He fought for me."

She had said it so matter-of-factly, like it was just a simple truth of life. Love wasn't easy. It wasn't just something you stumbled into. You had to fight for it. Hold onto it.

He thought about Meghan. About the way she pushed and pulled. The way she tested him, maybe without even realizing she was doing it. She was stubborn. Guarded. But he saw through all of that. He saw the way she softened when she wasn't thinking about it, the way she leaned into him when she thought no one was looking.

Maybe she was scared. Maybe she didn't even realize what she wanted yet.

But he did.

He wanted her. And he wasn't going to let her go.

The realization settled deep in his chest, warm and solid.

His father had gone after his mother in the pouring rain, chasing down that Greyhound bus like a fool in love. And Catherine had called him an idiot for it. But she had still stepped off that bus. She had still chosen him.

Tommy clenched the steering wheel a little tighter, determination setting in. Maybe love really did need a grand gesture. Not just words, but something she could see, something she could feel. Something that would leave no doubt.

By the time they pulled up to Two Bears Farm, the idea had already taken root.

It was a simple one, really.

Show her.

Not just tell her—show her what she meant to him.

When he got home, after lunch, he went straight to his basement workshop. He had work to do. It was time for him to embrace his art. To embrace a life with her.

Chapter 42

Tommy

Catherine came downstairs just as Tommy was packing up the last of his sculptures. He was using a large cardboard box—one Arlene had gotten from Amazon when she ordered a lamp for her room. It was big enough to hold everything he wanted to take to Meghan's gallery.

"What you got there, son?" she asked, peering inside.

Her gaze flickered around the room, noting the empty spaces on the shelves where his carvings had once been. Small wooden statues, once covered in dust, were now carefully nestled in the box resting in Tommy's arms. A knowing smile tugged at her lips.

"Figured I'd try something out, is all," he said.

"Good for you."

He shrugged. "They were just collecting dust. Might as well see if they're worth something."

She placed a gentle hand on his back. "Your dad would be proud," she murmured before turning away.

Tommy swallowed, his grip tightening around a small, painted figure—the third king from the Nativity set. His heart gave a dull thud. His father hadn't always understood his hobbies, but he had supported them. That had been enough.

Carefully, he placed the last piece—the baby Jesus in the manger—into the box, then grabbed the keys to the corvette. "I'll be gone a few hours," he called. "You gonna be okay?"

From the kitchen, Catherine's voice followed him. "Yes, I'll be fine. Don't worry about me."

"I'm taking dad's car," he told her.

She glanced up and said, "tell your future wife I said hello."

"She's not yet, ma."

Catherine just smiled and went back to fixing dinner.

She had been taking her medications, finally. The surgery to place stents in her arteries was scheduled for next week. If she stuck to her diet and kept up with her blood pressure pills, she'd be alright. She had told him just a few days ago, "I want to hold that grandbaby," and the determined glint in her eyes told him she meant it.

Chapter 43

Meghan

The doorbell dinged, and a figure stood silhouetted in the doorway, the bright afternoon sun streaming through the gallery's large windows. I really need to get shades for those, Meghan thought idly—until a familiar voice cut through her thoughts.

"Hey, hon."

For a split second, she thought it was Tommy. But when her eyes adjusted, she saw the truth. John.

Her ex-husband.

Meghan's stomach dropped. Her mouth tightened. What the fuck is he doing here?

John held up a bouquet of roses and a box of chocolates wrapped in familiar brown and gold packaging.

"Whoa," he said, stepping forward with that same old easy smile. "Before you go all crazy, just hear me out."

She folded her arms, bile already rising. Of all the nerve.

"What?" she snapped.

John exhaled heavily, like he was already exhausted. "Can we not argue? Just for a minute?"

She let out a short, bitter laugh. "I don't know, maybe if you didn't show up like a bad penny all the damn time, I wouldn't have to."

"It's only been twice," he pointed out. "This time included."

"That's two times too many."

"Just... give me a minute, okay?"

Meghan exhaled sharply and moved behind the counter, putting solid space between them. John had never been violent, but something about him still made her want a barrier between them.

"Fine," she said. "You have five minutes before I hurl, so—what do you want?"

John placed the roses and chocolates on the counter. "Peace offering."

She eyed the chocolates. The expensive kind from Luxembourg. Damn it. He remembered.

"You're not trying to get back with me, are you?" she asked suspiciously.

John chuckled. "No, Meghan, I'm not." Then, tilting his head, he frowned. "What do you mean, hurl?"

She bit her lip. Took a breath. Just say it.

"John, I'm pregnant."

His eyebrows lifted in surprise, and then—he smiled.

"Well, good for you," he said genuinely.

She blinked. Wait. What?

"John..." she hesitated, watching him carefully. "You're happy for me?"

"Yeah," he said with a small shrug. "I am."

Meghan crossed her arms. "Where is the real John Masterton, and what have you done with his body?"

He smirked, plucking at one of the roses. "I guess I deserve that," he admitted.

She eyed him warily. "So what's with the whole new-leaf thing?"

"You can thank Candace."

"Candace?" Her eyebrow shot up.

"Yeah," he nodded, a little sheepish. "She's something else. Challenges me. Calls me on my bullshit. Got me into therapy."

Meghan barked out a laugh. "You? Therapy? In the same sentence? Maybe I should thank Candace, then."

"Maybe you should." John glanced around the gallery, then back at her. "You're doing well for yourself."

"Yeah," she said simply. "I am."

Silence stretched between them.

He coughed, shifting his weight. For a fleeting moment, nostalgia flickered in her chest, but she shoved it down.

"Well, congratulations," she said briskly. "When's the wedding?"

John blinked. "Wedding?"

"Yeah, you and Candace."

"Oh." He rubbed the back of his neck. "She, uh... broke up with me a few weeks ago."

That surprised her. She thought Candace had him wrapped around her finger.

After another pause, John cleared his throat. "So, pregnant, huh?" His voice was softer now. "It's the farm boy's?"

Meghan stiffened slightly. "Yeah."

John studied her for a long moment, then sighed. "I think it's time for me to go. For good."

She nodded. "I think so too."

"I just wanted to stop by and say... I'm sorry," he said. "I'm heading back to LA in a few days. We just wrapped Diamond Girl, and I had some time before I fly back."

She looked at him, skeptical. "You? Apologizing?"

He nodded. "Yeah. I was an asshole to you, Meghan. And I'm sorry. For everything." He hesitated. "I got caught up in the whole new-kid-on-the-block, showbiz lifestyle, and I lost myself. It took therapy to find my way back."

She narrowed her eyes. "Still going?"

"Yeah. I have a guy in the city I do remote sessions with. Got another one next week when I get back."

"Huh."

He smiled. "What's that mean?"

"Nothing," she said, shaking her head. "Just... huh."

A small silence stretched between them again.

John cleared his throat. "Can I ask a favor?"

She tilted her head. "Depends."

"One last hug for the road?" He gave her a small smile. "After this, I promise—you'll never hear from me again."

She hesitated.

And then, finally, she saw him. The man he had been before Hollywood got to him. The man she had loved, once. The man she had hoped he would turn into.

Too little, too late.

But still—she nodded.

"Sure," she said.

He stepped forward, and she let herself hug him—just once, just for a second, just to let go.

"Thanks," he murmured.

And then—

A reflection caught her eye.

She turned.

Outside, parked right in front of the gallery—

The Corvette. Tommy. "Shit."

He stepped out, sunlight glinting off the white paint, his strong frame silhouetted against the bright day.

John chuckled. "Speak of the devil."

The gallery door swung open.

Tommy stepped inside, then stopped.

Meghan froze. Shit.

She looked down and realized too late that she was still in John's arms.

Tommy's expression darkened. His entire body went still.

Meghan quickly stepped back, but it was too late.

Tommy had already seen enough.

Chapter 44

Tommy

Tommy drove into town, navigating heavier-than-usual traffic.

Newton's Crossing had been growing fast. In the past few years, the town had offered economic incentives and lower taxes to attract businesses. New shops lined the streets—candle makers, art supply stores, a bookstore, even a small craft brewery that had been gaining traction over the last six months.

Still, he doubted anything would ever overshadow Angelo's. The Italian restaurant was a town landmark.

He pulled up in front of the gallery, shut off the engine, grabbed the box from the passenger seat, and stepped onto the sidewalk.

Then he froze.

Something in the window caught his eye.

Meghan.

His pulse kicked up. He took another step forward—

Then stilled.

Meghan. In another man's arms.

His stomach clenched.

John.

His grip on the box tightened.

Her ex-husband.

His lungs burned, like he'd forgotten how to breathe.

Meghan looked up, startled. Her expression shifted from surprise to something almost guilty.

"Tommy?" she said, her face flushing.

John turned, offering a handshake. "Hey, Tommy."

The box slipped from Tommy's hands, crashing to the marble floor. The sculptures inside rattled from the impact, some threatening to break.

His jaw tightened. "What the fuck?"

John hesitated.

Meghan's voice wavered. "Wait—" She forced a smile.

But Tommy wasn't waiting.

"God. Damn it."

He started for the door.

"Tommy, wait!" she yelled.

He didn't turn.

"Tommy!" That voice. The one that had the ability to stop his body in its tracks.

He turned. "What?"

She stepped toward him. His hands had turned to fists.

He glared at John, cold murder in his eyes.

She noticed.

"Tommy, just—"

"Just what?"

She let out an exasperated sigh.

This stubborn, hard-headed idiot.

"Stop being Tommy for one minute!"

She looked up at him. He glared down at her.

"What was that?" He motioned to the handsome actor standing a safe distance away.

"Nothing," Meghan said. She put a hand on his chest. "Please, just listen."

He looked down at her hand. The sincerity in her eyes.

The initial rage he'd felt began to ebb.

"Explain."

She sighed.

"First of all," she said. "Yes."

He blinked. "Yes what?"

She looked him in the eye, relief washing over her as she saw him finally calming down.

"Yes, I'll marry you, you stubborn asshole."

He stared at her.

His mouth opened, then closed—like he was processing what she'd just said.

"Yes?" he asked.

She embraced him, pushing her face into his chest. "Yes, I love you."

She hoped her words would get through his thick skull.

John, still watching, chuckled, seeing Tommy and Meghan wrapped around each other.

"Looks like I should take my leave now," he said, stepping past them with a wary posture—just in case Tommy decided to throw a punch.

"That would be a good idea," Tommy muttered. "We have a lot to talk about."

John smirked. "Yeah. You do."

He looked at Meghan. "We're cool?"

Meghan chuckled, looking up into Tommy's warm eyes. "We're a couple of Fonzies."

John laughed. "Good. Well, have a great life." He opened the door. "Call me if you need anything."

"Never," Meghan said.

"Got it."

The door dinged closed behind him, leaving Tommy and Meghan alone in the gallery.

Tommy exhaled. "I love you too." He paused. "I think I always have."

Meghan smiled. "I know. It just took me a while to catch up."

"I'm glad you did."

She smirked. "So what now?"

Tommy tilted his head. "What are you doing the rest of the day?"

Meghan arched a brow. "Closing the store?"

"Good idea."

She turned to the door, locked it, flipped the sign to CLOSED.

Two hours later, she was going to owe Reynaldo a lot more money.

Chapter 45

Tommy

They went back to the farm, found their picnic spot, and settled in.

She was his now, her body a testament to their shared passion. Her limbs entwined with his, her head resting on the pillow beside his, her legs slick with perspiration against his thighs. The muted sunlight filtering through the curtains painted her skin with a warm glow, highlighting the curve of her hip, the swell of her breast. He traced those curves with his hands, memorizing every dip and swell, every texture and temperature.

He recognized the rhythm of her breath, the soft moans that escalated into a symphony of pleasure. Her body arched, a graceful bow stretched taut, her lips parting to whisper his name, a prayer against his skin.

He moved within her, their bodies a symphony of motion and sensation. It wasn't just the physical act; it was a dance of souls, a merging of hearts. Their kisses were deep, their tongues entwined, their breaths mingling in the space between.

The heat between them built, a slow burn that ignited into an inferno. They were no longer two separate beings, but a single entity, bound by the invisible threads of desire and devotion.

Their climax was a symphony of release, a crescendo of shared ecstasy. It was a primal cry, a guttural moan, a whispered plea. Their bodies convulsed, their muscles contracting, their hearts pounding in unison.

In the aftermath, they lay entwined, their sweat-dampened hair mingling, their fingers tracing lazy patterns on each other's skin. The echoes of their passion and unspoken promises, whispered in the dark, filled the silence.

"You're mine now," he murmured, his voice rough with emotion. He looked into her eyes, cerulean pools reflecting the depths of his soul.

"I know," she whispered back, her voice thick with contentment. She nestled closer, her arm draped across his stomach, her fingers tracing the line of his hipbone.

With legs and arms and hearts entwined, they drifted off to sleep, enveloped in the afterglow of their lovemaking. Dreams of a shared future, a future where their bodies and souls would forever be intertwined, filled their sleep.

Chapter 46

Tommy

The gallery showing had been a damn success.

Meghan's newsletter, "The Fabulous Sculptures of Thomas Richards: The Reluctant Sculptor," had gone out to her entire mailing list—donors, collectors, art enthusiasts—and more people had shown up than he ever expected.

Trina and Reynaldo had been there, holding hands, whispering to each other like lovesick fools. Reynaldo had bought the lovebirds sculpture, and—because he was apparently the sentimental type—asked if Tommy could carve "Hen" and "Rooster" into them.

"You sure you don't want 'Lovebirds'?" Tommy had asked, raising an eyebrow.

Reynaldo had just smirked. "Nope. It's an inside joke."

Derrick had shown up with his wife, Carrie, and his daughter, Lizzy. She had practically raided the damn display—buying nearly every bird sculpture, plus the intricately carved castle.

"It looks like something out of a fairy tale," Lizzy had said softly, her fingers running over the fine details in awe.

Tommy had just nodded. "Yeah. Guess it kinda does."

By the end of the night, Meghan had found him, a check in her hand.

"How much?" he asked, wary.

Meghan hesitated. "You should sit down."

He frowned but dropped into the chair in her office.

She handed him the check.

He blinked. Then his eyes went wide.

"Shit." He whistled. "That much?"

Meghan smirked. "Yeah. That much."

He exhaled, still staring at the number. "And you didn't take a commission?"

Meghan gave him a look. "No, Tommy. You're my fiancé. It's our business now."

The word hit him like a damn truck.

Fiancé.

His chest tightened—not in panic, but in something deeper. This was real. She was real.

A slow grin tugged at his lips. "Well then... how about we put this toward the honeymoon?"

Meghan crossed her arms, head tilting. "Where were you thinking?"

He shrugged, trying to play it cool. "Paris?"

She pretended to think. "Paris is nice. But in that case, we'll need a little more than this."

Tommy leaned back, rubbing his jaw. "I have an idea of where to get it."

Meghan's smile faded.

"What idea?"

He met her eyes, steady. Unshakable.

"I have to go see Zion Rittermark."

Her breath caught.

"Tommy, no." She shook her head, stepping closer. "You don't have to."

But he just looked at her. That Tommy look—the one that meant his mind was already made up.

"Yeah. I do."

Her arms tightened around herself. "Are you sure?"

He gave her a slow nod. "Sure as the Pope wears a funny hat."

Chapter 47

Tommy

Tommy sat in the Corvette, a symbol of his family's past, while getting ready to shed his own past and that of his family's. A brief summer storm splashed on the roof. "It's now or never, buddy," he thought. The weight of his decision bore down on him. He asked himself if he wanted to do this and what it would do to his family. He and Arlene had talked about it. He would put a provision in the sale where she would live in the house for another year until she decided to move out. He remembered their discussion.

"You really want to go through with this?" she had asked.

"Yes, it's not ours anymore. I'm moving with Meghan somewhere else, to a simpler and easier life," he had told her.

He had offered it to George, but the foreman said, "No, I'm about to retire." Tommy told him that he would give him an excellent severance, and George agreed. "Yeah, hard work isn't my thing anymore. Time to move on."

With all the people in his life telling him this was the right decision, he had accepted it. It was time to go forward with the sale.

The Rittermark farm was a testament to everything new about farming. The long rows of chicken barns, the industrial facility where crops were harvested and prepared for shipping, even the large house, not a farmhouse but a mansion of brick, three stories of wealth created through generations of Southern money.

He got out and ran through the splashing rain to the front entrance, a canopy that held back the worst of it. He knocked on the door. A young woman answered, wearing a black and white maid's outfit.

"Can I help you?" she asked.

"I need to see Zion Rittermark. Is he home?" Tommy said.

"Sure, come on in. Should I ask who's calling?"

"Thomas Richards," he said. "Junior."

A few minutes went by. He looked around at the large living space. To the right was a large industrial kitchen with white countertops, a marble-topped island, and gleaming pots and pans hanging above it. Silver appliances punctuated the large space. Soon, a man came out of an office, the same office where Tommy had to confront old Gideon Rittermark. The bald-headed man with gray hair and a tan suit came to him, and the men shook hands.

"Tommy," said Zion Rittermark, the new head of the family. "To what do I owe the pleasure?"

The two men had been friends for a long time, though Zion was twenty years older and much more patient and grounded in the modern era than Gideon, his father.

"Can we talk in your office?" Tommy asked.

"Sure, come on in."

Tommy remembered this office, the study where he had to sit as a nineteen-year-old to tell old Gideon about the possible marriage to his granddaughter Trina and how he was going to end the engagement.

The study was better lit than that day, with corner lamps and a bright lamp on the desk. The blinds had been opened, letting in the grey light of the cloudy, rainy sky.

Zion sat down and offered Tommy a seat. Tommy took a seat in the red leather chairs in front of the desk, looking Zion in the eye.

"So, I've decided to sell the farm."

Zion cocked his head. "Really?" he said. "That's a big decision."

"And one that doesn't come lightly."

"Why now?"

"Mom's getting sicker. Arlene has some issues going on, but she's looking for a new place. I'm getting married, and I just don't want the responsibilities of farm life anymore. The place has become more of a burden than anything."

"So, who are you going to sell it to?"

"You," Tommy said. "I was hoping, anyway. I was going to give you the right of first refusal, considering..." His words hung in the air, letting the weight of their shared family history through the years sit in the silence between them.

"What are you looking to get out of it?"

"Well, you know what it's worth. I was thinking of letting you give me an offer, and we could go from there," Tommy said.

Zion sat back, thinking. "It's a nice property."

"One that would add to yours in a good way, I'm thinking. Since we have been neighbors for a while, you know."

"Yes, I do," Zion said. He pulled out a sheet of paper from the printer behind the desk. "I'm going to write a number, and that's my starting price. You can take a minute to think about it. Maybe talk it over with your sister. Come back to me."

"She's given me permission to barter without her."

"Good." Zion wrote a number, folded the paper, and handed it across the desk.

Tommy looked at the paper and smiled. He looked at it again, considering, then back up at Zion.

"Well?" Zion said.

"Sold." Tommy handed the paper back.

Zion grinned. "Didn't think it would be that easy."

"My life is all about being easy from now on," Tommy said.

"You sure?"

"Absolutely. Get the paperwork ready." Tommy said, oh yeah, I want a clause in there about the house."

"What's the clause?"

"Arlene and my mother get to live there. Rent free. In perpetuity."

"Its always your house," zion said. "We'll keep it that way."

"You get the land, and when they leave it, you get it all. How's that?"

"I can work with that." Zion said.

"Good," Tommy said, getting up from the seat. "Now, let's get it in writing."

Zion stood up and shook Tommy's hand. "I'll have my lawyers draw up the paperwork and bring it to the house tomorrow."

"Thank you."

"You're very welcome," Zion said as he escorted Tommy to the foyer. "Thank you."

Tommy shook the man's hand again, his chest lighter, happier. A part of his life was over, and he was ready to start a new chapter with a wife, a child, and a family.

He left the house. The storm had abated. He went to the Corvette, started it up, let it rev, smiled, and pulled out of the Rittermark farm road, ready to start a new life with new potential.

He now had a wedding to help plan. And judging by that bulge in Meghan's midsection, it would have to be soon. He smiled, driving down the road. Really smiled, for the first time in a long while. Missus Meghan Richards. He liked that idea. Liked it a lot.

Chapter 48

Arlene

The sun dipped low on the horizon as the reception began, casting the farm in a golden glow. Wedding guests mingled under the open sky, tables adorned with wildflowers and simple lanterns. Laughter filled the air as people danced to live country music, clinked glasses, and exchanged stories.

Arlene sat at a table in the corner, her sponsor Dana beside her. The two women watched the revelry, cider glasses in hand.

"You know," Arlene said, swirling her glass, "for me, it all started with a wedding."

Dana raised a brow. "Do you want to leave? You don't have to stay."

Arlene shook her head, a small smile tugging at her lips. "No. I can finally come to a wedding without wanting a drink. I think I'm on the other side of this now."

Dana nodded approvingly. "That's good. Keep it up."

"Yeah." Arlene let out a soft laugh. "Weddings were my Kryptonite. Not anymore. Thank God."

Catherine ambled over, leaning on a cane, long hair beautiful in the summer light, tied with a pink bow. "You doing okay, sweetheart?" she asked, leaning a soft hand on Arlene's shoulder.

"Doing great, mom." Her hand went to her mother's and tightened around it. "I'm glad you were able to see this."

"I am too. They look happy."

"They are," Arlene said. "They really are."

She raised her glass, clinking it lightly against Dana's, and together they sat, content to watch as Tommy and Meghan danced under the twinkling lights, their arms wrapped around each other, the embodiment of love, hope, and new beginnings.

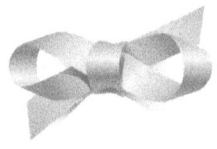

Chapter 49

Meghan

The cake had been eaten—three tiers of perfection, purple and gold accents, half chocolate, half vanilla. White frosting, thick and sugary, handcrafted by Catherine and Arlene.

Tommy sat beside Meghan, watching as she reached for a small box wrapped in red-and-black checkered paper, the pattern reminiscent of a Scottish Highlander's kilt. A frilly red bow topped it off.

"Who's this from?" she asked, tugging at the ribbon.

He swallowed hard, his throat tight. "It's from me."

She peeled back the wrapping, lifted the lid, and gasped. Inside, nestled in soft tissue paper, was a cardinal perched on a twig, its lifelike green leaves curling naturally around the base. Her fingers trembled as she pulled it out, eyes shining.

"How did you—?" she started, but then she saw it. The tiny, almost imperceptible crack along the wing. The legs, once broken, now lovingly restored. She ran her fingertips over the careful repair, a choked breath escaping her lips.

"I went to the guy you sold it to," Tommy said, his voice thick with emotion. "Made him a replacement."

Her head snapped up. "But... why?"

He reached for her, brushing a loose strand of hair from her cheek. "Because this is yours," he said softly. He kissed her forehead, then whispered, "Well, actually... it's ours."

She let out a small, happy sob, pressing a trembling hand to her mouth. Tears spilled over, and she tried to blink them away.

"You didn't have to."

He smiled, wiping her tears with his thumbs. "Yeah," he murmured. "I did."

She couldn't hold back anymore. She threw her arms around his neck, kissing him long and deep, pouring everything into the moment.

The crowd sighed and smiled. Arlene clapped, misty-eyed. And from the back of the room, George's voice rang out with a teasing, drawn-out—

"Awww."

Laughter rippled through the guests, but Tommy barely noticed. He was too lost in Meghan's embrace, in the warmth of her lips, in the feeling that, for the first time in his life...

Everything was exactly as it should be.

As they drove from the farm, he stopped and placed a small carved statue of a girl riding a bike at the white cross on the side of the road. The words written on the cross: "Maggie Grace, taken too soon."

He nodded in silent prayer, then walked back and got in the car.

"Is there something you'd like to tell me about that?" she asked, her eyebrow raised in concern.

"Maybe one day," he said, his eyes glassy.

"Okay," she smiled.

"Let's go to Paris."

Chapter 50

Tommy

Tommy leaned against the wrought iron balcony, gazing at the Eiffel Tower, its golden lights shimmering against the velvet night sky. He still couldn't believe he was here.

"It's so different from the books," he murmured, taking in the grandeur of the city beneath him.

Meghan, standing beside him, wrapped in a soft white robe, sighed contentedly. "It's lovely," she whispered.

He slid an arm around her waist, pulling her close. "I know something else that's lovely."

A blush crept onto her cheeks, her lips curving into a satisfied smile.

"You flatter me too much," she teased.

"Not enough."

Moving behind her, he slid the terrycloth strap of her robe aside, exposing the damp skin of her shoulder. She leaned into his embrace, inhaling the scent of him—fresh soap, coconut, and vanilla, a far cry from the earthy scent of the farm he usually carried.

His breath was hot against her neck as he brushed aside her wet hair. The warmth of his lips met the curve where her neck met her collarbone, his kiss slow, deliberate. A shiver rippled through her, and she exhaled a soft, breathy moan.

"Again, huh?" she murmured, melting against him.

"Isn't that what honeymoons are for?" he chuckled, his voice rich with amusement.

His hand glided down, resting over the slight curve of her stomach—their baby, growing within her. He traced slow, lazy circles over her skin, his fingers trailing lower.

"Can't get enough, huh?" she teased, though she made no effort to pull away.

His hands skimmed over her hips, firm yet reverent, and he gave a small, playful pinch to her ass.

"With you?" His lips brushed her pulse point, sending another shiver down her spine. "It's never enough."

She turned in his arms, sliding her hands up over his broad shoulders, pulling him into a kiss. Slow at first, then deeper, more urgent.

"Good thing I feel the same way," she whispered, her lips grazing his.

They kissed on the balcony. The hum of Paris faded in the streets below them. Catcalls in the night, music and laughter, and the occasional car horn added to their moans of passion and pleasure while the lights of the Eiffel Tower lit up the night sky, and the stars high above twinkled in a clear summer sky.

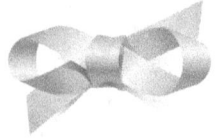

Chapter 51

Arlene

The house was empty.

Not just quiet—but hollow, the kind of quiet that leaves you alone with your thoughts. The kids were in Phoenix with their dad. He'd texted earlier to say they'd landed safely. They'd be with him for a month.

Tommy and Meghan were in Paris, overlooking the Eiffel Tower. Lucky them. They'd be gone for two months, a whirlwind honeymoon across Europe and the Mediterranean, finishing in Key West. Tommy had always dreamed of going there.

George was taking care of the farm, though most of the land was his now. Tommy had sold it, keeping only the barn and the house. But George was rarely around these days.

The house groaned and ticked like old houses do—sounds swallowed when laughter, running feet, and life filled it. But now, every creak echoed, stark against the silence.

Arlene ran a bath in the clawfoot tub, sinking into the sudsy water. Heat pressed against her skin, loosening her muscles, but not her thoughts. For the first time in over a decade, she was truly alone.

Single. Alone. In a house too big for one.

Afterward, she microwaved frozen lasagna, eating it in half-hearted bites before leaving the fork in the sink. Her hair was still wrapped in a towel, damp strands framing her tired face. She'd glimpsed herself in the bathroom mirror earlier—lines carving deeper into her cheeks, weariness dulling her eyes.

She'd opened the medicine cabinet, hesitated, and pulled out a pill bottle. Tommy's name was on the label. Now, she sat at the kitchen table, the bottle in front of her, next to a glass of water.

Her phone buzzed with a screenshot of the kids on the farm, grinning and covered in mud. She smiled despite herself.

It's just one, she thought. I have a headache. It's been a stressful day.

The rationalizations came easily:

One won't hurt. No one will know. Dana's not here. I don't have to tell my sponsor. Besides, it's not alcohol. Pills aren't the same.

She twisted the cap, staring at the white ovals inside.

Her phone buzzed again. She ignored it.

I'll go to a meeting tomorrow. It's fine. Just one.

She tipped the bottle, a pill sliding into her palm.

"Fuck," she whispered, her voice trembling.

Her hand hovered, shaking.

The house creaked.

She reached out.

Chapter 52

Tommy

He set the last moving box down with a grunt, wiping the sweat from his forehead with the back of his hand. "That's the last of it," he said, stretching his back. "Unless you're hiding more in the truck."

Meghan smirked, standing in the middle of their new apartment, hands on her hips. "Nope, that's it. Promise."

The place was small but cozy. Just enough for the two of them—and the little one on the way. The walls were still bare, the furniture mismatched from both of their old places, but it already felt like home.

Tommy glanced toward the extra room down the hall—the one they'd painted a soft sage green the week before. The nursery.

He exhaled, walking over and leaning against the doorframe. The crib was already set up, though still missing a mattress. A rocking chair sat in the corner, a hand-me-down from Catherine, and a mobile of little farm animals hung from the ceiling.

He turned to Meghan, his chest tightening in a way he wasn't used to.

"What are we gonna name him?" Tommy asked, running a hand through his hair.

Meghan raised an eyebrow, crossing her arms over her belly. "What makes you think it's a 'him'?"

Tommy blinked, then chuckled, rubbing the back of his neck. "I dunno, just a feeling."

She stepped closer, resting a hand on his chest, fingers lightly tracing the collar of his t-shirt. "You're gonna love them no matter what, aren't you?"

He nodded without hesitation. "Yeah. With everything I got."

Before Meghan could respond, the front door swung open, and Trina waltzed in, balancing a box of what looked like bathroom essentials. She set it down with a huff. "Alright, that's the last of what I am willing to carry."

Meghan grinned. "You sure about this move, Trina? Or do I even need to guess who you're moving in with?"

Trina shot her a knowing smirk. "No. You already know."

Right on cue, Reynaldo strode in, a box of Meghan's books in his arms. He set it down, dusted off his hands, and walked straight to Trina, sliding an arm around her waist. With effortless confidence, he leaned in and pressed a slow, deep kiss to her lips.

When he pulled back, he smiled down at her. "Come, mi gallina—you and the rooster have plans for dinner."

Trina melted just a little, her usual sharp edge softening around the man who clearly worshipped the ground she walked on. Meghan watched the way her best friend looked at Reynaldo—the kind of look that said she was exactly where she wanted to be.

Meghan raised an eyebrow. "You sure about this?"

Trina glanced at Reynaldo, her smirk turning into something softer, something real. Then, without hesitation, she answered.

"Oh, hell yeah."

Meghan and Trina shared a knowing smile.

Tommy chuckled, shaking his head. "Well, I guess we all got our happy endings, huh?"

Meghan leaned into his side, her hand slipping into his. "No," she murmured, looking up at him. "This isn't an ending, Tommy."

She glanced toward the nursery, her heart full.

"It's just the beginning."

.. ᢙᢙ ..

Months later

THE GALLERY WAS QUIET, the last few patrons having left an hour ago. Tommy moved through the space, turning off the lights, checking the locks. It had been a good night. Sales were strong, the art spoke for itself, and Meghan...

Meghan.

She'd been glowing. Laughing. Holding court like she was born to do it. Seeing her in her element made something settle deep in his chest—like a puzzle piece finally clicking into place.

As he reached for his keys, his phone rang.

Arlene.

He answered immediately. "Hey, what's up?"

"Hey." Her voice was steady but urgent. "I'm at the hospital. It's time."

A pause.

Tommy exhaled, his pulse kicking up. "Already, huh?"

"We've known this could happen for a while now, bro."

Yeah, but knowing it and feeling it happen in real-time were two different things.

"How's she doing?" he asked, already grabbing his jacket.

"She's ready, but she's in a lot of pain."

His stomach clenched. "Okay, I'm two minutes away. Tell her I'm coming."

"I will." A beat. "She knows you love her, but she's saying some... unkind things about you right now."

He let out a breathless laugh, running toward the car. "She's delirious?"

"You don't want to know."

He didn't ask. He just hung up, threw himself into the Corvette, and drove like hell.

The hospital parking lot was a blur. He skidded into a spot, barely remembering to throw the car in park before jumping out.

Arlene was already waiting by the entrance.

"Where is she?" he asked, out of breath.

"Come on."

She turned, leading him through the bright white corridors at a half-run. The scent of antiseptic and something else—something warm and alive—filled his lungs.

They rushed to Meghan's room, pushing through the door.

She was sitting up in bed, hair damp with sweat, watching TV. For a moment, it almost looked normal. Like she was just relaxing after a long day. Then her face twisted, her body tensing.

She looked up at him, her eyes wide with pain.

"There you are, you son of a bitch! What kept you?"

Tommy blinked. "Traffic?" He shot her a crooked grin.

Her glare could have peeled paint. "A likely story."

She gripped the side rails of the bed, let out a low, guttural groan.

Tommy rushed to her side. "How far apart are they?"

She exhaled, breath shaky. "Every—" She suddenly cried out, gripping his wrist.

He winced. "Okay, got it. Every few minutes."

Meghan let out a shaky breath, nodding. "This boy is coming fast."

The door swung open. Two nurses and a doctor entered, checking the monitors.

"Alright, Mama," the doctor said, scanning her vitals. "You're progressing quickly. Let's get you to the delivery room."

They started unlocking the bed's wheels, prepping to move her.

Meghan shot Tommy a glare, reaching for his collar. "You are not leaving my sight, do you hear me, farm boy?"

"You got it, city girl." he said quickly, holding his hands up in surrender. "Wild horses couldn't stop me."

She let him go just as the nurses started wheeling her out.

Tommy followed, but as he turned toward the door, the TV caught his eye.

Entertainment Tonight. On-screen, John Masterson, grinning like a damn fool, had his arm wrapped around a blond, buxom woman.

A headline scrolled across the bottom:

John Masterson & Charity Moore: Hollywood's Hottest Couple!

The host beamed. "So, Charity, What's this movie about?"

On screen, John said, "Well, it's a romantic comedy about a woman who runs away from her husband, comes back years later and they reconnect. It really is a happy ending..."

Charity said, "Yes, It's something I've wanted to make..."

Tommy barely heard the response. Because honestly He didn't care. Not about John. Not about Charity. Not about whatever tabloid nonsense the world was eating up.

His wife was about to give birth to their son. That was real.

He turned his back on the screen and followed Meghan down the hall.

Machines beeped and monitors hummed.

And in the center of it all was Meghan. Sweaty, flushed, wild-eyed.

"There you are !" She turned her head and snarled, "You did this to me asshole!"

Before she could lay into him further, a contraction hit.

She groaned, head rolling back, gripping the rails of the bed.

Tommy stood by her side, his hands holding hers. "Sorry? Not sorry?"

"Fuck you."

"I think that's how this started," he joked. She looked at him.

"You're doing great, sweetheart," the nurse soothed, checking the monitors. "Just a short break before the next one."

Meghan exhaled hard, sweat glistening on her forehead. "Jesus. Give me a minute."

Tommy wiped a damp strand of hair from her cheek, watching as she sagged against the pillows. Her breathing slowed, her body sinking into a momentary lull between pains.

Before either of them could say another word, the doctor's voice cut through the moment.

"Alright, Mom. It's time. You'll need to push."

And just like that—everything else faded away.

She sucked in a breath, braced herself, and bore down.

A sharp, guttural groan ripped from her throat.

Then—a cry.

A high, piercing, beautiful cry.

Tommy's heart stopped.

"Congratulations," the doctor said, holding up the squirming, red-faced baby. "It's a boy."

The room blurred.

Tommy stared, chest swelling, pride and love crashing over him like a wave. He turned to Meghan, grinning. "Told you so."

She let out a breathless, teary laugh.

He leaned down, kissed her, his lips lingering against her damp forehead. "I love you."

She exhaled, spent but soft with love. "I love you too. But don't do this to me again."

Tommy chuckled, brushing sweaty strands of hair from her face. "Simon needs a sister eventually."

Meghan's head snapped toward him. Her exhausted glare was deadly.

"You want to die tonight, mister Richards?"

He held up his hands in surrender. "Okay, maybe in a few years."

She exhaled, closing her eyes for a second.

Then—softening.

She cracked one eye open, voice a whisper. "Yeah... maybe."

Tommy smiled.

A nurse walked over, placing the tiny, wriggling bundle into Meghan's arms. Their son. Simon Peter Richards.

Meghan looked down, eyes glassy with wonder.

Tommy leaned in close, tears in his eyes witnessing so much beauty in such a small thing, and pressed a kiss to his son's feather-soft head.

Later, in the quiet of the hospital room, Catherine finally got her turn.

Meghan, exhausted but glowing, had just finished breastfeeding when she looked over and smiled.

"You want to hold him?"

Catherine grinned, eyes shining.

"Sweetie, you'll have to shoot me if I ever say no to that question."

Meghan gently placed the baby into her arms.

Simon, small and swaddled, nestled against Catherine's shoulder.

A moment later, he let out a soft burp right onto her back.

"Oh no—sorry!" Meghan gasped, sitting up straighter. "I thought he was done."

Catherine beamed down at him.

"Honey, it's not the first time a baby's burped on my back."

She looked at Simon—dark hair, bright blue eyes—and kissed his tiny forehead.

"And it sure won't be the last."

. . ᨏ . .

The End

. . ᨏ . .

www.ingramcontent.com/pod-product-compliance
Lightning Source LLC
Chambersburg PA
CBHW070303260626
47160CB00003B/697